dogged

Thank you...
to everybody who has ever come to one of my performances
and supported me by buying books or employing me to do
writing-related things; in particular Writing West Midlands,
Poetry On Loan, Fair Acre Press, Offa's Press, Multistory. To
Simon Fletcher for encouragement and opportunity over the
years. To my mum and dad who didn't bat an eyelid when I
announced I wanted to be a writer. Thanks to Helen Cross
for mentoring. To those friends who have always taken an interest in what I'm doing. To Linda Nevill and John Brook
for help with early drafts. To Paul Francis for always being so
honest and giving of his time. To Dave Pitt and Steve Pottinger
for being them. To Jean Hampton for seeing something of
the writer in me and making me think I could. To Margaret
Holroyd for kind words about my prose writing which kept
me going.

dogged

Emma Purshouse

Ignite Books
2021

ISBN: 978-0-9932044-8-7

Typeset by Steve at Ignite.
www.ignitebooks.co.uk

Cover design by Alex Vann.
www.alexvanndesign.co.uk

Author photo by Nicole Lovell.

Printed and bound in the UK by
CPI Group (UK) Ltd
Croydon. CR0 4YY.

"You have talked so often of going to the dogs –
and well, here are the dogs, and you have reached them,
and you can stand it."

George Orwell
Down and Out in Paris and London

i.m. Doris and Tom

Nancy stands on the step. Her shoulders have been aching all night. Years of scrubbing quarry tiles up at the Dartmouth are taking their toll. She rolls her shoulders forward and twists her head to peer over towards her back. A lump has started to form under her overall. "Wot now? If it ay one thing, it's summat else." As she watches, the lump starts to bulge, move, and rupture the skin. She hears Mr Maddox's voice.

"If God'd uv meant uz to fly, e'd uv givun uz wings."

The voice is accompanied by the sound of a trickle of whisky being poured into a glass.

Her emerging wing – just the one – unfurls itself in a grand gesture and then flails against her back. It is large and black. It is oily, tarry, nicotine-stained, and the feathers are stuck together. It hangs like wet washing in a back yard on a windless day. "Sort of bost," says Nancy. "Shit!" she thinks, as Marilyn comes out onto her step and waves. Nancy tries to wave back without showing her new wing.

"Is that....?" says Marilyn screwing up her orange lips into the shape of a cat's arse.

"No!" says Nancy, cutting her off in mid question. "It ay!" The conversation is ended.

"Bloody dreamin agen," she thinks as she awakes. Yesterday, their Vee had been in a dream she'd had. At one point, Nancy had been flying in a big plane. There was only her in it and she didn't know who was piloting the thing. It wasn't too bad, she recalled. If that was what flying was really like, maybe she wouldn't be scared of it. Scared. Nancy is shocked to realise that she might be scared of something. She doesn't usually feel anything much. She's too long in the tooth for feelings. She sits up on the sofa in the dark and tries and tries to remember when she had last been scared but she can't.

Her head aches.

Nancy sometimes feels like she is about to spontaneously combust. She's seen a programme on the telly about it. The wick effect, they call it. She feels like her wick is burning very slowly and that one day she'll vanish in a haze of cigarette smoke, leaving her old trainers and maybe a Bic lighter inside the pocket of her smouldering blue overall.

Nobody knew how much Marilyn's bingo win was, but everyone knew that she'd had one. Doreen, from up the top shop, reckoned she knew someone who knew someone who was there at the Gala when Marilyn had won. "It was the National Game! 54k!" Doreen said. Nancy Maddox wasn't really sure if Doreen knew what the phrase *54k* actually meant.

Bernice down the pub said she'd heard the win happened online. Nancy knew this was rubbish, but couldn't be bothered saying so. Like Nancy herself, Marilyn Grundy didn't have a phone, let alone a computer.

Reeta from Sangha's shop, at the bottom of the street, said that she'd heard that Marilyn had won at the Mecca and it was only fifteen thousand. "Only!" thought Nancy. She could think of one or two things to do with "only" fifteen thousand pounds, even if Reeta couldn't.

Nancy is considering the bingo win as she stands on the step outside her front door. She takes off her glasses and huffs hot air onto each of the oval lenses, the left one first and then the right. The lenses are held in horn-rimmed-effect plastic frames. She stole the glasses out of a bin in Specsavers ages ago when she used to clean there.

Nancy didn't see it as stealing, because nobody wanted them. She can see quite well out of the glasses. Better with than without.

The wall behind her is a mixture of red and brown brick, soot-stained by the industry that used to happen here or hereabouts. To the right of the door frame, at chest height, is the number fifty-seven. It is daubed in cream paint. Underneath the number, in little black letters made in marker pen, a child has written, DAVY WOZ ERE.

Nancy polishes the lenses on her cardigan sleeve before putting her glasses back on. She tucks a stray strand of hair behind her ear, the arm of her glasses acting like a grip to hold it in place. She takes a half-eaten piece out of her pocket and rips away the remaining crusts. She starts mouthing the cloying combination of corned beef, marg, and white bread. She places the crusts back in the pouch pocket of her blue overalls as she eats.

Nancy's teeth are worn down, like those of an old sheep. Bloody useless! Nancy doesn't do dentists or doctors.

She walks forward off the step, and as she does so she puts her hand to her back as if something cracks or jars. Nothing shows on her face.

She has second thoughts about the crusts; she retrieves them and throws them over towards some pigeons which are scratting in the gutter. The birds flutter up and land again. "Vermin!" She hears Billy's voice in her head. "Ferals!" she imagines him saying.

Nancy eyes the plumpest pigeon. It gazes back. They lock beady eyes. And then, almost as if it doesn't like being stared at, the pigeon takes flight. Straight up into the blue yonder. Nancy watches it go, wonders what the view is like from up there.

If the pigeon had chosen to communicate, he might have told her that one of her ridge tiles was loose, that the skylights in the old factory roofs were all smashed, that the newbuilds and warehouses looked the same from any angle, that the temple domes and the church spires were beautiful, that he could see "the man on the oss" from where he was, that the self-harming Black Country wore its scars of road, rail, and canal like badges of honour, that there were more green spaces than she imagined, that she was a speck in a tiny rockpool, that the further you went the better it looked.

But Nancy picks up none of the pigeon's messages. She takes a packet of fags from her pocket and undoes the cellophane wrapper. She removes the foil and puts the rubbish in the pocket of her overall to throw away later. She fishes out a Bic lighter. She has a house full of Bic lighters. Bernice sells them cheap behind the bar at the pub. Nancy buys one nearly every day when she cleans and forgets to take one of her own. This one is green. Nancy spins the wheel and makes a flame. A fag now droops at her bottom lip. She's smoked roll-ups in the past when times have been harder.

It's more difficult to suck the smoke in than it used to be. She coughs and her shoulders hunch round. Her body is still racked with coughs as she puts the lighter and fag packet back in her overall pocket. Two or three drags later the coughing subsides, as it always does. The thought of giving up doesn't cross her mind. Nancy knows her own mind. Thirty years or so ago they told her she had two weeks to live, but there was their Chrissie and Davy to rear, so she discharged herself from the hospital and ate winter cabbage. Nothing but winter cabbage for six months! She put on three stone and brought her kids up. "Bugger the doctors!" she mutters. "Still 'ere, ay I?"

Marilyn comes out onto the step of the house opposite. She shakes a tatty old red rug into the street, and the dust cloud she creates blows up in the air and away. Marilyn waves to Nancy, who lifts her head in a sort of acknowledgement.

"Had a bit of a win!" shouts Marilyn, beaming.

"Ar, I 'eard."

"Nice surprise," Marilyn adds, still beaming.

Nancy says nothing.

The postman comes down the street like he's on speed. Perhaps he is. His toes are turned out and his shoes are squelching. They squelch even though it hasn't been raining. He hands Marilyn her post and she goes back in.

The postman squelches across the street. He doesn't smile at Nancy as he thrusts a fistful of letters in her direction. Nancy doesn't smile either. She nubs her fag against the wall and puts it in her pocket; there are strands of tobacco hanging untidily

11

out of the end and when she goes to smoke it again later, the tobacco will have fallen out completely and she will curse.

She takes the letters from the squelching postman and rifles through them. One of the letters has a gaudy Australian stamp on it that makes Nancy wrinkle up her nose. She stuffs another one of the letters into her overall pocket. Billy doesn't know that she hasn't paid the council tax. If he were to find out, Nancy wouldn't be able to explain to him what on earth she was playing at. She knows it is something to do with not being satisfied with the services that are being offered. She also knows that she'd better sort it or there'll be hell to pay.

Nancy is thinking of going back inside when an ill wind blows down the street. She shudders as Daniel Grundy appears in a swirl of grit at the top of the road. He is unsteady on his feet; for a second it seems like he will keel over but he rights himself. His eyes seem to be rolling in his head.

Bits of Daniel Grundy have come loose.

He walks a wavering path down towards Marilyn's closed door. Even after all these years he knows the door, even though it is the same shape and size and colour as all the other council doors in the street.

Instinct.

"Now 'ere's trouble if ever ar sin it," says Nancy under her breath to the greasy breeze.

Daniel sniffs the air. It smells of chip fat and tastes of dust. Nothing changes. *Tang! Tang!* The four cans he is carrying are held together by linked plastic circles. He has two fingers tucked through the gap in the centre and curled under part of one of the plastic rings in order to carry his load. As the cans bounce together they sound like the alien spaceship noises off some TV show that he used to watch every week when he was a kid; a kid with a lazy eye and a patch. Daniel remembers the laughter and the prodding, poking, and kicking that the other kids gave him at school because of his eye. Daniel thinks about the aliens that still wait in space. They are waiting to land and probe Daniel Grundy, abduct him and suck out his brains.

Aliens. He shakes his head as if to shake out a memory. His eyes don't feel quite right; they don't move as quickly as his head does.

Daniel is hungry and thirsty, but he doesn't know this because he's forgotten it. The rattling takes priority, priority over everything. He sees a staring woman. A staring, stary woman standing on a step; she is swaying. She looks familiar.

"Had a good look?" he shouts, before he rattles the letter box on his mother's front door. The whole world rattles.

He stoops and shouts through the flap. "Mom!" His voice drops onto the mat. Here's the junk mail Marilyn Grundy never expected. She's not seen him for...how many years is it? Maybe she never expected to see him again. Don't give junk mail house room, Marilyn. Rip it up before it's opened! Bin it! If you don't, before you know it, piles of junk mail will stack up and then spill over your table, take over your sofa, fill up your house with unwanted things.

The door opens a crack, the smallest crack. A dirty yellowing dog's muzzle sniffs at the gap and then Marilyn Grundy's washed-out face appears a few feet higher up above it. She has dirty yellowing hair that matches Toby's muzzle. Toby and Marilyn both stand and blink in the light.

"Hello, Mom."

"Daniel?" A look of shock spreads across her face briefly like a cloud might cover the sun as it moves through the sky. The cloud passes quickly and joy shines through.

Daniel doesn't let on that he overheard some old dears in the doctors who'd been talking of his mother and her win. Marilyn tells herself that Daniel couldn't possibly know about the money. They both pretend that he's come to see her for herself, to give his old mother a kiss, and make up for the lost time. They pretend that he isn't junk mail. Daniel even gives her one of his cans. They sit on the settee together drinking strong lager out of dusty wine glasses. Chit chat. Marilyn is careful not to scare the lad with questions. She's tempted to ask about her grandkids, but changes her mind. She's pleased to have him home. Toby the dog is in front of the fire, Joey the canary with his head under a wing snoozes in his cage, and Marilyn's long lost boy is back. All is right with the world.

When Daniel Grundy wakes up he doesn't know where he is for a few moments. He sniffs the air. He smells dog and Pledge. He's still rattling and bits are still loose. The drink has worn off and now he needs both drink and a wrap of brown to smoke. Smoking heroin is Daniel's latest trick. It stands to reason if the house still smells of dog and Pledge, like it always did, then his mother's housekeeping money will still be in the same place as it always was. Maybe the bingo winnings will be there too, all sitting together in neat little rolls secured with elastic bands. Job done, on his way.

Upstairs, Marilyn sleeps silently under blankets and candlewick. The strong lager has got the better of her. As Daniel creeps up to her room, she is curled up like a mouse in a nest.

In the back of her wardrobe is a hat box; inside the hat box is a tin. The key is always in the lock of the tin. It is a green tin with little slots for posting money. They are all labelled: *gas, electricity, water, coal.* Daniel opens it quietly and finds thirty quid, *for emergencies.* "Well, it's a start," whispers Daniel to his sleeping mother. "And this is an emergency," Daniel thinks, as he grinds his teeth without realising he's doing it. The dog has followed him up the stairs and is staring at him

14

with mournful, brown eyes from the doorway.

"Fuck off, Fuck Face," Daniel whispers as he passes the dog. He goes back down the stairs and the dog follows with a wagging tail and a misplaced sense of loyalty. Daniel stands in the lounge and fishes a mobile out of his pocket. He can't use it – no credit. He scrolls through the contacts list and writes some of the numbers down on the wallpaper next to his mother's mirror. Daniel Grundy is paranoid in case he loses his important numbers. The canary makes a *peep-peep* sound. It is an uncertain little sound as if to say, "I don't think you should be writing on your mummy's wallpaper, Daniel." It is like the sound an ineffective nursery school teacher might make.

"Ahrr! Ahrr!" yells Daniel Grundy at the bird. Its feathers shake and its little heart beats fast. Daniel opens the small barred door and puts his hand in the cage. He closes his fingers around the bird, feeling the pulse beating against his fingertips. He knows he could crush the thing and take its life if he wished.

Daniel leaves the house and heads up to the phonebox on the Vicarage Road. It's still quite early in the evening. The voice on the phone tells him to meet him on the car park at the Black Horse. A pair of mournful, brown eyes watch from the other side of the road as Daniel makes his call. A feathery, wagging tail waves from left to right as if to say, "Here I am, I'm over here."

The dog's mournful, brown eyes haven't looked on the world for seven years. The world smells nice. The mournful, brown eyes blink and a rough, pink tongue flops out and starts to rasp at a dry nose, dry from years in front of a gas fire. The dry nose sniffs the air and smells chips and earthy vegetables piled up outside corner shops. It smells curry and bacon and eggs and petrol fumes.

It smells other dogs.

The dog trots off up the road on his four little white legs, stopping every few seconds so that one of the white legs can cock itself at every tree, lamppost, electricity box, wall, and telegraph pole.

In the distance the traffic on the Birmingham New Road whirs, and hums and sirens wail.

Back at the house Marilyn is still sleeping like a mouse, while outside in her back yard cats yawp like banshees. Marilyn and the canary shudder at the sounds they hear in their sleep and somewhere in their subconscious they both wonder why the dog isn't barking.

Marilyn wishes now that she'd bought tinfoil when she went to the shops earlier in the day. Not that she knew she needed any because up until that very afternoon she'd lived on her own and rarely used it. She never has a roast dinner any more.

"It is for want of tinfoil the kitchen got smashed." The thought is like a poem she remembers from school. About Richard the Third was it? Or was he the rainbow one? Richard the Third Gave Battle in Vein. No, that wasn't right. Marilyn is sure veins are important somehow.

She tries to imagine a rainbow as Daniel smashes and clanks and screams and shouts and trashes her kitchen. It is midnight. What on earth does he want foil for at this time? She has a nagging recollection of some feature on breakfast telly that she'd watched, but covers it quickly with other telly thoughts, and remembers instead when Daniel and Shane had saved tin foil for the *Blue Peter Appeal* when they were little. The whole family had saved all the foil they had in a plastic bag that she'd hung on the handle of the back door. She'd tried with them, she really had. *Blue Peter* wanted the foil for

African kids, or was it to buy Guide Dogs for the Blind?
    That was it...dogs!

"Where's the dog?" says Marilyn.

Toby Grundy was at that moment whimpering under the large hands of a kindly vet. Blood splashes and sploshes on the stainless steel table. The kindly vet knows the dog probably will not live, but he has to try. Something about the creature reminds him of a mutt he'd had as a kid. It's a tough call; the damn club will be shut by the time he finishes operating and he's sort of agreed to meet a man in The Greyhound. A man with a nice smile. He looks back at the dog and sighs. "I'm missing out on a hot date for you." The dog whimpers again.
    The veterinary nurse grins at the vet. "Soft git," she says.

Half an hour later a white leg is lying in a bin of waste. It is the same white leg that had, only hours before, cocked its way all along the road down to the Black Horse, only to cock itself one final time up a gatepost before running out into the road to try and keep up with Daniel. Daniel was all that Toby had in the outside world and Daniel was disappearing rapidly, a shape in the distance turning a corner.
    When the car reversed from the car park and hit the dog there was a lot of yelping and a screech of brakes as the car wheel spun away. The driver drove off, seemingly oblivious. The landlady of the Black Horse saw the incident as she took the bins out. It was the landlady that phoned the vets. It was

the landlady that jotted the bright green vehicle's personalised number down, and then paused, before binning the scrap of paper; she didn't want any trouble.

Daniel hadn't seen his dealer accidentally run Toby over. He was already a quarter of a mile away. The little bag of brown was nestling in Daniel's tracksuit trouser pocket; the feel of it against his leg, reassuring.

Nancy had the urge to go over the road and knock on Marilyn's door. Check there hadn't been any bother. But she thought it might be too early to call on Marilyn. She was wrong. Marilyn has been up since before first light.

Daniel's banging about had subsided eventually, once he had found an old unopened bottle of cooking sherry, although not before Marilyn had got in the way of one of the cupboard doors as she tried to reason with him over his fruitless search for foil. After that, Marilyn had slept for a couple of hours, waking up every now and again to look out onto the darkened street in the hope that Toby would reappear. But as yet, no sign.

Marilyn has checked every room twice, and looked in the back yard too many times to mention, in case he's found his way home. She's even absentmindedly looked in the washing machine, the fridge, and the oven.

"Marilyn, Marilyn, Marilyn. Look at you," Marilyn says to herself as she stares at her reflection. The mirror she is peering into is a 1930s one. Marilyn doesn't notice the crack any more. She fixes on specks of what look like mildew. The mildew has also been there for years, like the crack, but she hasn't noticed it before. She rubs her finger over her mirror teeth, then rubs her finger over her non-mirror teeth. She's not quite sure where the mildew is. She runs a lipstick quickly around her lips. It runs smoothly, like a train on a track. The lipstick has a huge depression in it from years of use. She smacks her lips together as she turns the end of the tube to wind the lipstick back in. "It's hard to find orange lipstick," she says to Toby. But Toby isn't there.

Marilyn gingerly powders under her eye. She goes to pat Toby's head but Toby still isn't there.

"Where did my smile go, Toby?" she says sadly, looking back into the mirror. If Toby could have spoken he might have said that it disappeared with the last bus driver that came through these parts, 1979 or thereabouts, but luckily for Marilyn's feelings, Toby couldn't speak because he wasn't there.

As Marilyn turns away from the mirror, she notices some strange scribbles on her wallpaper. She's not entirely sure but she thinks they look like numbers. How long had they been there?

"Peep-peep," the canary says, drawing her attention. Marilyn plays her fingers along the bars of his cage. She notices that he's made a brown worm of excrement in his drinking water.

"Tut, tut, naughty Joey." The bird is going bald at the back of his neck. "Perhaps we'll have to take you down the PDSA," she says as she lifts the plastic tray out to change the water. "But first things first," she pauses to imagine where she might look, "we need to find Toby."

Daniel moves on the sofa. Marilyn jumps; she has quite forgotten he is there. "Sorry about the dog, Mom," he says as he looks at her with a pathetic expression. Marilyn doesn't answer him. She takes her lipstick off the mantleshelf and puts it back in her flowery make-up bag, which she zips up as tight as her lips before putting it on the armchair. She heads out in search of the dog.

As soon as Daniel hears the front door click shut, he grabs the make-up bag and tips the contents on the floor. "No money in there," says Daniel as he pokes about amongst the dried-up cosmetics. So now he knows for sure the money isn't where his mum usually keeps her money. It isn't anywhere in the kitchen, because he'd searched that with a fine toothcomb last night, killing two birds with one stone as he took the room apart in his quest for foil, and it isn't in her make-up bag. "Front room?" says Daniel to the canary. The canary stays schtum. "It'll wait," Daniel mutters. "Gotta go see the doctor fust." He can't believe that smoking his brown last night had been impossible. "This must be the only house in the world that doesn't own a roll of tinfoil."

He undoes a bottle of nail varnish remover as he speaks and sniffs hopefully at the fumes.

"Peep," says the canary.

Marilyn has a picture of Daniel on his first birthday. It's a black-and-white photo with one corner bitten off. Nobody knows who bit it off. In the photograph Daniel is sitting in a high chair and there is a cake. His eyes look crossed. Round the table are his grandparents and his dad. It was taken a couple of years before his dad had left them, which had been before Shane was born. In the photo, Daniel has a shock of white blonde hair. It went brown before he was seven, a ratty brown like all the other kids' hair in the area.

Something about that place seemed to colour everything, to sort of tarnish the houses and the people that lived there. Perhaps his blondeness was due to the way his mum dyed her hair? Perhaps the peroxide had got into Marilyn's bloodstream and then by osmosis it had transferred itself to the placenta and that's why Daniel's hair was white-blonde and then ended up brown?

There is a knocking at the door. When she gets to it, Nancy is standing there, glowering. Marilyn is a bit scared of Nancy, but she still smiles.

"How are you?"

"More tuh the point, ow um yow? What ya done tuh yower fairce?"

Marilyn reddens and touches her cheek.

"I give it a bit of a knock on the kitchen cupboard."

"Wheyer's yower Daniel?" says Nancy, indicating that she knows exactly what kind of kitchen cupboard Marilyn means.

"He's gone out somewhere."

"Wheyer?"

"Dunno."

"Is e cumin back?"

"Dunno. He's left a bag here. He might have gone to look for the dog. Toby got out last night. Accidentally. Daniel's a good lad really," says Marilyn half-heartedly, trying to defend her son against something that hadn't yet been said.

"Yow wanna watch aht fuh yower winnins," says Nancy, straight to the point. In Nancy's opinion, Marilyn is puddled, and she's betting the flighty piece will not have put the bingo money in the bank, however much it is. She probably doesn't even have a bank account. Nancy is judging Marilyn by her own standards. Nancy hasn't got a bank account, but then what would be the point? She doesn't have any money.

"Ohhh! Our Daniel wouldn't." Marilyn stops herself as she remembers the thirty pounds that Daniel has evidently borrowed while she was asleep. She thinks about the empty green tin lying on the bedroom carpet. She is sure he'll put it back when he signs on and gets some money. Nancy raises her eyebrows and blinks a number of times, as if she's reading Marilyn's mind, before cocking her head to one side and squinting. Marilyn thinks about the mess in her kitchen, the hieroglyphics on her wallpaper and the contents of her make-up bag, now inexplicably strewn about the back room floor.

"Wait there!" says Marilyn. Nancy waits. She hears some clanking and one or two curses. Marilyn rummages about in the glory hole set into the wall in the passageway between the front room and the back. Nancy can hear lots of grunting and items being moved about.

When Marilyn comes back she's pulling an old tartan shopping trolley. One of the wheels is missing. She looks up and down the street and says in a hushed voice, "Look after it for me." Nancy seems uncertain. "I trust you!" Marilyn says.

Nancy nods, takes the handle of the trolley from Marilyn. The axle scrapes the floor as she pulls it over the road towards her own house.

Toby Grundy has been getting used to walking with three legs and is doing rather well. He hasn't been discharged from the vet's; he's left by a back door. What is it with Toby Grundy and open doors? This time it's the vet's new receptionist who's been careless. She'd been asked to feed him and had done so, but she was in a hurry to go outside and make a call.

Sheryl is leaning against the wide open fire door to stop it from closing and locking her out, smoking with one hand and now texting her good-for-nothing boyfriend who hasn't answered his phone when she tried to call. Toby Grundy slips past her and limps off down the drive towards the street.

When Sheryl goes back inside she immediately notices that Toby's cage is empty, and goes cold. She needs this job. She's put a deposit on a new three-piece suite and the monthly repayments aren't going to be cheap. She has a quick scout round for Toby before going back to reception. She is looking shifty and doesn't quite know what to do. She smiles at a woman with a rabbit. It's unlikely that anybody will notice that Toby is missing, not for a while. Everybody is busy with their appointments.

Sheryl decides to play it cool. She takes a couple of calls, shuffles some forms about, looks at the in-tray on the desk and then decides to update the vets *Lost and Found* Facebook page with details of all the injured animals that have been brought in. Sheryl's fingers busy themselves on her keyboard. She is very diligent, gets them all done quite quickly, bar her one deliberate omission. Well, it would be awkward if somebody called up looking for the "white, wire-haired, cross-breed dog found in Parkfields". The one that she'd let loose.

Toby Grundy is supposed to be on regular antibiotics and painkillers, but Toby Grundy doesn't know this. He had thought, when he got into the street, that he might look for the lady with the bird but he doesn't know where to start so instead he heads for the nearest lamppost.

Toby Grundy isn't disappointed to find he can't cock his leg any more, because he hasn't realised it's missing. He cocks his imaginary leg and urinates before he trots off around town to sniff at Wilkos' door, bark outside the ladies gym, and then run over the road without waiting for the green man to flash. It isn't Toby Grundy's fault. They don't teach road safety in front of the gas fire.

He runs in the library door behind a tall man who smells of labradors. Toby stands in the cold foyer, and barks at a flustered-looking librarian who is trotting down the grand stone steps. The librarian will go home later and write a poem about a three-legged dog.

Toby Grundy sniffs until he is sure there is no food here. He runs back out of the library. He sniffs the air again. Meat! He runs up Market Street towards the kebab shops. He begins to run from one end of a plate glass window to the other. Backwards and forwards, backwards and forwards as people point and laugh.

It's not often you see a three-legged dog dancing in front of a window.

A man, who's just been served, comes out of the kebab shop. He has one tooth which wobbles in his head as he laughs at Toby Grundy. He gives Toby Grundy some kebab meat. "Come with me, Tripod," the man says. Toby/Tripod Grundy will go anywhere and do anything if there is meat involved, so he follows the man without a second thought. If a change of name is in order then so be it. The man sits down on the floor outside a boarded-up shop to eat his food, sharing the odd strip of meat with Tripod. He's recently got into town and doesn't know the place. He's lost, and therefore has a lot in common with the dog. The man takes his hat off and puts it out in front of him before telling Tripod Grundy to sit by the upturned baseball cap. Lots of people start to drop money in the hat. They, "Ahh," and pat Tripod Grundy's head. Tripod Grundy likes the head patting, but he is thirsty now. The man with one tooth says kindly, "You thirsty then, Tripod?"

He goes in the shop again and when he comes back he has a bottle of water. He opens it and tries to tip it into Tripod Grundy's mouth. Tripod laps clumsily at it. The man takes a swig himself and pats Tripod Grundy's head. "You're good earning potential you are, Tripod."

When the man goes in to the Tap and Spile to spend some of the dog's earnings, Tripod Grundy sits outside and waits for his new master. He is very loyal and has adapted quickly to his new name, but he whimpers a bit as his painkillers start to wear off and his missing leg begins to hurt him. Tripod lies down. He wants more kebabs and more bottled water so for the time being he forgets about the lady and the bird and he waits.

The lady is at home now. She's bought a paper so that she can look through it for the lost animals. There are only two listed, a lost Lhasa Apso from Bilston, and a tabby with a white bib, missing in Rowley Regis. She's happy to think that there aren't too many lost creatures in the world. The lady doesn't know about Facebook groups that reunite the plethora of anxious owners and their wayward pets, and if she did know she doesn't have any computer skills. Or, for that matter, a computer. So there she is, looking in the rag of her local paper for a four-legged dog called Toby. The lady has got it all wrong.

She gets sidetracked by the headlines. She reads about the people who have been injured in a terrorist attack in London. She sheds a tear or two as she reads about the carnage and the chaos. She feels for them all and for their families. She sheds a few more tears, some for the missing dog, some for herself, and a few more for the unknown people in the capital.

Marilyn goes to the phonebox and phones the town vet's to make sure that something bad hasn't happened to the dog. The woman on reception, who is very short with Marilyn, has a nervous cough. She assures Marilyn that no dog of that description has come in and puts the phone down quite quickly. It's a shame Sheryl hasn't taken Marilyn's number, but she isn't to know what will happen next.

Marilyn is relieved in one way that the dog isn't at the vet's because perhaps that means he's still OK. She phones Sunnyside Dog Kennels too, but no sign of Toby there either. Marilyn nips back to the top shop and buys a jumbo roll of tinfoil.

Later, when the one-toothed man wobbles out of the pub he notices that the dog isn't very well. He is a kind one-toothed man and in spite of the earning potential that Tripod Grundy has, the one-toothed man realises the dog needs treatment. The one-toothed man can't afford a vet. Even Tripod Grundy hasn't got that much earning potential. The PDSA would need benefit information. The one-toothed man can't get benefits because he doesn't have an address and he's using a false name. He picks up Tripod and walks up the road until he notices a Doctor's and goes in to ask if anybody knows where the nearest vet's is. The receptionist is very pleasant and directs him back the way he has come. If only all receptionists did their job that well.

The one-toothed man carries Tripod all the way to the vet's and when he gets there he opens the door and puts the dog down before shooing him in on his own. The dog looks at him with big, brown, mournful eyes. The one-toothed man looks back with equally big, brown, mournful eyes.

Tripod Grundy totters in and slumps in front of the desk, where the receptionist looks at him with a mixture of disbelief and relief. Her new three-piece suite, which had seemingly vanished into thin air less than two hours ago, is now very much back on the cards.

She rushes the dog through into the back, puts him into his cage and locks it up with only seconds to spare before the kindly vet comes through to give Tripod his next injections. The vet gives him two shots. The dog licks the vet's hand. The vet pats the dog's head. The vet thinks of the man with the nice smile who he'd stood up the night before. Tripod Grundy yawns and goes to sleep.

Sheryl has returned to reception, allowing herself a sly smile. She is happy that nobody is any the wiser. The slight pangs of guilt she might feel about the owner missing her pet will soon disappear when she takes delivery of her new leather-look suite and corner unit.

Later in the day, the man with one tooth will get a good kicking off some lads on a stag night. He will lose his last tooth and end up in A&E where he will go to sleep for five hours before the doctors see to him. It will be nice and warm, although there will be nothing to eat and he will have to ask for some water because he will not be able to afford to buy anything out of the drinks machine.

"Daniel Grundy!" the doctor shouts. It is the second time she's shouted the name. She will be cross if she has to walk out into the waiting room. "Daniel Grundy!" she shouts again. A flat-capped old man with droopy eyes points over to where Daniel is slumped. There is an exclusion zone around him. Even in the packed waiting room nobody has chosen to sit by him. Daniel Grundy smells. He hasn't changed his socks or his underwear for weeks; it isn't really on his list of priorities. The doctor walks up to him and gives Daniel a prod. He wakes up, eyes rolling as he tries to focus.

"Sorry," says Daniel. Daniel uses the word a lot. Although there are a few people who might say, "He doesn't know the meaning." In the surgery Daniel pours out his carefully under-prepared lies. "My bad back, doctor, it's getting wuss. I need more painkillers. I lost some of the ones you give me last time." Dr Ram looks at Daniel, sighs, and then puts on her glasses so that she can see his notes.

"You missed your appointment yesterday, Mr Grundy."

"Yeah, soz. Somefin came up."

"According to our records, it is your leg that is giving you pain." The doctor has continued to read, ignoring Daniel's feeble apologies.

"Uhhh."

"Your leg, Mr Grundy. The thing attached to your hip." Dr Ram hadn't used to be prone to sarcasm, but a town centre practice right next to a shelter for the homeless had become somewhat wearing.

"Yeah, it's spread. It's in my back as well now," says Daniel, thinking on his unwashed feet.

Dr Ram toys with the idea of playing the game and offering to send him to the hospital for an X-ray but it seemed wrong to waste other people's time when she could get rid of him. She writes out a prescription for dihydrocodeine.

"I'm still feeling depressed too. It's the pain."

"It's the drink that's making you depressed. You need to cut it down."

"I haven't had a drink for weeks." The smell of the chronic alcoholic fills the room as Daniel speaks. It makes Dr Ram feel queasy. She remembers the stink of hyenas.

"I fink I need strong tablets for my depression," Daniel continues. He's not even sure why he's asking for the tablets. He's taken them in the past and he didn't feel any different. Whatever the anti-depressants had done to his serotonin levels, at the end of the course of treatment he'd still been Daniel Grundy. There didn't seem to be a cure for that.

"Are you using drugs, Mr Grundy?"

Daniel puts on the face of the mortified. It isn't a very good face, not particularly convincing, but Dr Ram doesn't see it because she is busy prescribing Seroxat. She wants Daniel out of the surgery. She's not a bad doctor, but it's easier this way. She doesn't want an argument as it will hold the appointments up. She has people with real problems to see.

As Daniel leaves with his prescription, a man comes in to the doctor's carrying a three-legged dog. "Do you know where the vet's is?" the man asks. Dr Ram can see it is going to be one of those days and returns to the comparative safety of her surgery to spray some air freshener around as the receptionist starts giving directions.

Daniel doesn't recognise the dog at all, although Tripod recognises a familiar smell as Daniel walks past him. It makes him think of the lady, the bird, and dog food.

28

Daniel goes to Boots and gets his prescription. He asks for some needles too. Maybe it's time he bit the bullet and started injecting. Smoking uses too much.

He grabs a bottle of water off the shelf by the sandwiches and swills down three of the painkillers immediately, and then a couple of anti-depressants for good measure. "They'll stop me rattling for a bit," he thinks, before he puts the opened, part-drunk spring water back on the shelf he'd taken it from.

The painkillers won't hold him for long and he's conscious that the bag of brown won't last for ever, whatever he decides to do with it. Where is she keeping her winnings? Once he gets back and gets himself sorted, he'll start on the front room.

Nancy has decided that the letter with the Australian stamp has already waited a day, so it can wait until after tea. She has done a Fray Bentos pie with some spuds and gravy. Billy moans, claiming the pie is cold in the middle. If he'd eaten it when it was ready, instead of insisting on reading the sports pages first, it wouldn't have been, but there was no telling him. Billy has been right for sixty years of marriage and he wasn't going to stop being right now.

Nancy takes the tray back off him, goes in the kitchen to put the plate under the grill and heat the food through again. Nancy flicks a two-fingered V from behind the kitchen door, which makes her feel better. When she goes back through, she picks up the letters from yesterday and looks at them again.

The Australian stamp is more gaudy and colourful than she remembered. Their Vee often writes, but Nancy isn't one for writing back.

She opens the letter and reads slowly, mouthing the words to herself. *Dear Nance, G'day from Brisbane.* The opening salutation annoys Nancy more than the stamp has.

"G'day! Thinks er's bloody Australian now," she says to herself as she folds the letter up without reading any more of it and puts it in her overall pocket. She goes back in the kitchen to start washing up. She'll read it properly later.

"Wos yower Vee av tuh say fuh erself?" Billy shouts through from his chair.

"Usual," says Nancy without giving anything away, although in her head she is still fuming. "Bloody G'day!" Nancy mutters as she scrapes gravy off the plates. Billy doesn't pursue his line of questioning.

The *Emmerdale* theme tune begins. "Bloody rubbish! Dunno wot we pay the licence fower!" chunters Billy. Sometime, somewhere down the years, they'd both started speaking in exclamations.

After she's washed up, Nancy goes upstairs into Davy's old room. The tartan shopping trolley is propped up against the wall. She'd snuck it up there while Billy had been snoozing in front of the midday news. She stares at the trolley and then she gets Vee's letter out of her overall pocket again. She lights up a fag to smoke as she prepares to read.

"Dear Nance, G'day from Brisbane."
Nancy steels herself before reading on slowly and aloud.
"How's things with you? Hope Billy is AOK. And Chrissie and the kids. Everyone here is good. We've had a new kitchen since I last wrote and Norman is talking about putting in a games room for when the grandkids come and visit. The weather is hot, hot, hot.

30

Much better for the old joints than the English damp. I don't miss England. I miss you though. I wish you'd come and visit. I know you'd love it here. We've got plenty of room and Norman said to tell Billy that the fishing is great."

There is more but Nancy can't continue. She feels choked. She misses Vee, too. She's almost forgiven her for the G'day thing, but then she gets cross again when she thinks about Vee's unreasonable request. "Bloody visit!" It was as much as she could do to get Billy out of his chair. How the bloody hell would she get him on a plane? She remembers the line that Billy had said in her dream, "If God'd meant uz to fly e'd uv givun uz wings." Nancy rubs her shoulder blade. She is stiffening up again.

Maybe she should go on her own. No, she couldn't do that. Could she? Vee would probably offer to pay. "Charity case, is it now?" says Nancy. She directs it at the shopping trolley as though it's another person in the room. She remembers the "G'day" and starts to fume. Nancy puts the letter down on Davy's bed. She stands, and goes over to inspect the tartan shopping trolley more closely. She empties the contents out onto the floor; a mouldy onion rolls across the carpet and hits the skirting board with a thunk. The trolley appears empty now. Nancy reaches into its lopsided carcass. There is a square of black plastic in the bottom, put in by the manufacturers so that the bag can keep its shape. She gets her fingers under it and lifts it, pulls it out and throws it on the floor. She picks up the trolley and turns it on its end and shakes. A flutter of notes appears at her feet. Nancy looks a little guiltily at the door, pauses briefly to blink a few times, leans the trolley back against the wall before licking her finger and beginning to count the money. It doesn't take her has long as she'd hoped it might.

"Huh," she says to the onion as she finishes counting. "Theyer's uh lesson in listenin tuh rumours." She feels slightly cross with Marilyn, even though Marilyn had never once claimed anything about her win, other than that she'd had one. Nancy puts the notes back into the trolley before hiding the whole thing in the cupboard which leads to the loft.

Billy is snoring when she goes back downstairs. Nancy's feeling slightly more sluggish than she had been. She clicks the telly off, and the light, then sits awake in the dark, listens to him breathing, and recalculates her thoughts about the difference Marilyn's money could make to Marilyn's life based on her recently accrued knowledge of the woman's apparent worth. There'd certainly be enough to do something nice. A few swanky holidays, a trip somewhere. But a life changing amount for Marilyn? Nancy's mind wanders back to Australia and Vee's letter.

Weren't there spiders in Australia that could kill? she thinks. "An' dogs that ate babbies," she mutters. "Worram they called?" Nancy nods off in spite of her aching shoulder and she dreams again. She dreams of Meryl Streep giving her a shopping trolley with a baby in.

In the morning she doesn't remember the dream. She wakes Billy up with a start. "Wottisit?" he says as he eases his head off the back of his chair and looks over at her. He is sure the mad woman has just shouted, "Dingo!"

Daniel has locked himself in the toilet. Surprisingly, once he'd got back from the doctor's he'd fallen asleep, his pain taken away for longer than he'd expected. It was another day entirely by the time he'd woken up! Now he's sitting on the pan and looking at his needles. He looks at the roll of tinfoil that his mother has bought specially for him. He found it, waiting for him in the kitchen. "Smokin is a waste," he reasons. The trouble with Daniel is that he has a problem with needles. He shudders as he uncaps a micro fine and looks at the point. Daniel makes a decision. He gets off the toilet, half pulls his trousers up and goes out into the kitchen. He holds the top of his trousers with one hand to stop them dropping and he uses the other to open the kitchen drawers and rummage.

He finds a Bic biro and rushes back into the toilet. He sits on the pan again allowing his trousers to fall. He pulls the pen insert out of its plastic tube and bites the little blue stopper out of the top. He puts the empty pen tube between his teeth, empties some of the brown on the foil and heats the underside with a lighter. As the powder turns to liquid he sucks the smoke up through the makeshift pipe and breathes it in.

"Daniel." A timid little mouse voice squeaks on the other side of the door and interrupts his concentration. "You going to be long, love?"

"Fuckin hell, mom. I'm on the bastard bog. Can't I get any fuckin peace anywhere?"

It goes quiet. Daniel calms himself and begins to breathe in the smoke again. "Bloody hell. It's good stuff, this."

Daniel falls asleep after a while, still sitting on the pan. He dreams of the day his dad's dog had bitten him. Daniel was three, or maybe four. The creature's jaws had locked onto his arm. His dad had to stick a garden fork into the dog's back to get him off. They had to put the dog down. His dad had never forgiven him. Then Daniel had to have a big needle at the hospital and it hurt and the doctor had promised him a lollipop for being brave. It was to be a special lollipop that made a whistle sound when you blew in it, the doctor had said. Then the doctor realised that they'd run out of lollipops with whistle sounds, and so Daniel had the needle and had to go without.

His dad left not long after. His mother said his dad had got another dog. Daniel was afraid to go and visit his dad and his new dog, who was a redhead named Sheila Anderton.

Daniel stays in the toilet for four hours and Marilyn has to go in the mop bucket.

"Ar've allus liked Rhyl," says Nancy as she smacks Tyrone on his head. Patting is too soft for Tyrone. He is nodding with his eyes half-closed, making little whining noises. He is hoping she will polish his collar. She blows a coil of smoke out of her mouth and carries on smacking him. Tyrone squints in the smoke, but doesn't move. "Ower Vee wants me tuh goo tuh Australia," the old woman says and Tyrone turns his head slightly. He likes the smacking but what he really wants is crisps. He tries to smile at her. She stops smacking him, so he noses at her hand. She stands up and brushes her overall down. Tyrone sniffs around at her feet for crumbs. There are none. He barks. It is the bark for crisps. But she doesn't seem to recognise that. She's thinking of the shopping trolley in her cupboard again, as she smacks him on the head absentmindedly. Rather like Tyrone and the crisps, she can't quite get it out of her mind.

Bernice appears behind the bar. Tyrone does his crisps bark again. "Yow alright, flower?" Bernice looks at Nancy with a questioning smile. Nancy feels un-nerved by Bernice asking how she is. "Crisps!" barks Tyrone again, but nobody is listening. He snuffles off behind the bar.

"Ar, ah'll carry on now." Nancy starts brushing up the bits and pieces off the pub floor. She uses a full-sized broom, holding the handle part way down to sweep the debris into a dustpan.

"Yower Billy alright, is he?" asks Bernice.

"Ar. Same as ever."

"Chrissie?"

"Ar."

"How's her Neil's health and temper?"

"Ffft. Usual."

"Yow could do with an oliday," Bernice says. It isn't really astute, it's the kind of thing that people say to other people who look fed up and won't give the game away as to what's pissing them off.

"Couldn't we all," says Nancy as she clatters about. She doesn't say anything else and manages to keep on the tip of her tongue the line, "On wot yow pay me?"

Bernice goes out to supervise a delivery from the brewery. Her pleasant behaviour is down to the brewery delivery. The appearance of the butch dray woman, who Bernice rather likes, always puts a smile on her face. She is sometimes very pleasant to her staff if anybody who she half likes is in earshot.

Bernice stands in the street and admires the strong arms and thighs of the butch dray woman, who is humping barrels about. The butch dray woman always asks about Tyrone. She's got one of her own. It's a Staffy thing. People with Staffies have their own little club. Dog owners sniff each other out, nuzzle up to each other's arses, smiling with one another when they find a shared breed. They talk about their dog's behaviour like proud parents might talk of their children. The butch dray woman's dog has had puppies. Bernice imagines the dray woman's puppies and gets hot under the collar.

At ten to eleven, Johnny the Maggot walks in to the open bar where Nancy is wiping down the tables.

"Er ay open yet," says Nancy.

"Ar've cum to pay off mi tab."

"An start another no doubt." Once, Nancy would have laughed at this, but her laughter's dried up like a sun-baked puddle.

Johnny the Maggot shrugs, embarrassed, and heads for the bar. He raps his house keys hard against the drip tray. "Shop! Anyone abaht?"

There is a scuffling and a snarling as Tyrone appears, doing a convincing impression of *Dr Who*'s dog *K9*. A square body with a rectangular head. Tyrone has stuck his face in the hole of an old smoky bacon crisp box and now he can't get it off. He tries his crisps bark again but he deafens himself. Johnny the Maggot laughs, puts his keys in his pocket, and waits for Bernice. He isn't really in a hurry.

As Nancy leaves the pub, she feels the sun on her back, so she sits on the low wall that belongs to the terraced house next door. Decides to enjoy the heat for a bit. Another fag is in order. Nancy looks up at the blue sky as she smokes. It is a perfect sky. There are no clouds, no birds that she can see, and no vapour trails. If she had floated off then she wouldn't have minded. It is the kind of blue that should make a person think about going somewhere, probably abroad, or to the coast. Maybe to Cannock Chase, a park, or a beer garden. Or...Australia.

Her attention is bought back to earth as Bernice opens the sash window. "Let's gerra bir'ov air in," she hears her say. The window is positioned above the plastic letters that stretch over the pub doorway to read   ARTMOUTH ARMS. Somebody had stolen the D years ago. Bernice had blamed their Davy.

"There's other folk uz names begin with D," Nancy had argued. Although secretly she kept an eye on Davy, looking for indications that maybe Bernice was right. Nobody had bothered to replace the D in all those years. That's the thing round here, when something goes it goes for good; nobody has the energy to put things straight. Apathy.

Nancy douts her fag and decides to go up the town. She thinks that maybe she will sort out the council tax problem. She's not sure how it's happened, but when she stops to consider how often somebody comes round to borrow money maybe it's not so surprising. One day it will be their Chrissie coming round and asking for a sub until pay day, the next a grandkid will turn up needing money for college stuff, or one of the great grandkids will have to have money to go on a trip from the play group or for a new pair of designer kids' trainers. It's never ending. She's sure if she talks to them at the council that she'll be able to find a way of paying some extra off each week. Maybe she could ask for more hours from Bernice, or approach another pub. She checks for the council tax envelope that's still hidden in her overall pocket and notices the betting slip. She'd found it on the floor in the men's, tucked it away in her pocket. Wouldn't that be a stroke of luck? A winning betting slip, providing the right amount of money to pay off her dues.

Nancy hasn't been up the town for ages. It feels funny as she walks towards the shops. Was it last Christmas maybe? She doesn't really need to go to town usually; she can get everything she needs off the Vicarage Road or out of their Chrissie's catalogue. What's the point of going up town? She ignores the question and crosses the ring road anyway. Their area, their turf, is sectioned off by main roads like a little pocket of life trapped in a rock pool.

She crosses Sainsbury's car park and passes the vet's where Tripod Grundy is taking his antibiotics like a good little dog. She walks down towards the library and crosses again. She goes in the main shopping centre. The crowds feel too much. The chrome and glass make her disorientated. Upside down. She heads out onto Dudley Street and up towards the civic centre before changing her mind to turn up King Street and walk to the end where the betting shop is. Three young men stand in the doorway. Nancy barges past them with her ticket in hand and marches up to the counter. "This win?" she says to the woman.

"Blimey, this was a while ago, flower." The woman says as she checks her records.

The woman smiles. Nancy's heart lifts for a split second, "Pulled up, love," and then sinks. Bloody typical, knackered before it even managed to get to the end of the race. She gives a sigh. She knew how it felt. Wouldn't it have been nice, just for once, a bit of good fortune.

Nancy leaves the bookies and crosses over towards the job centre, perhaps she can pick up some extra work from there. She looks at the jobs in the window and catches sight of her reflection. Would they let someone of seventy-nine register for work? She decides she doesn't want to find out, and heads back past the bookies towards the civic centre. She fully intends to go and sort it out now, that is until she walks past the post office. She stops to catch her breath.

She doesn't know what's got into her as she stands in the queue. A little kid in front is playing with the plastic posts of the make-shift fence designed to keep the queue in order. He's found out how to unhook the retractable fabric barrier and is whizzing it in and out of its housing in the post.

"Don't do that," says his mother, with no authority. The kid carries on and the mother ignores him. Nancy gives him a look, and he stops.

The queue moves quite quickly. Queues seem to move faster than they used to. A robot voice shouts out numbers. *Cashier number seven. Cashier number five. Cashier number two.*

Nancy goes to a window.

"Ar'd like uh passport form please. No," she corrects herself, "Ar'd like two passport forms." The woman in the window looks at her like she's stupid.

"They're on the shelf at the back. You didn't need to queue." The woman points a prettily decorated, squared-off nail in the direction of the passport forms.

"Funny avin' square nails," thinks Nancy. "Ar bet ower Vee'ud av square nails done." Nancy feels cross again.

She goes over to the pigeonholes and attempts to read the labels, but some of them have peeled off and in the end she has to pull the forms out one by one. "HGV licence... driver's licence... passport." She takes two. Then she goes back and takes two more. With her spelling she is bound to make a mistake or three.

As she passes back by the counter, she waves the forms at Square Nails. "How much? A passport?"

The woman tells her. "Bleedin 'ell," says Nancy.

Nancy goes back into the melee of the shopping centre. She stops outside a travel agents and peers through her glasses, and then on through the cluttered window of late deals at the girls in their uniforms sitting at desks with computers. They look like they are busy doing nothing. Nancy has never been in a travel agents. She doesn't quite have the nerve today. She reads the window deals. She notices a special offer flight to Melbourne. She doesn't know if it is close to Brisbane or not but she knows it is in Australia. It's sure to be a rough guide to a price. It isn't as much as she'd thought it would be. But on her wages and their pension it might as well have been a million pounds, or 54k, or 15 thousand.

The various rumours about Marilyn's bingo win run through Nancy's head again. She could put them all straight. Not that she would, she isn't one to tittle tattle. As she turns from the window she collides with a woman pulling a shopping trolley and they both mumble apologies. The woman's trolley isn't tartan, it has flamingoes on it. Nancy wonders idly if Australia is where flamingoes come from.

When Nancy gets to the top of their street, Marilyn is helping Daniel out of a taxi. He is shuffling like a little old man.

"Wos up wi' him?"

"He had a little accident."

"Oh ar. Wot little accident?"

"A funny turn. He took summat."

"Wot kind of summat?"

"I am here, you know," pipes up Daniel. Then he starts coughing for effect.

"Better get him in," says Marilyn. "Before he catches his death."

"If only," thinks Nancy as she leaves them to it and heads into her own house. She shuts her front door behind her, feeling kind of guilty... guilty about wishing bad things on Daniel, and guilty about skulking off after work without telling Billy, guilty about continually thinking about shopping trollies with less money than they might have been expected to have. "Ar've onny bin tuh town," she says to herself, defensively.

Billy is, of course, in his chair when she gets back.

"Wot yow got theyer?"

"Doh miss a trick yow, do ya? I jus' got sum passport forms."

"Who fower?"

"Uz."

Billy's jaw drops. "Yow wot!"

40

Thirty yards or so up the street, Nigel Clancy's dog Duke and Mrs Elwell's mutt Terence square up to one another. Who's left the the back yard gate open? It doesn't matter now. The fact is the gate is open and that is that. Duke bares his teeth. Terence's hackles start to rise. They go for each other's throats.

"I'll do you a nice bit of marg and jam on a piece, shall I?" Marilyn is spoiling Daniel rotten. Maybe that has always been the problem. Maybe Daniel is spoilt. She is treating him as if he has the measles or the mumps rather than treating him like the useless article that he really is. Perhaps if she treats him well and spoils him a bit he might think more of himself. He might save himself, get off the wrong path he's taken.

"That'd be nice," he says politely.

He is still feeling sorry for himself. The hospital had been off with Daniel. Marilyn had found him passed out in the toilet, rung an ambulance, gone in with him, and then come home when she was sure he'd gone to sleep. Then when the hospital called to say they were releasing Daniel, she'd gone to fetch him. Daniel had been very grateful, thanking her repeatedly all the way home in the taxi. He sounded like a very forlorn parrot.

"Thanks, Mom." He'd kept nodding off, then jolting awake. "Thanks, Mom," he'd say again.

Daniel knows he still has some brown left so he can be nice to people for the time being.

"Wanna cup of tea, love?" Daniel nods. He sits and watches *Doctors*. He likes the look of one of the woman characters. He tries to tune into her accent. He's still a bit disorientated but he thinks it might be an Irish accent.

He remembers when he was five and he went to the O'Riordan twins' birthday party. Their mother was a nice Irish lady. Lovely voice. "You want a sandwich, Daniel? You want a piece of cake, Daniel?" She made the other kids let him join in. They all played pass the parcel. Every layer was a different sheet of newspaper, the parcel done up like a packet of chips. And the excitement was the same as when you opened a packet of chips, because between each layer of Mrs O'Riordan's parcel was a little present. And when the music stopped a kid had to tear off a layer and they'd find one of the lollipops she'd wrapped into it. Daniel got anxious. The music never stopped on him. Near him but not on him. All the layers had nearly gone and he hadn't got a lollipop yet. No lollipop again. Mrs O'Riordan was in charge of turning the music on and off. She was looking in the window reflection to see who had or who hadn't won. She fixed it. She fixed it so Daniel Grundy got the biggest bar of chocolate he'd ever seen in his life.

"Ah, the poor little mite. Him with his lazy eye and dem national health glasses. And his daddy gone like that," she said to her husband later.

Daniel smiled so big he could have fit the bar of chocolate in his mouth in one go. He thought his face would crack in two. And somehow, because he was a winner, the other kids let him play with them for the rest of that day. They didn't even have to be told to let him. He joined in with everything. It was the happiest day of his life. He took the chocolate bar home with him and kept it under his pillow. He had a piece every night for a week and a half and he never shared it with a soul. Then one night, after a particularly warm day for April, Daniel went to his stash and found it had melted leaving brown stains on the sheets under his pillow. They looked like shit stains.

Daniel was devastated. He went off chocolate after that.

Mrs O'Riordan was a good woman. She didn't regret having Daniel round to the party and letting him win the pass the parcel, even when the twins got a ringworm a piece from getting too close to Daniel Grundy.

Daniel wakes up and finds that *Doctors* has finished and *Coronation Street* has started. He doesn't remember going to sleep. He doesn't remember anybody changing channels. He eases himself up off the sofa. His mother is snoozing on the other end of it, curled up with her feet tucked under her. Daniel waves his hand in front of her face to check she is out of it and then he goes into the front room. He smokes some of the brown. Now, he only has a bit left. He needs a drink too. Where is the woman keeping her winnings? He's been through her purse of course. He's looked under her mattress. He slowly takes the front room apart. He opens drawers and tips out the contents. He picks up ornaments quietly and looks in the holes underneath as if his mother might have used each one like a money box. He feels down the back of the sofa. Nothing. It's nowhere to be found. He looks through papers he finds in an old briefcase, but it's birth certificates and death certificates and there's no mention of bank accounts. Perhaps it isn't true. Perhaps she hasn't won. But deep down he knows she has.

He decides to go back through and try and scrounge some money off his mother for a drink. He's been through the glory hole before, but something makes him look again. And there it is against the skirting board, a crisp new ten pound note like the sort banks issue. It's not the worn sort that you'd get in change.

Daniel sniffs at the note, decides it is evidence of there being money and that it has been here in this house.

Daniel is sweating and shaking now; he's not sure if it's the excitement of knowing the money is real or if it's because he needs a drink. He scuttles through to where his mother is sleeping. "Need a drink!" he shouts at the canary as he goes back in the middle room with his crisp ten pound note now tucked down his boxer shorts. The canary wakes up shaking. "Need a drink!" he shouts at his mother, who also wakes up shaking.

"I'll put the kettle on!"

"A proper drink!"

"You want to borrow a couple of quid?" she says, keeping a jolly tone in her voice. She looks towards the kitchen cupboards and their dangerous doors. "Pass me my purse." Daniel grabs her purse off the mantleshelf from under the photo of his first birthday and throws it at her. If the characters on the photograph could, they would close their eyes or busy themselves cutting cake or start to clear up but they can't, so they watch. The purse is old-fashioned, a little metal clasp bent in an arc around a saggy brown leather bag. She's had it years and years and years. The leather never used to be that brown; it's worn that way. It never used to be that soft; it's worn that way. It's stretched leather and it feels like old skin, like the skin that hangs on the underside of arms. Old saggy skin. Bingo wings. Marilyn is taking too long, so Daniel snatches the purse back from her.

"Yeah! I want to borrow a couple of quid!" he shouts as he tries to open the clasp but he can't.

"Daniel Grundy can't open a simple clasp."

He imagines the characters on the photograph are whispering and sniggering behind their hands. He rips the clasp away from the leather and the money spills and flies around the room. The canary starts shrieking and fluttering around the cage, wispy wings knock against the bars; the fluttering sound gets in Daniel's head. It's the dragons. The dragons are circling. He starts to scream and scream and scream. Marilyn lies back on the sofa looking at him in terror, curling up more. Daniel grabs the mirror off the wall and smashes it. He upends

44

the chair under the window. He runs in the kitchen and swipes at the pots and pans and the crocks on the drainer. He kicks at the toilet door. He kicks and kicks and kicks until he smashes one side of the hardboard and creates a hole. It is shocking this violence, but Marilyn is numb. The action seems to be unreeling like a film in front of her eyes. There is a dis-connect. She stares hard at the hole Daniel has just created. Perhaps she could get in the hole and hide in the door, run along the inside of the walls behind the skirtings, be like a little mouse again. All the time his screams are getting worse and worse.

He comes back towards his mother. Lucid. He sees her and says, "Lend us a hundred quid. You've had a bingo win. You're good for it. I'll pay you back." She tries to get off the sofa and head for the stairs door. She might be going to escape. She might be going to get money from the bingo winnings stash. As she attempts to stand she puts her foot heavily on a glass that is lying on its side. It has been spilt in the kerfuffle. What a nice word kerfuffle, so gentle. As she goes over on the glass, her ankle twists. The noise of the snap of the glass stops them both. A tableau is formed. Daniel wakens from his frenzy and shakes his head. He looks at his poor mother's foot. He goes outside and asks a passer-by to phone an ambulance for his mother; there is some decency in the lad.

He comes back in and picks up the coins. There are seven pounds. He gives three to his mother and takes four for himself. "She'll need a bit of money to get back after," he thinks. So thoughtful. He waits for the ambulance to come, even though it is inconvenient and he is shaking and sweating. One of the ambulance men recognises Daniel and his mother from the day before.

"She trod on a glass," Daniel says.

"I trod on a glass," Marilyn echoes. And they are, in fact, telling the truth. Many household accidents are silly.

Daniel waves the ambulance off, and heads up to the shop to buy cans with the four pounds. He will be able to get a tenner's worth of brown now too, but that won't be enough because he'll need it again later. He's got habits to feed. He watches people as they walk past. Women with bags over their shoulders, kids with mobile phones clutched to their ears. How easy would that be? It would be stealing from people though, and he was never bought up to steal, not from people. It doesn't occur to him that he's stealing off his mother. She's family and she should give him things. Shops didn't matter, because that wasn't really stealing from people. He was scared of the bogeyman that comes to get you if you steal off people. Daniel Grundy wasn't brought up to be a bad kid.

Maybe he can pay for some of the brown and get a bit more on tick. He scrolls through the numbers on his phone – no credit again. He goes to the telephone box, feeds it a quid and punches in the number. The dealer gives him a time and a place. Daniel goes to the offy and then home to kill a couple of hours with a can.

Billy and Nancy are sitting in silence, licking their wounds. The argument had developed into a violent tongue-lashing. Verbal recriminations cutting through the air like fencing foils. Every jab, thrust, and barbed comment hitting home. Years of petty marriage misdemeanours flung backwards and forwards. Cutting. They were both still stinging like salt had been rubbed in their re-opened sores.

Nancy doesn't really know why she'd even brought it up, let alone actually fetched the passport forms. What was she thinking of? "Seventy-nine," she reminds herself. How had that happened?

There is a tapping at the front door. It is after nine o'clock! They exchange glances. Nobody in their right mind answers the door after dusk here. The council have put a peephole in, but the street is so dark you can't see anything through it. Nancy gets up and goes into the front room to stand behind the door and then puts her ear to it. "Oo is it?"

"It's Marilyn from over the road."

Nancy tuts. "Ow many Marilyns does er think ar know?" says Nancy to herself. And then she tuts again, because she's tutted like Billy does. Perhaps she's caught tutting off the miserable old goat in the other room. Nancy is about to open the door when Marilyn does another whispery kind of a shout.

"I'm a bit short for my taxi."

"Taxi!" thinks Nancy. "Wot's er doin' avin taxis agen? That's the second in one day."

"Owd on." Nancy pulls across the curtain that covers the door to stop draughts, and opens the door a crack. She eyes Marilyn up and down as if she thinks it might be someone else doing Marilyn Grundy impressions so they can get in and steal things. If it is, perhaps they can take the old goat and his chair.

"Only 50p," says Marilyn.

Nancy stares out at a fidgety-looking taxi driver parked up outside the Grundy house. Happy enough to drop off, not so happy to wait. A lot of the drivers wouldn't pick up or drop off from houses round their way. Nancy ferrets around in her overall pocket but can't find any change.

"I ay got none, cock," she says, stubbornly deciding that on no account is she going to ask the old goat if he's got any change because that would mean being the first to speak. Being the first to speak constitutes an apology and there will not be one of those any time soon.

"You'll have to get some out my winnings," says Marilyn.

"Ang on." Nancy goes back through into the middle room and opens the stairs door. The old goat doesn't look up but

47

she can tell he's dying to ask what's going on. Nancy goes upstairs to the shopping trolley and pulls out a ten pound note before coming back down to give it to Marilyn. As she does so, Marilyn's front door opens and Daniel appears on the step before slamming the door behind him. He's got an appointment to keep and he's running late. He is surprised to see his mother and the Maddox woman in the street and wonders what they're up to.

Nancy keeps one eye on Daniel and watches as Marilyn winces and then limps towards the waiting taxi to hand over the crisp new ten pound note. Daniel, maybe for show or maybe because he cares, walks over to his mother and gives her a hug. He looks at the crisp new note that Nancy has given his mother and makes a mental comparison with the crisp new note that he'd popped down his pants earlier. Coincidence? Daniel thinks not.

The driver takes the money through a barely open window before handing back change and driving off, looking relieved.

Daniel's head is whirring and whistling with thoughts as he kisses his mother on the head and says, "Gotta dash!" He looks over at Nancy and points two fingers to his own eyes before pointing a single finger back at the old woman. The gesture is wasted on Nancy, and she looks at him like he's deranged. Daniel runs off up the street as his mother limps towards the closed door.

"Wot the bloody 'ell uz the daft mare done now?" thinks Nancy. She tuts because she knows she's going to have to help, and then she goes to Marilyn, takes her arm and offers her support. Nancy takes Marilyn's key off her and opens the front door.

"I'll be alright from here," says Marilyn as they cross the threshold. Nancy ignores her and clicks on the light in the neat front room. Except it isn't neat, there are bits and pieces from upturned drawers all over the sofa and ornaments lying amongst them. It is cold and feels unlived in. Two downstairs rooms and still none of the older generation can bring themselves to use the front one for anything else other than best. The glory hole door is open so Nancy pushes it to, and they struggle through the gap into the middle room. A wave of warmth hits them. Marilyn has left the gas fire on.

"Yow got money to burn?" says Nancy as she clicks on the light.

The room is trashed. Nancy sighs. Marilyn bursts into tears. She is still sniffling as Nancy helps her to sit down on the sofa. Nancy, embarrassed at displays of emotion, busies herself, picks up all the strewn bits and pieces. She wraps broken mirror shards in newspaper and pulls the cover over the bird cage when she notices Joey lying stone dead in the grit on the bottom. Which is kind; it is more than Marilyn can deal with today. The room looks like a bomb has gone off.

Nancy fetches blankets from upstairs and covers Marilyn up. Marilyn is holding a handkerchief up to her eyes. It is sopping wet, a little blue *M* embroidered on one corner. Once Nancy has cleared the kitchen she makes a cup of tea. There aren't many drinking vessels left. She serves Marilyn a strong cuppa. "Yow orright, cocka?" she says, as she passes her the cup. She immediately realises her mistake, it's a stupid thing to have said. Marilyn shakes her head and the sobbing starts again.

Nancy pretends the crying isn't happening, tells Marilyn she'll be back in a bit, then goes back over to her own house. Stupidly she's left the door ajar. She wonders if maybe someone has gone in during her absence and taken Billy and his chair. But no, there he is, right where she'd left him.

He is still so angry he doesn't even ask her why she is rummaging about in the glory hole. And when she comes out with an old walking stick he is curious, but the stubborn old goat still won't ask, not even then. She is tempted to whack it over his head and knock some sense in. Then she remembers she is seventy-nine. Perhaps she should be knocking sense into her own head. She imagines the headlines. *Seventy-nine year old Wolverhampton woman beats herself to death with walking stick.* Then, underneath, in small type *Husband refuses to comment.*

She goes back over the road to Marilyn's. She shuts her own door this time and takes her key.

She leans the stick against the mantleshelf where Marilyn will be able to reach it. Marilyn looks like a poorly kid lying on the sofa. Nancy pulls a vacuum cleaner out of the glory hole and hoovers up the remaining smaller fragments of debris. "Yow be orright gerrin tuh the toilet?" Nancy shouts over the noise of the hoover. Marilyn comes out from behind her hankie and nods, looking embarrassed.

"Shuwah?"

Marilyn starts to cry again. Nancy has noticed a mop bucket outside the toilet door so she goes to get it. She clicks the pull switch in the bathroom and the light comes on. There is a piece of foil, blackened, and a pack of needles. The Miss Marple in her didn't need many more clues than this. It was like a game of Cluedo. It was Daniel Grundy in the bathroom with the hypodermic.

She puts the bucket next to Marilyn. "Ar'll be back fust thing tuh sort yower breakfast aht. Ow long yow s'posed tuh stay off it fower?" Nancy nods towards the foot, and Marilyn shrugs.

"It's not broken," says Marilyn. "A bad sprain, they said."

Nancy nods and then goes without saying goodbye.

"Oh, Joey," says Marilyn to the bird in the covered cage. But Joey couldn't answer because he was as dead as any stressed canary could be.

Daniel Grundy didn't come home that night so that was one small mercy in the day.

Now Tripod Grundy is well enough, the soft-hearted vet takes the dopey-looking dog home with him. He can't help himself. He reminds him so much of the dog he'd loved as a kid. The vet has started calling the dog Sebastian which is the same name as his special childhood pet. The vet even bought Sebastian Grundy a large tartan bed, a bowl, some toys (although Sebastian Grundy doesn't know what to do with them), some treats and a flea treatment.

Sebastian Grundy also doesn't know what to make of the wood floors in the vet's house; they are skiddy, especially for a dog with three legs. They feel like outside, so Sebastian cocks his imaginary leg and pees. Luckily, white leather designer sofas wipe down well. Sebastian slumps down in front of the log burner and stretches as he lays on his side. He yawns and falls asleep.

When he awakes sometime later, the vet is on his knees performing oral sex on a man with a nice smile. "Oh, he's awake!" the man with the nice smile says. The vet says nothing for a moment, at first he thinks the man with the nice smile is making fond references to his own cock. The vet stops what he is doing, turns and is quite relieved to find the man with the nice smile is talking about Sebastian. The vet rubs his jaw and moves the bottom mandible from side to side.

"He needs his antibiotics," says the soft-hearted vet and on that he trots off into his designer kitchen.

The man with the nice smile lies back in the leather chair, crosses his left leg over his right knee and works on maintaining his erection. Sebastian Grundy sees the opportunity for fuss and in one bound he sticks his head in through the leg-shaped triangle, jumps up, and ruins the vet's evening.

The man with the nice smile screws up his face and doubles up with pain, pushing the dog off. He eventually manages to get dressed and, with the nice vet still making all sorts of apologies from the doorstep, he drives off into the night.

The vet comes back in and looks at Sebastian Grundy sitting there with his tongue out, his electric hair standing up on end, his one leg missing, and the vet laughs. Sebastian appears to be laughing too, although he doesn't really know why.

Marilyn Grundy wakes up on her sofa. Her foot is hurting. She stretches and sits up. There is a knocking at the door. She looks at the clock. It is a quarter to six in the morning. "Who on earth would be knocking this early?" Marilyn stands, gingerly. "Hold your horses!" She reaches for the stick and tests it out. Her back won't straighten and her foot is agonisingly painful. Overnight she's gone from a reasonably active seventy-or-so-year-old to a shuffling elderly woman who fears she may never leave the house again. The door is still being knocked. It takes Marilyn four and a half minutes to get to it. When she opens it, Nancy Maddox is standing there with a bowl of something steaming in one hand, and a shoebox tucked under her arm.

"Come in," says Marilyn. She doesn't really need to, because Nancy is already in. They both go through into the middle room. Nancy looks for signs of any more trouble and sniffs the air. Marilyn sits on the chair.

"Car stop. Gooin' up the Dartmouth." She makes Marilyn sit with a look, and hands over the bowl, which contains porridge. In the box are a few crocks, oddments that Nancy has had lying about. She puts them on the drainer in the kitchen. Then she fetches out some sandwiches wrapped in cling film.

"Dinner,"says Nancy.

"You're too kind," says Marilyn.

"Well I ay gonna let yow starve, am I?" says Nancy crossly. She doesn't like it when people compliment or thank her, it makes her inexplicably agitated.

Then she fetches out a thermos. "Tae," says Nancy. "Ar put sugar in. Ar day know if yow did or if yow day, burrit's good fuh shock, ay it."

Marilyn isn't sure what Nancy means until she asks if she'd mind taking the cover off Joey before she goes. Marilyn cries into the sodden hanky again. Nancy takes the stiffened bird and puts it in the shoebox. The little yellow corpse rattles around in the box and finally nestles in a corner where, if it hadn't have been dead, it might have felt safe.

"Ar'll be back at tae time. Bring yow sum cod an' parsley sauce." She says this as if it might have been Marilyn's favourite. It isn't. It had been Nancy's boy Davy's favourite. Nancy looks in the box at the dead canary and she feels sad. More feelings. She leaves Marilyn sniffing on the sofa.

When Nancy gets up to the Dartmouth, Bernice is in an arsey mood because Nancy is two minutes late, and then she can't get started quick enough for Bernice's liking because her shoulders ache. Tyrone is in an arsey mood too, because Bernice has still forgotten to get any crisps in. He doesn't like scratchings. When the nice lady puts her box down on the seat he noses the lid off. Tyrone thinks it might be his lucky day as he sticks his head in the box once the lady has taken her mop and bucket off into the toilets. "No crisps. Damn." He eats the canary anyway. A little yellow feather will stay stuck to his jowls all day until Bernice notices it after closing. "What yow got 'ere?" she will say as she pulls the tiny fluffy feather off and lets it float away out of the bathroom window.

"Crisps!" Tyrone will bark.

"Blast," Bernice will say, "I forgot to pick up the crisps from the cash and carry." She will wonder why she's only just remembered. Tyrone will fart as he laps at his water dish. He will be disappointed but not unsurprised that there is no smell of smoky bacon.

Daniel Grundy is off his head. He's been out all night living the dream in a crack house down Parkfields. The dealer was impressed with a crisp ten pound note, albeit a rather sweaty, smelly one, but perhaps he was more impressed by the fact that Daniel is the son of the bingo-winning woman he's heard so much about recently. To be fair, most of what he's heard had been off Daniel himself as he wheedled and whined to be allowed to indulge himself to his heart's content without paying up front.

When Daniel wakes up in a dog basket on the floor of the crack house, with a disgruntled Akita looking at him, he is shocked to find that he's run up a fifty pound bill.

"Yuh was up for it, man. There was no stopping yuh. Puffin' away like a lickle steam train, yuh was."

Daniel remembers being passed another can, and smoking a little bit of something, but fifty pounds worth...? He was already drunk when he'd got there so perhaps they are right. He'll have to take their word for it.

"Did I have a good time though?" Daniel laughs, trying to be cool. His laugh sounds like a bird being strangled.

"The best," one of his hosts answers, smiling with his mouth but not his eyes.

"Yuh've got until 5 o'clock to pay up!" whispers the dealer as Daniel leaves. "I know where yuh live, man!"

Daniel feels panicky and pukes up in the privet hedge which is at the bottom of the path that runs from the crack house to the street.

An old man wearing a blazer with some sort of regimental badge on the pocket is standing on the step of his home next door, smoking his pipe. He watches Daniel on his way. He's fed up of living next to a crack house; he thinks he would like to live in a country fit for heroes instead. Spain, perhaps.

Daniel Grundy's state has worsened by the time he has walked up Thompson Avenue and along Steelhouse Lane. He cuts through the scrubby park to Vicarage Road and is sick again by the children's swings.

When he gets to the shops, he discovers the shopkeepers aren't too pleased to see him and will not serve him. He stands in Jackson's shop shouting, "I want! I want! I want!" over and over. He's forgotten what he wants and then he sees the cans. He grabs at them and tries to pay for them with a bottle-top and a small stone that had taken his eye as he'd been looking in the gutter.

He is thrown out onto the street by a man in a bright orange turban. This isn't Mr Jackson. Mr Jackson sold up thirty years ago but his name remains, people unable to call the shop anything else. Mr Jackson would have thrown Daniel out too and probably given him a clip round the ear. The tall Sikh, who isn't Mr Jackson, goes back into his shop holding his nose. Some might say he was over-dramatising the smell but he really wasn't. Daniel stunk like a dead dog.

"I want! I want! I want a pound!" Daniel shouts at the passers by. "Go to the shop for me. They won't serve me. Pound! Pound! Pound!"

"Where did you get your hat?" he says to a big man with no smile. The hat is knitted. "It's stupid colours. Cat in a hat," thinks Daniel Grundy. "Green eggs and ham and a can," he shouts a shopping list.

Poor Daniel Grundy's head is caving in. "Pound! Pound! Pound!" goes his head. "Pound! Pound! Pound!" shouts his mouth. Daniel Grundy's world swirls. The man in the hat melts away without leaving a pound.

Two neighbourhood wardens pick him up. "You're nearly police and nearly traffic wardens," says Daniel. "You're nearly people." Daniel laughs at what he perceives to be wit. But all the neighbourhood wardens hear is a gurgling sound. They prop him up against a wall.

"Do you think we should call in for an ambulance?" says the one to the other.

"Dunno," says the other. "Can you hear us, mate?" he asks, touching Daniel's face. Daniel feels hot. He is burning up in the desert sun. He wants to dive into a pool, into a cool oasis pool.

"I need a drink," thinks Daniel Grundy's brain. "A nice cool drink of water-water-water-lager." When Daniel opens his eyes he doesn't see the neighbourhood wardens, he sees lime-green leaves spiralling on a distant tree and a sky empty of colour like a Tupperware box lid. Daniel Grundy is trapped in a lunchbox. "I'd like a sandwich," says Daniel Grundy, suddenly speaking clearly.

The neighbourhood wardens look at one another. "Maybe we'd better get an ambulance. His mouth's bleeding."

"Sandwich," says Daniel.

"He's wet himself," says the other, covering his mouth as the smell grows riper.

"Sandwich," repeats Daniel.

"Don't touch him then."

"Sandwich!"

"Can we have an ambulance? Vicarage Road. Top end by Sutherland Place."

"Sandwich!" screams Daniel. The crackling of the warden's radio is freaking Daniel out.

"Looks like he's fallen over. Drunk, yeah." The neighbourhood man in his fluorescent jacket looks at Daniel as he waits for a reply. "OK," he says into his radio. He turns to his buddy. "It's on the way."

Daniel fades out again, and dreams of the cat in the hat. He read it when he was six. It was the first book he ever read. "Well done, Daniel Grundy." It was also the only book he ever read all the way through. It gave him nightmares. It was like a bad trip. It never seemed to get anywhere. Played on a loop. Cat in the hat, hat in the cat. Daniel Grundy feels like he is playing on a loop, too.

The ambulance men recognise Daniel; it's been three times in less than a week. They scoop him up off the pavement. Bin men. Rubbish.

In casualty they say he's had another fit and there's nothing they can do for him if he doesn't stop drinking and doing drugs. Daniel Grundy isn't really listening. A fit is no good to him. He's had a fit but no sandwich, no beer, no brown. He'd been two hundred yards from his mother's where he would have got a sandwich, beer, and possibly brown, and then he fell. And now the hospital have let him go. He's three miles away from where he started. One step forward, three miles back. He walks home along the canal. It takes him four hours and thirteen falls, none of which, unluckily, had been into the cut. He is in such a mess he doesn't even notice the three-legged dog chasing the ducks. It is a funny sight. Daniel would have laughed if he'd noticed. Anyone would.

A woman with two black-and-white cats, each in their own basket, makes her way through to the vet's surgery. The cats have first names, middle names, and surnames; maybe the woman has too much time on her hands. She's called them Nicodemus Septimus Theobald and Barabas Archibald Blake. Who on earth do they think they are? Cats with middle names and surnames, it's ridiculous.

They are cats from two different relationships.

Nicodemus has had an accident in his cage. The vet lifts him out and weighs him on the scales before scooping up the bullet-hard shit. The cat does more hard shits which bounce on the stainless steel table, like peas in a colander. Bounce, bounce, bounce, three little bombs bouncing about the room.

Barabas, the other cat, has got wax in his ears. The kindly vet puts drops in and rubs them. "It's OK, sweetheart," says the vet to the cat. The woman stifles a giggle. It seems funny him calling Barabas, the cat that pisses up everything even though he's been done, "sweetheart". The vet says the cat has behavioural problems, says she needs to try a cat pheromone dispenser to calm him down. The vet shows her the little device that will plug into her mains and tells her it's only thirty-six pounds with a ten pound refill every few months.

When the vet turns his back to sort out a booster injection, Barabas bats his ears with his paw. Bat, bat, bat; a glob of ear wax flies out. Splat! It hits the wall. The woman goes to say something, then changes her mind. What should she say? "Excuse me but my cat, the one with behavioural problems, has batted ear wax up your wall." Some things are better left unsaid. She notices another shit bullet on the floor under the table. She reddens, and wants to get out as quick as she can. The vet sticks two needles, one for each cat, into the rolls of fat on the back of each of their necks. He disposes of the needles safely.

The woman leaves, taking the missile-firing cat and the cat with behavioural problems with her, and stopping at reception to buy the pheromone dispenser. Later in the week she will discover that Barabas has started pissing up that instead.

The vet watches her go and thinks about Sebastian waiting at home for him, and he smiles. Except Sebastian isn't at home! Sebastian Grundy has behavioural problems of his own. Separation anxiety! The vet had left the conservatory door open for Sebastian so Sebastian could have the run of the garden, but poor Sebastian Grundy doesn't like it when he can't see a human.

For a little while he was OK. He chewed up a couple of cushions off the cane furniture in the conservatory to keep himself occupied. Vets do work such long hours. Sebastian trotted round the garden and he howled a bit. Then he howled a bit more. Then he howled and howled until the neighbours twitched curtains and moaned about, "That gay vet bringing his work home with him again."

Sebastian Grundy can still dig even with three legs. He is very resourceful. He dug a hole at the back of the garden under the fence, which is stained blue because gardens are another room. He dug out onto the canal which runs at the back of the vet's house.

The dog is not really enjoying his freedom. He's still lonely. He misses the nice man who calls him sweetheart. He runs along the towpath. There aren't many people around at all. Sebastian is feeling sadder and sadder, and then he sees them. Ducks! He's never seen ducks before. What fun. When he barks, they quack. Ruff, quack, ruff ruff, quack quack. Sebastian likes the noise. He chases them up and down and into the water, then he hides in the bushes waiting for them to come back onto the path. When they do, he chases them again, taking a flying leap in the direction of a shocked mallard. Splosh! Sebastian Grundy falls in the canal. He doggy paddles about. He doggy paddles after the ducks. What fun. He doggy paddles for ages. When he's finally had enough, he can't get out. The bank's too steep. Poor Sebastian Grundy. What will he do?

Marilyn Grundy's door has been knocked more times in one day than it had been in a year. She'd answered it less than fifteen minutes ago when Nancy delivered the cod in parsley sauce, as promised. It is typical, she's not finished her tea, she can hardly move, and there is more knocking. It is an impatient, rude sort of knocking. Now there is shouting.

"Grundy. I'm gonna kick yuh white ass from here to fuckin kingdom come. Yuh hear me, Grundy. Yuh owe me, man." Marilyn shivers from her washed-out hair down to her twisted ankle. Even her white ass shivers. The voice is rich and full of something. Malevolence. Marilyn Grundy doesn't know the word but she doesn't need to know the word to know that the voice scares her.

Later, the knocker goes again. "Mom, it's me. Daniel." Her boy sounded childlike and she forgot for a second that he was a man, a man who had wrecked her house. Blood is thicker than water, everyone'll tell you that. It takes Marilyn five minutes to get to the door this time. She is slowing down. She should be speeding up.

Daniel comes in looking dreadful. He stinks. He walks past her, and when she gets back into the middle room he is sitting on her sofa eating the sandwich that Nancy had put up for Marilyn that morning. Marilyn hadn't felt like eating it, and had been saving it for supper. She looks at Daniel. She looks at the empty cage. She looks at the space in front of the gas fire.

"What happened to you?" asks Daniel. He eats, slapping his lips together. There is blood on the sandwich where he's bitten into it with his battered mouth. Marilyn can't believe him; doesn't he remember what happened the night before?

She musters all of her courage and says, "You can't stop here anymore!" That was it. "Well done, Marilyn Grundy," she thinks. "Go, Marilyn Grundy."

Daniel burst into tears, big snotty sobs running all over the sandwich. "I've had a fit. I need help. I've got nowhere to go." Whaaa, whaaa, whaaa. It's an act, Marilyn. It's an act. The Amazing Wailing Daniel Grundy.

Marilyn looks at her son. He is seven again, crying on the sofa. Crying because the kids at school had given him a kicking behind the big oak tree on the playground. They'd kicked him, broken his national health glasses and then he'd fallen on a tree root and cut his leg wide open. He'd come home that day and sobbed for hours and hours and in the end she'd had to hold him and rock him and rock him until he couldn't sob anymore. She'd kept him off school for a week, then she'd got scared the wagman would come looking for Daniel and so she sent him back. But Daniel hadn't gone back, instead, he'd walked in the front gate and had gone over the fence at the rear, heading for the canal. The canal was better than school. Daniel would spend many more days down the cut before his school days were over. He never wore his glasses again after the beating, and his eye strengthened. Every cloud.

Daniel Grundy has made himself seven again. Daniel is still sobbing. She sits on the sofa and puts an arm around her sad, smelly son. "I need help, mom." Marilyn nods. She is thinking the doctor. He's thinking £50 to pay off his debt. Make it £80 so that he can score some more and get a drink.

"We'll sort something in the morning, son." Marilyn is still thinking help from medical professionals. Daniel is thinking crisp new ten pound notes. Daniel finishes his sandwich and starts on the remainder of Marilyn's cod in parsley sauce.

That night, Marilyn sleeps on the sofa in the lounge and Daniel sleeps on the sofa in the front. Neither of them can manage the stairs.

It's 5.45 in the morning as Nancy knocks the door, a bowl of porridge in one hand. It is burning her, but she's tough. She has asbestos fingers; perhaps that is the source of her cough. She has a thermos flask which she has put down on the floor at her feet so that she can lift the knocker. Sandwiches are tucked in her overall pocket. Marilyn gets to the door in under four minutes, the sleep has done her good.

Nancy comes in. There is a shape on the sofa under a blanket in the front room, and the floor is littered with cans and other paraphernalia. Daniel hasn't heard the door. Not that Daniel would have got up off his good-for-nothing arse if he had.

"I told him he's got to go soon," whispers Marilyn.

The two women go through into the middle room. Nancy sets up everything Marilyn will need for the day and then clicks Marilyn's radio on. "Birra company. Summat tuh keep yow occupied."

When she leaves, Daniel is still asleep on the sofa in the front room. He is snoring now. Nancy slams the door to the middle room behind her and doesn't change her stride at all, in fact, if anything, she walks a little heavier. "Lazy bugger," she says out loud.

When Daniel finally wakes up and is coherent again, he wanders through to the middle room. His teeth are chattering and there is sweat on his forehead. His mother starts telling him about a local radio item, about how a fire crew had rescued a three-legged dog after it became trapped between a towpath and a 20ft wall. He is about to tell her to shut up but then he has a change of heart and listens.

"Perhaps they need a home for it," says Daniel.

Marilyn looks thoughtful. She looks at the space in front of the gas fire. "Do you think they might?"

"I could phone for you."

"Phone who?"

"The radio station, RSPCA, I dunno. Reckon I could find out where it's gone." Daniel gets his phone out of his pocket. He knows full well he hasn't got any credit.

"Oh dear, no credit," he says. Marilyn looks at the space in front of the gas fire again. She wouldn't mind a three-legged dog. It would be quite apt, she was without the use of a leg and the dog was without the use of a leg. And if Toby ever came back they could be company for each other.

"I've got a pound, I could go up the phone box," says Daniel. What a thoughtful boy he's becoming, spending his last pound on his mother.

"How much would it cost to get some credit on your phone?" asks Marilyn.

"I can get a ten pound top-up card."

There goes Marilyn, reaching for the purse. Marilyn, who has hardly got any money left in the house. She's already started on the bingo winnings.

"I've only got the change from my taxi."

"That'll do," says Daniel. "I'll get five pound." Off he goes, out into the early morning to get a five pound top-up. Top-up of Tennants Extra.

Marilyn doesn't get her hopes up too much because somebody else might have phoned about the three-legged dog, or maybe they'd found its owner. "That would be nice if they found its owner and it could be reunited with its family," she thought. Happy endings and all that.

Somebody else has heard the radio report and has phoned up. The kindly vet fetches Sebastian in his nice 4x4. Sebastian is sick on the leather seats and then he falls off them and bangs his stump when the vet goes round a roundabout. Once they get home the vet locks Sebastian in the house and he fills in the hole by the blue fence.

Sebastian looks out of the window, his electrified hair standing up on end. The vet looks back towards the dog, wistfully. He will have to find a better arrangement than this. He'll need to find Sebastian a better home; Sebastian needed to be with people who could be around more. The vet's lifestyle isn't much good for a dog. The vet's lifestyle isn't much good for anybody really. He is working too hard, and the man with the nice smile and the squashed genitalia isn't returning his calls.

Nancy curses. "New fangled bloody nonsense." She twizzles the seat round and round then sits on it. Now her eyes are above the green light. She stands up again and twizzles the seat the other way, two turns. She sits back down. Better, but still not level with the eyes on the screen. She stands up again and gives it another turn. She sits back down. For a second she is dizzy and she starts to cough a little. The automated voice starts talking to her. She listens and puts her money in when instructed, a two pound coin. She sits back and waits. She looks at her darkened image. Flash. That was one taken. The machine asks her if she wants to accept or reject the image. She looks at it. The light is shining off her glasses. She takes another. Flash. This time she's got her head tilted at a strange angle. She looks at the woman in the picture. It looks like her own mother staring at her. She accepts the image.

She waits outside the booth for the photos to be delivered. She takes them and looks about her, ashamed. She opens her jacket and sticks them in her overall pocket, tries to forget about them until she gets home.

It had happened again. She'd gone up town with every intention of sorting out the council tax problem and she'd ended up back in the post office. She'd spent two pounds on the photos and another 53p on an envelope that she didn't need so that she could get change. Now she's got £7.47 left. It seems like a silly amount to go and offer the council tax people so she decides to wait until she can get the money back up to a tenner.

On the way home she bumps into Emily who is up town shopping. "Orright, nan. You ay got a tenner you can borrow me, av ya? I've seen these trackie bottoms in Primark."

"Ar've onny got £7.47," says Nancy.

"That'll do. I'll rob the rest out of the money I've got put up for the rent. I can always put it back later in the week."

That night, after Billy has gone to sleep in his chair, Nancy goes into their Davy's room and sits on his bed. She gets the forms out and starts filling them in. Her hands feel cold and unbending. The pen sits awkwardly in her left hand. She never uses pens much except to write the odd betting slip or birthday card. She fills out her name, her address, her date of birth. It is going well. Her hand soon gets into forming the letters. She reads the instructions. "Counter-signing the photo," she says out loud. She reads the instructions again. Then again. She gets the photos out of her overall pocket and stares at them. She lights up a fag and coughs. The room is colder still and feels a bit damp, which makes the coughing worse.

She reads the instructions yet again. She looks around the room. She looks at the walls as though searching for a divine source of inspiration from the wallpaper. There is some grafitti of their Davy's done in biro near the ceiling. The word has spiky little letters: SLF, it says. What was that? Some band he'd been into. Something to do with fingers. She flexes the fingers on her one hand.

She re-reads the instructions about certification. It seems that she needs a professional person to sign the photographs. A professional person who knew Nancy and could say she was who she claimed she was.

"Bloody professional!" Who did Nancy know? Bernice had known her a good forty years. Marilyn had. Billy had. But publicans, depressed temporary agoraphobics, and retired foundry workers can't sign passport photos.

Nancy's shoulders feel stiff again. She rolls them round and round and bones crack. She lights another fag. Nancy has reached a hurdle. She isn't sure how she is going to get over it. She'll need a good run up. Nancy isn't sure she even wants to get over it. Australia. What if she didn't like it when she got there? If she got there!

She puts the passport forms and the photos inside the trolley in the cupboard. They sit on top of the bingo winnings with the mouldy onion.

"Well, it looks like er. Ar car be shuwah though," says Billy.

"The glasses aren't quite right," says Marilyn.

"That could be er overall. Check the pockets for a Bic lighter." Bernice comes right up close to Nancy and peers at her. Nancy is dumbstruck. She's standing in the dock in a court. There's a judge, complete with red robe and a wig. Her Vee is in the witness box.

The judge is a woman, wearing half-glasses and looking over them at Nancy like she's looking at a piece of abstract art and she's trying to get the measure of it.

"We only need one of you to sign to say it's her. Then she can go free," says the judge.

"I ay signin nothin," says Billy firmly, folding his arms defiantly. "I'm not sure either," says Marilyn, who for some reason is now wearing a pair of Mickey Mouse ears.

Nancy turns to argue with them.

"See! Tay er!" shouts Billy triumphantly. "Er never ad a wing!" Nancy blinks awake. "Tay the bloody photos uz need certifying," she thinks.

On Saturday morning holy hell descends on the street. There is such a caterwauling and a to-do going on that even Billy leaves his chair. He and Nancy stand on the step, their mouths open at the sight that meets their eyes.

A tall man with very defined muscles is bouncing Daniel's head off the lid of the green garden waste dustbin outside his mother's window (the council had insisted that the people in the street had the bins and no amount of explaining to the council that the houses didn't actually have gardens could make them take them away again, so it was nice in some small way to see them being used for something). The tall man is wearing dungarees which have the straps hanging down from his waist. He doesn't have a shirt on, which presumably signifies that he also knows how defined his muscles are. The tattoos on his skin have no colour, form strange tribal shapes as he moves.

Daniel is screeching, even though the banging of his head on the bin probably looks worse than it is. Marilyn is on her step waving a walking stick about, trying to get a strike in. "Leave him alone!" she cries.

"Is that the stick aht uv ower glory hole?" says Billy.

67

"Yes," says Nancy. It is the first time they've spoken properly since the row. Neighbours from up and down the street peer from doorways and windows. The smart green car is parked at an angle across the street. A red-skinned older man with knotted hair leans on his car door watching on approvingly. He puts his sunglasses on the top of his head. "Was fifty pound. Now it's a hundred pound, for the inconvenience."

"Mom, pay the man!" Daniel shouts. "Pay him...you wanna see me dead?"

The second man walks over to Marilyn. "Ah heard yuh 'ad a lickle win. I suggest yuh pay up, or yuh son gets it." He turns to his counterpart. "Show her, Colin. Show her how he'll get it." Colin puts two hands around Daniel's head and lifts it away from the bin before smiling at him and smashing Daniel's face into the brickwork next to his mother's front door. There is a collective wince from the onlookers.

"That's got to hurt," says Mrs Elwell, with relish.

Colin lets Daniel fall to the floor. The two men look around at the people calmly as if challenging them to say something or do something. The spectators start to drift away and go back inside.

Before the men get back into their car, the man who's clearly in charge walks over to the crumpled heap on the floor that is Daniel and, so that his mother can hear, says, "The alley behind the houses at 5pm. Give yuh chance to sort the money out. Don't make me come lookin again. Yuh know what arm sayin!"

Daniel scrapes himself up off the pavement and crawls back into the house. "You said you'd help me!" he accuses his mother.

Marilyn looks confused. "I meant I'd help you to sort yourself out, phone a doctor or something. I didn't mean I was going to pay for your drugs."

"Bitch!" spits Daniel.

Nancy walks over to them. Billy has gone inside in disgust. "Yow orright?"

"Yes, no thanks to this bitch," says Daniel. Blood is pouring from his nose.

"Ar wor talkin tuh yow." Nancy looks at Marilyn. Daniel goes into the house. "Wos tuh be done?"

"I'm going to have to pay them off. I don't want him dead."

"If yow pay em once, they'll cum agen."

"I'm frightened. I'll never forgive myself if something happens. I'll pay up, and then he's got to go. I'll give him until next Friday, the end of the week. Give him time to sort somewhere else out...with a friend maybe."

Nancy isn't convinced. Daniel didn't have any friends, she was sure of that, and if he did then they were as good for nothing as he was. "Ow yow gunna get the money to em? Yow car goo walkin abaht on that."

"I'll get Daniel to take it up."

"An then it woh get theyer, will it? E'll be off spendin it with sum other dealer an yow'll be back tuh square one."

Nancy shakes her head, she knows she shouldn't be getting involved. "Ar'll tek it," she says. Marilyn looks at the woman and thinks she is either very brave or a little mad, but she is grateful, nonetheless.

At 4.55pm precisely Nancy walks up the street, turns left, goes under an overgrown buddleia which is awash with white butterflies and heads up the alleyway which then turns to run between the back of a row of terraced houses and a line of filthy garages, many of their metal doors gone, tatted in years ago. The green sports car is parked up at the far end and the two dealers are sitting on the bonnet.

"Who's this? Granny smackhead?" The two men laugh.

"A debt's a debt," says Nancy, feeling slightly hypocritical. She's one to talk, what with the council tax in arrears. She really must sort that out on Monday. Nancy tries to ignore her thoughts about her unpaid bill and continues. "Ar'm here tuh pay off Daniel's debt. £100, courtesy of his mother." She fetches the money out of her overall pocket. It is wrapped in a Lidl carrier bag and she hands it over. "Count it!" she instructs.

"Nah, I trust yuh. Yuh've got an honest face. Innit, Colin?" The two men laugh at the old woman.

"Count it!" she says again.

Something about the way she says it makes them do it.

"It's all there!" Colin says to his boss.

"Doh sell Daniel anythin else. There's no mooer where that cum from. If yow sell im mooer stuff then it's on yower own head because e ay got the money tuh pay for it."

"What?" says Colin. "You can't speak to the man like that." He makes a move towards Nancy.

"Leave it. Let her go. Be off with yuh, lady, before I change mi mind."

Nancy stands her ground. "Doh sell Daniel anythin else. Ar want yower word."

The man that isn't Colin shakes his head in disbelief. He didn't know that old white ladies could be quite this feisty. Old black ladies yes, but not old white ladies. "Alright, yuh got mi word."

"Tell em all, Daniel Grundy ay gorrany money, norra bean. Tell em all not tuh gi' im anythin withaht the money up front."

"Yeah, I got yuh."

Nancy, not wanting to turn her back on the men, walks past them both to the other end of the alley and turns left onto All Saints Road and left again back onto Vicarage Road. She stops off at the chippy. "Pie un chips three times," she says to the man behind the counter. She's worked up quite an appetite. She treats Marilyn and the old goat to a portion each. She doesn't get much change from a tenner. "Three hours cleanin fuh a chip supper," she thinks to herself.

In the alley Colin is thinking his boss might have gone soft as he tries to justify himself. "Grundy's a fuckin pest, man. No skin off my nose not to supply him. It's more trouble than it's worth, dealing with boss-eyed bwoy."

On the quiet, he's a little phased, he's not used to dealing with people who aren't scared of him. Colin is relieved when his boss pulls the gun out of the back of his jeans where it's been tucked and waves it about. "Come on, nah. We got some overdue rents to get."

Nancy knocks on Marilyn's door. Daniel answers it. "Is it paid?" Nancy is taken aback. She hadn't realised that Marilyn would tell him that she was sorting it out. She nods. Daniel smiles. "She must trust you very much, to have given it to you." Nancy ignores him and walks through to the middle room.

"Brought yow sum chips un uh pie. Day know if yow liked salt and vinegar so ar gorrim tuh leave it off. There's a tub of mushy paes theyer too."

"I don't know what I'd do without you at the moment."

"Nor me," Nancy says. "E woh be gerrin' anymore stuff unless e pays furrit up front, so if yow doh gi' it then he car gerrit!" Nancy says this loud, so that Daniel can hear. "D'yow ear that, Daniel Grundy?"

Daniel comes in the room, laughing. "They ay gunna stop giving me stuff cos you say so."

"We'll see," says Nancy. "We'll see."

Nancy goes home and in to her own middle room.

"Where yow bin?" he asks.

"To gerrus sum chips. Un a pie." She gets a plate apiece and they eat chips and pie out of the paper, like they're on the seafront somewhere. There is a melting of iciness as Billy finds the pickled egg she's brought him. He thinks it's her way of saying she's sorry about the passport thing. He's wrong; it's her way of saying she's sorry for sloping off and facing down armed gangsters, but he isn't to know that.

Their Chrissie turns up before dinner time. It is Sunday. Nancy hasn't even started the dinner; she's only just got back from cleaning. It's taken her longer than usual but they'd had a stripper on in the back room at the Dartmouth and Bernice was worried about the baby oil being a trip hazard. Bernice had recently been on a health and safety course at the brewery and was up on all the lingo. Nancy ended up scrubbing the tiles twice.

Chrissie suggests that her parents should come to hers for Sunday dinner. She's done a roast and it is ages since they'd all sat round for a meal together. Billy, predictably, says it will be too much of an effort to go visiting, and anyway he prefers Sundays in his own house.

"Ar'll cum even if e woe," says Nancy.

Billy raises his eyebrows as if he is going to say something. He feels guilty, and remembers the pickled egg from yesterday.

"Ah, goo on, Dad." Chrissie smiles at him half-heartedly, knowing full well he won't. Nancy thinks about the passport forms again and the gangsters and then she feels guilty too. She is about to do a U-turn, to stay in and get his dinner, when another bomb goes off.

"Orright, we'll booth come, cock," Billy says.

Nancy and her daughter both make the same shocked face at one another, and in that moment they look alike.

"Abaht an hour then," stutters Chrissie, still taken aback. Billy looks at her. How had his little girl become a grandmother? She smiles back at him. "The kids am coming too with the littluns," she adds. "Thought we might go down the Monkey House after," says Chrissie, pushing her luck. Billy thinks about buying crisps and pop for Chantelle and Wrayon.

He smiles, and the two women exchange another look.

Nancy wonders, as she gets herself ready, if maybe the old goat, having got out of his chair twice in a week, might be overdoing it in his attempt at a hat trick. She puts on a smart skirt and a matching lavender jacket, and pins a small cameo to the neck of her blouse. One of their Davy's girlfriends had bought it for her. Which one was it? She can't remember now. As she pulls a pair of cream heels from under the bed, she even starts to wonder again about getting Billy to go further afield. It might be possible. She tries to squeeze her foot into one of the shoes. Her feet have spread out in her trainers. She looks at her trainers and puts them back on. She puts the shoes in a plastic bag. She could probably manage to keep them on through dinner, but walk in them? Torture! Perhaps she could put them on before they went in the pub, too.

When she gets downstairs Billy is sitting in his chair also trying to squeeze his feet into shoes. "Ar've put mine in a bag," she says.

"Ar car goo up the row'ud in mi carpet slippers, con I?"

Nancy goes in the kitchen and finds a shoehorn from the cupboard under the sink. She walks back in and gives it to him. Even in a sitting position he can hardly reach to get the horn in between the back of his shoe and his heel, but he manages it. "Bleedin 'ell," he says as he stands up. Nancy is unsure whether he's cursing about his tight shoes or the effort of being upright.

"Oh shit, ar ought tuh tek er uh sandwich or summat... I wuz gunna do er uh portion uv ower dinner," says Nancy, talking about Marilyn.

Billy tuts. "Ar cor abide waitin," he says to the back yard through the window, which is a strange thing for a man to say who sits all day in his chair doing nothing else but.

They knock Marilyn's door and hand her the sandwiches, explaining that they are going out for the day. "Don't you

73

both look nice," says Marilyn, beaming. Nancy has got some beetroot on her blouse and is trying, in vain, to scratch the stain off. They walk up the road in silence. Chrissie's is only a few streets away. Nancy realises it has been ages since they've gone to Chrissie's.

Billy has lifted the door knocker when Nancy stops him. "Owd up," she says. She kicks her trainers off and puts the court shoes on the path, stepping into them. "Jesus!" she says as she gets them on. She is putting the trainers in the bag when Chrissie opens the door and lets them in. When they walk in, the house is full. The kids are all already there. Neil takes their jackets. Billy is given the best chair and Nancy goes in the kitchen. She opens a window to let the steam out. Emily is stirring something.

"Orright, nan," she says smiling. "I ay got ya tenner yet." Nancy has forgotten about it; she didn't expect to get it back anyway.

"Yow've got summat on yower tooth," says Nancy. "Cabbage or summat."

Emily runs her tongue over her teeth.

"Has it gone?" Nancy peers at her again.

"No. Still theyer."

Emily keeps running her tongue over her teeth and smiling. "Has it gone now?"

"No!"

"Nan, it's my tooth gem!" Emily laughs and gives a wider smile to show it off.

"Yower wot?"

"Like teeth jewellery," says Chrissie as she comes into the kitchen. It was like the old days; it was nice to be around family, you could always be cheered up by the madness.

"Yow 'eard this, Billy?"

"Wassat?"

"Tooth jewellery. Show im, Emily." Emily rolls her eyes

74

but goes in and smiles at her grandad.

"Looks like uh birra cabbage."

"Thas wot ar said," Nancy agrees.

"Youse lot know nuffin about style," she says, and goes back to stirring the custard for the trifle.

"I'm thinking of having my belly button pierced," says Chrissie.

"They'll need to use a harpoon!" Neil smirks, and the boys all laugh. Chrissie flicks him with a tea towel and he feigns being injured. They smile at each other. Nancy watches them. Things had settled out. There'd been badness in the past but maybe they'd grown up or grown together or something. They seemed content.

Dylan's phone goes. "Back in five," he shouts, "Jus' gotta go out." Nancy likes being around the to-ing and fro-ing. Billy is balancing Chantelle on one knee and Wrayon on the other. He looks happy in a little world of his own with the children laughing and the adults smiling and joking. Nancy wishes she was up home so she could go out on the step for a while. It wouldn't seem right going out on somebody else's step.

When the dinner is done they all sit round where they can. There is no table; it wouldn't have fitted in the room. Dylan comes back and fetches his plate out of the oven. He crouches up the corner with it balanced on his knees and starts to tuck in. His phone goes again. "Yeah, yeah. Sorted. Ten." He stands up and puts the dinner back in the oven. "Gotta go." Nancy doesn't mind the coming and going. She likes the action.

Neil looks at Dylan. "Can't you give it a rest for five minutes? Your nan and grandad have come!"

"You doh mind do you, nan?" says Dylan with a cheeky grin. He can get round his nan. She's a bit soft with him. It is something about his smile. She shakes her head. "See, dad, nan don't mind. I'm only going for five minutes."

"Make sure you save a little ting for me," says Jackie.

"What you want?"

"Ten. Nah, make it twenty."

"Twenny wot?" asks Billy.

"Fags, grandad," says Jackie with a smirk.

Neil looks cross. He is turning into an old man, thinks Nancy. He'll be sticking to his chair before Chrissie knows it.

The tension doesn't last long. As soon as Dylan is gone the easy-going air returns.

After pudding they all head off down the Monkey House. They have to wait for Nancy to change into her trainers for the walk. Dylan gets back in time to make some wisecracks about "Nans in Nikes." He takes off his baseball cap and plonks it on his nan's head backwards. The family laugh at her again.

They say that cleanliness is next to godliness and there must indeed be some truth in the rumour. It's Sunday, the Sabbath, and Daniel Grundy is in the bath. How he's got there is a mixture of desperation and cunning on Marilyn's part.

The smell was starting to overwhelm her. She suggested politely that he might like to relax in a hot tub of soapy water and that she'd put the immersion on for him if he'd like. Daniel had refused quite politely, saying he was shaky and didn't feel able to go to the bathroom. Marilyn had pressed the point by saying that she really couldn't stand the smell any longer, to which Daniel had responded, "What smell?"

"Daniel, if you take a bath I'll give you ten pounds!" She couldn't help it. She was feeling stick to her stomach. The magic words lit up his eyes and in the next stale breath he was up and into the bathroom. He had peeled off his clothes, quite literally peeled, or that's how it appeared to Marilyn; she was trying not to look but she was determined to get the clothes in the washing machine and needed to see when they were off his back. They were almost stuck to him; his trousers turned inside out as he took them off and the smell seemed to get worse as if little pockets of stench had been trapped between skin and fabric.

He'd lowered himself into the hot water. He was skinny and looked like those living skeletons they pulled out of the piles of bodies in the concentration camps. Marilyn had seen the footage of them. His shoulders, shoulder blades, elbows, pelvic bones, knees, ribs and vertebrae stuck out, protruding from his pasty skin in an obscene manner. His penis was dark and shrivelled up. He didn't try to hide himself from her; he had no shame, it seemed. How had he got like this? Those people in the death camps had ended up like that through evil forces unleashed upon them, through no fault of their own; Daniel had done this to himself, through choice it seemed. It was offensive.

Marilyn gets a bar of soap from the cupboard. She takes it in and hands it to him. "A tenner, you said," says Daniel, refusing to take the soap until she nods. The bath water is already grey. Marilyn hobbles back through to the kitchen, pulling the bathroom door to.

"Don't fall asleep in there." She puts on rubber gloves and grabs his clothes off the floor, putting the whole lot in the washing machine, trainers and all.

She puts the dial to sixty degrees and pours in three times as much powder as she usually does. She adds a capful of Comfort.

Daniel stays in the bath for a good hour and a half. Marilyn goes in from time to time to make sure he hasn't drowned and to let a bit of water out and top it up with some fresh warm. She even adds a drop of disinfectant. He's dozing rather than sleeping and she's not too concerned that he'll drown. By the time he comes into the middle room wrapped in a towel, his clothes are hanging in front of the fire on a clothes horse. They're steaming, and so is the cup of tea that's next to them. A couple of pieces of buttered toast are also waiting for him. Marilyn's ankle is now raging from standing up for too long to prepare drink and food that Daniel doesn't deserve.

Daniel seems quite refreshed, almost normal. He's even attempted a shave of sorts. There are pieces of toilet roll stuck to his face where he's bled. He doesn't even moan when she asks him to put *Songs of Praise* on the telly. Daniel plugs in the TV then sits back down and eats some of his toast and slurps his tea. Marilyn studies him, it's almost like he's losing his faculties one by one. He eats like his brain isn't really working; it's very strange to watch her adult son regress into something almost apelike. Subhuman is the word that comes to her mind as she watches him. His toenails need cutting, they're curling over, almost like claws.

"Gis it then," Daniel says. He's after his tenner. The light appears in his eyes again, proving he's not quite dead.

"Cut your toenails first," says Marilyn.

"Ya day say I had to cut my toenails," responds Daniel.

"Part of having a bath," she replies. She hands him some nail clippers. Daniel cuts the nails on his feet slowly and painfully, making a song and a dance about having to do them.

When he's finally done, Marilyn tells him to lift up the one end of the telly and there underneath is a crisp flat ten pound note. He's shocked. He'd never of thought of looking there. Daniel stands up, goes through into the kitchen. "Where's me clothes?"

"They're here, Daniel. Right under your nose."

Marilyn points towards the clothes horse as Daniel comes back in and looks at the garments as if he doesn't recognise them. He starts to put them on.

"They're still wet, Daniel."

He ignores her and continues. She gives up. She's learning that there's no point arguing. Perhaps she should pay him another tenner not to put them on until they're dry.

Daniel is dressed. "He looks quite respectable," thinks Marilyn optimistically. She considers her son again with a more realistic eye and revises her thoughts. "Well, he looks cleaner than he did," is all she can really say about the matter. He is steaming a little as he takes his mother's tenner and heads for the street.

Once he gets out into the road he makes sure no one is looking and tries the Maddoxes' front door. His mother had casually mentioned in conversation, one-sided conversation, that they'd gone out for the day. He goes up the alley between the houses and puts his hand over the gate, feeling for the bolt. He shoots it back and gets into their yard. He tries the back door. Lucky for them they've been careful. He thinks about smashing a window and going in, but the tenner, already in his pocket, is nagging away at him. But he'll come again; he'll get that money somehow.

Back in the Grundy house, Marilyn is spraying the sofas and carpets with Febreze. She's not sure what's in it but it works. The smell of Daniel is gone by the time the *Antiques Road Show* starts. Marilyn imagines an ad campaign where a glamorous seventy-something-year-old mother of two sprays her alcoholic, drug addict son with a bottle of the wonder chemical and he comes up clean and smelling of roses. They both smile for the camera and little starbursts flash off their ultra-clean teeth.

The Monkey House is lively for a Sunday. The Maddox family (Chrissie would always be a Maddox and so would her kids, even though she'd married a Jackson) are all sitting in the kids' room. There are a few families in and all the kids are playing together, running outside to the play area and running back to blag pop and crisps off their parents who give in every time. Nancy watches Billy playing cards with Neil, Liam, Dylan and one of the Flanagans (she's not sure if it's the one who won the pools or the one who went to prison for blackmail).

She's had a couple of barley wines and is feeling relaxed. She's kicked the cream shoes off under the table and is talking to their Chrissie. Rubbish really, chit chat, family gossip. Chrissie thinks their Dylan has got a girl on the go, can't work out who and she's worried about how Chantelle isn't speaking very early but she doesn't want to upset Emily by saying anything in case she starts thinking the kid is backwards or something. Nancy says truthfully, "Yow day spake propa till yow was three!" which shuts Chrissie up for a second. She changes her track of conversation but still keeps looking at Chantelle fearfully for signs of a special school future.

"Yow heard from Auntie Vee?" says Chrissie, smiling. Auntie Vee always brought a smile to the kids' faces. They loved her.

"Ar," says Nancy, trying to leave it at that.

"Well. How is er?"

"Orright, ar'spose."

"How's Norman?" Aunty Vee had re-married in her sixties to Norman, who was a self-made man. An Australian! How she'd managed to meet a self-made Australian man down Low Hill had been something of a puzzle to all the family but she had, and that self same self-made man had whisked her off Down Under.

"Purrin uh gairms room in fuh their kids, e is." Chrissie and her mother both look around the Monkey House family room. There are two Disney posters and a chalk board. The cards Billy and company are playing with can be borrowed from behind the bar, as can the set of dominoes, but the double blank is missing. It disappeared in June 2003 when a toddler from Myatt Avenue found it on the floor one night. When nobody was looking she toddled off outside, and buried it under the slide in amongst the shredded bark.

"That'll be nice for em," Chrissie says. Nancy and Chrissie sip their drinks but say nothing for a while.

Whether it is the barley wine or the nice family atmosphere making her feel secure, she isn't sure, but whatever the reason Nancy lets her mouth run away with her. Well, not run exactly, but walk a little too far.

"Asked me an yower Dad tuh goo ova." Chrissie doesn't say anything. She knows her mother and dad wouldn't go. Not that far. Never in a month of Sundays. "Ar've got the passport forms." Chrissie looks sideways at her mother. A brief glance. Never in a million years.

"Doh know oo tuh get tuh countersign the photos, though," says Nancy, almost to herself.

"Countersign?" says Chrissie. This was new. This was month of Sunday stuff, million years stuff.

"Hey, Dad!" shouts Chrissie. She had been going to say, "Wot's this about you pair gooin to Australia?" But Nancy pre-empts it and grabs Chrissie's arm.

"Sshhh!" she says, digging her nails in hard without meaning to.

"Oww!" Chrissie pulls away from her mother's grasp.

"E doh know."

"What? He doh know he's gooin to Australia?"

"E ay gooin. Says e doh wannu. E doh know ar'm agooin!"

At that moment Lizzie comes over, bored of chatting up the barman, and notices the awkward silence between her mother and her nan. "Wot's up?"

"Your nan's pissed," hisses Chrissie, looking away from Nancy before leaning her elbow on the table and resting her head on one hand.

Daniel Grundy has got himself a woman! He's found her on Vicarage Road standing on a corner. It is raining. A thunder storm has broken the warm spell. It is pouring down and she is standing there drowned, like a little rat. He stares at her for a bit from out of the phone box. He is part sheltering and part wondering who on earth to phone next. His dealer isn't answering the phone, which rings out and out. Surely that Maddox woman doesn't have this kind of power. "Witch!" thinks Daniel.

He waits a while longer and watches the girl pacing up and down. He starts to feel quite sorry for her. That's not true, he is desperate for a hit, and what he actually starts to feel is like he might have found another meal ticket. Daniel saunters over. In his head at least it's a saunter, in reality it's more of a shuffle.

"You want business?" she asks.

"Nah," says Daniel. "Wanna come to mine for a warm and a cup of tea?" She looks at him as if trying to work out what he's about. She works it out quite quickly.

"You got any gear?" she asks. Daniel looks her in the eyes and notices they are a bit crossed, like his own. For some inexplicable reason it makes him want to tell the truth.

"No," he says. "I was hoping you might have some." She looks at him again. She notices that his eyes are slightly crossed, and for some reason she wants to tell the truth.

"I have," she says. Daniel's pulse quickens and his stomach turns over. It's love. The brown is in sight and it's love. They walk down to his mother's. It is embarrassing not having a key and having to knock. Daniel thinks to himself that if he had all of the bingo winnings he wouldn't be beholden to his mother. That he wouldn't have to beg for money. He could clear off, taking the money with him, and sit pretty for the rest of his life. He looks at his new girlfriend; maybe he would take her with him and they'd both sit pretty. Three and a half minutes later Marilyn's face peeps round the door.

"Oh it's you, Daniel." She looks at the girl standing with him.

"This is my mate," he says, struggling for a name. Millions of girls' names, and he can't think of one. "Haven't seen her for years," he adds, trying to sound convincing.

Marilyn has seen her more recently than that, only a couple of weeks before, standing on the corner of Raby Street, but she doesn't say anything. She isn't judgemental. How can she be? She's had her bus driver phase. It wasn't for money or anything, but she had to admit she'd had one or two free bus rides out of the experience. Marilyn opens the door and starts to hobble off, leaning heavily on her stick.

"Oh, what you done?" asks the girl who hasn't been introduced because she doesn't have a name.

"Trod on a glass," chorus Daniel and his mother.

Daniel reaches behind the sofa in the front room and fetches out the tinfoil as the girl follows him in. His mother is still hobbling off. "Hang on, what about my cuppa?" says the girl with no name to Daniel.

"Fuckin 'ell!" growls Daniel, getting narkey because he's rattling.

The girl with no name makes for the door, heading back on to the street. Daniel sees his meal ticket escaping and goes on a charm offensive. "Sorry," he says. "You know how it is!" The girl with no name nods. She does know how it is, but luckily she has her habit under control now. She paces herself and knows how much she needs, takes it at regular intervals.

She sells herself to meet her habit. She doesn't have to steal anymore, she just has to sleep with men, sell the bits that men want. Simple. Sorted.

"I'll put the kettle on," says Marilyn. "You look drownded. Come in here and sit by the fire a bit." The girl with no name follows Marilyn through into the middle room. She sticks her tongue out at Daniel. He follows the girl with no name to make sure she doesn't escape.

"You should sit down," says the girl with no name to Marilyn. "I'll stick the kettle on. Make you a cuppa. Shouldn't be walking on that foot." Marilyn relents and sits, turning the gas fire up to full beforehand. The girl with no name busies herself in the kitchen and finds everything she needs. "There aren't many cups," she comments. Marilyn looks at Daniel but says nothing. The girl with no name brings two mugs through and hands one to Daniel and one to Marilyn. She goes back and fetches her own tea which is in a china cup. She doesn't sit in a chair, she sits as close as she can to the fire. Daniel is fidgeting. The girl looks at the empty cage with the open door. She looks up around the room at the curtain rails as if searching for the missing bird. She doesn't ask. Marilyn watches her as she does it, looks at Daniel, and thinks about the canary.

The one side of the girl's hair starts to dry and as it does it kinks up a little into waves. The other side still hangs poker straight and wet. A girl with no name is in front of the fire in Toby's space, and Marilyn quite likes it. It feels like family. She thinks about the grandchildren again, until Daniel goes and spoils it.

"Come in the front now," he says. The girl rubs her hands and her face as though trying to rub feeling into the numbness. She has felt the family thing too, but now the spell is broken. She is torn between the fire and the front. The front is close to the street. The fire is close to memories of a time when things had been more normal. She chooses the front room

84

with Daniel, back to the colder air, and the draughts from the street which remind her that her new life is not far away.

Daniel starts ripping off a square of foil. "I'm not smoking it. It's a waste. You got any works?" she says. Daniel shakes his head, thinking about the unused needles in the bathroom. She opens her bag and takes out her own needle, and the bag of brown. The beautiful bag of brown. Daniel is in love again, stomach flipping and turning. She takes out a little brown bottle and shakes it holding it up to the light. "Shit," she says, ascertaining there is none left. "You got any citric?"

"Uh?"

"Lemon juice. Anything?"

Daniel goes back into the middle room where Marilyn is sitting staring at the place where Toby had used to lie and where the girl with no name had been sitting. "You got any lemon juice, Mom?" She looks at him, puzzled.

"Pancake day," she says dozily.

"Uh?"

"In the fridge, left from pancake day."

He runs to the fridge and finds a Jif plastic lemon wedged at the back behind some margarine. He shakes it. It's nearly full.

He goes back through to the front. "She likes lemon in her tea," he comments to his mother in passing, by way of explanation. He gives the girl with no name the plastic lemon. She looks at him and then laughs at his eager face.

"Come on! Come on!" he says.

"Calm it down. You're like a Jack Russell with a cloth."

Daniel passes her a lighter. It is a yellow Bic lighter he's found on the shelf where the mirror used to hang. He doesn't know where it's come from, because his mother doesn't smoke.

The girl isn't prepared. She'd planned to go home and take her next fix. "You got a spoon? An' a belt?" Daniel is spinning the wheel on the lighter but nothing doing. "And another

85

lighter by the look of it," she says sarkily. She is starting to rattle now too and getting angsty. Daniel is going mad with the anticipation. He runs back through to his mother.

"Matches?" he says.

"No, love."

"Fuckin 'ell! Candles?" says Daniel in desperation.

"In the drawer," his mother says. She hears cutlery clanking as Daniel grabs a spoon. "Not that drawer, love, the one with the pens and the batteries in." The candles he finds have been there since the winter of discontent; all those bread strikes and power cuts it was good to be prepared, you never knew when these things might happen again.

Marilyn is more than half asleep now. She is pleased Daniel has got a new friend. "That wouldn't have happened without him having that bath," she congratulates herself. "Maybe a little romance would do him good, straighten him out." She thinks Daniel wants the candles to create a bit of mood lighting. Wrong again, Marilyn.

Daniel finds the candles and lights one of them off the gas ring before running back through to the middle room and heading upstairs, dripping wax on the carpet as he goes. He finds a belt in his mother's wardrobe. It is a pretty, spangled affair. He can't imagine her wearing it now. For a second he gets an image of a blonde woman in a roll-necked sweater with a belt round her nipped-in waist, and a smile on her face. He shakes his rattling head and the image is gone, like a fruit machine nudge. Beautiful blonde lady. Nudge. Washed-up bedraggled woman.

Marilyn wakes a little as he comes back downstairs. Tin foil, belts, disappearing lemon juice, candles and teaspoons. The boy's gone mad.

Back in the front, the girl with no name puts the brown and the lemon juice into the spoon and holds it over the candle. She takes a fag out of her bag and rips some of the filter out, puts it in the spoon. The tip of the needle nestles in the filter. She draws back the plunger and takes the liquid up into the microfine.

"I've only ever really smoked," says Daniel. She looks at him. "I don't like needles," he says.

"Well, you better get used to it."

She points the point upward. Flicks her middle finger against the plastic. Air bubbles rise to the top, she presses the plunger to release them. She believes him about not using needles. "You better have the first hit," she says.

Daniel takes the belt and ties it around his arm tightly. He squints for a second as if he can't look but then focuses and watches fascinated as the veins in his arm come up easily. He allows her to stick the needle in, pull the plunger back until blood appears in the barrel of the syringe and then he allows her to press the plunger gently, lovingly. His fear of the needle evaporates with her in control. 1 second: she takes the needle out of his arm. 2 seconds: she undoes the buckle of the belt. 3 seconds: she slips the belt off his arm. 4 seconds: Daniel sits on the sofa. 5 seconds: she slips the belt up her own arm. 6 seconds: she tightens it. 7 seconds: she tightens more. 8 seconds: BANG! Daniel Grundy is in heaven. Orgasm. Love.

The girl has her own fix. It takes her a while to find a vein. She injects herself left-handed. Laying the needle upwards. Towards her. Two fingers hold the cylinder. A thumb pushing the plunger away from herself. A spot of blood. An expert thumb pushes the plunger in. She waits for her hit.

The kindly vet had been out for a pub lunch with the man with the nice smile, and tried to rectify the squashed genitalia incident. They were at least talking. They talked over a carvery and a very nice bottle of red. Then they went walking alongside a river, and maintained a truce. They even managed a quick fumble in the woods. The kindly vet received most of the fumbling because the man with the nice smile still wasn't up to it.

The man drops the vet off, but says he won't come in. He's peering towards the house as though looking for signs of dangerous dogs lurking. The vet is disappointed, but waves him off and then goes inside.

Sebastian Grundy has eaten a cushion. A cushion hand made by the girl who works in the art gallery shop part time and does textile design the rest of the week. It had been a very nice felt cushion. Everybody always commented. Sebastian Grundy had liked the cushion, too. He was getting into the toy thing but he wasn't yet able to distinguish between toys and soft furnishing. The cushion didn't have eyes or a squeaker but Sebastian Grundy often didn't pick up on the little details of life; like missing legs, for example.

The vet sighs and makes a decision. He phones his mother. "He's a lovely dog. He needs more company than I can give him."

It is a long conversation but by the time he comes off the phone he's talked his mother into giving Sebastian Grundy a go.

It is pouring with rain when they leave the Monkey House. They hadn't meant to stop out so late, but it had been such good fun. It is nearly ten o'clock as they walk down the road in silence, the rain running off their faces and down inside their collars but even that doesn't seem to dampen the mood.

The light is on in the bottom shop. "Ar'll get some fakes

fuh mornin," says Nancy. As they go in, Reeta is mopping the floor, and her husband is pulling the security grille down on the cigarette counter.

"Only just!" he says amiably. He reaches in and pulls out ten fags and puts them on the counter. A little girl comes through from the back room and smiles at Nancy.

"Which one's this un?" says Nancy.

"It's Kuhli's eldest. Say hello to Nancy, Ravinder," says Reeta coming up to the counter. The little girl smiles a gap-toothed shy smile and then runs off back the way she came through a curtain of fine pink chains.

"Er's a pretty little wench, ay er?" says Nancy.

"Takes after her grandad," says Reeta's husband laughing. "Big family celebration tomorrow," continues Reeta's husband, puffing up his chest. "Everybody is back home to see Pritvi graduate. First class degree."

"Law," says Reeta, almost as puffed up as her husband.

"Oh ar," says Billy, not really listening but registering enough to realise he is supposed to react.

"Remember uz to er," says Nancy.

The rain is slowing as they walk the last few yards up to their house from the shop. When they get in, Billy makes a cup of tea. The day is full of surprises. He puts three sugars in Nancy's tea. It's been ten years since she's taken three sugars but she doesn't say anything.

Nancy puts the fire on and she goes to draw the curtains. As she does so, something catches her eye. There is a shape in the dark; it looks like a man lying on the shed roof, a man with a strange-shaped head. She stares through the oval lenses of her glasses and on through the window, cupping her hands around her face to stop the reflected light. "Con yow see summat on the roof?" Billy comes to the window and looks.

"Wheyer?"

"Theyer!"

"The kids frum ova the back uv probly kicked uh ball on theyer or summat." Nancy is not satisfied with that explanation and goes out of the back door. Billy follows, tutting. They set next door's security light off as they get outside. Next door have become very security conscious since they started growing cannabis in the loft.

"Towd ya. Nothin theyer. Ow many uv them barley wines did yow av?" He is right, there is no sign of a ball, or a man's head. Shadows. Tricks of the light.

They go back in.

Daniel Grundy has grazed his nose as he slid down in between the back of the shed and the fence to hide. He's skinny enough to fit almost anywhere. Rats. Drainpipes. He waits for the lights to go out in the Maddox house and then pops his peanut head out from behind the shed to make sure the coast is clear. He forgets about the security light and it comes back on. He freezes, but the Maddoxes are both snoring, out like lights as soon as they sat in their chairs, not even managing to finish their teas.

Daniel makes a run for it but he'll keep watching them, he'll wait and he'll get his chance. Today had been brilliant. Today the girl had helped him overcome his fear of needles and that hit had been the best thing he'd ever known. He would take her away from all this and she would inject him every day, living happily ever after off his mother's winnings.

Nancy isn't entirely sure if she has dreamt the answer to one of her problems so much as figured it out as she's woken up. She has some recollection of a dream where she was wearing one of those daft hats that the teachers used to have on their heads in the cartoon strips, the ones the kids wear when they finish university. In the dream she'd been sitting on a bus going somewhere and everyone was staring at her hat. She felt trapped, like if she took it off then she'd draw more attention to herself, but if she left it on then every new person that got on the bus would point and then the attention would start again.

Daniel Grundy is attempting to mither his mother to death. "Go on. I need fifty quid. I owe someone else, big time. Not the guys from the other day, some other people. Some other people who are worse." Daniel spits as he talks, and white slime collects in the creases where his top lip joins the bottom one. He is very focussed on his story. He's repeated it so often in the last three hours he almost believes it himself.

Marilyn is trying to watch the television, trying to ignore the mithering. "Fifty quid won't kill ya." The news is intercut with his whingeing voice. The newsreader blah blah blahs on about inflation. Daniel blah blah blahs on about fifty quid to pay a debt. The newsreader blah blah blahs on about falling crime rates. Daniel blah blah blahs on about how he will soon be found dead in a gutter. He asks his mother how she will feel then. The newsreader blah blah blahs on about the weekend football results. Daniel blah blah blahs on about the kicking he will get. Graphic details of spilled guts and snapped bones are shared with his mother and the newsreader.

Marilyn tries to get out of her head the malevolent voice that shouted through her letterbox, and the scene in the street on Saturday.

"Daniel, for mercy's sake! I don't have any money in the house." She finally snaps and engages in his, up until this point, one-sided conversation. Mistake.

91

"Well, go and get some then. From her over the road. Your best mate."

"She's not got any money there now," Marilyn lies.

Then Daniel plays his trump card. "I bet you'd give it to our Shane. You've always preferred him to me."

Both of their minds flit back to the day that Marilyn had taken a sickie. The day she'd thought he was at school but he wasn't. The Wednesday in question, Daniel Grundy had wagged, as he often did since the glasses incident, but it was freezing cold so he'd gone home, watching from the back yard until his mother, who was hoovering and tidying, went upstairs for something. He had crept in through the back door, snuck through the kitchen into the middle room and hidden in the glory hole. He'd fallen asleep under some coats which smelt like old tents, but had awoken when he heard voices. He had strained to hear, tuning in to pick up his mother and a man talking. He heard the man say, "Why don't you come away with me for the weekend?"

Daniel had frozen in horror. "I can't," he heard his mother answer. "The boys."

"Leave em with someone," said the man. Daniel's heart had started to thump in his chest.

"They wouldn't stop with anyone," Marilyn said, and then she paused as though she was thinking. "Well, Shane might. But Daniel..." His mother didn't complete the sentence.

"He's a bloody mummy's boy, that kid," the man had said.

"I do sometimes wish he was more like Shane."

Daniel felt sick. He started to panic. He wasn't sure how long he'd been standing their reeling before he heard his mother making animal noises. He came out of the cupboard and peeped in through the door. He saw the man lying on top of his mother. She had one leg up on the sofa and the man was pounding away at her. Daniel thought his mother was hurting, the noise she was making. He was scared, he wanted to protect her. He wanted to drag the man off his mother. But his mother wanted him to be Shane. His mother loved Shane more than she loved him.

Why wasn't the dog barking? The dog lay quietly in front of the fire throughout the incident. In Daniel's imagination, it was Sheppie. In his mother's it was the one before that, Judy. But both of them remembered the dog sleeping in front of the fire. Daniel also had the clear image of his mother being fucked. Marilyn's picture is one of Daniel, standing screaming while she stares at him helplessly from underneath the bus driver whose name was... she can't remember now. She can only remember that he drove the 79, mostly, and that his wife didn't understand him.

Marilyn didn't even realise what Daniel had heard. She didn't mean she loved Shane more. She didn't say it that way. She hadn't known Daniel had been in the cupboard. The bus driver had cuffed Daniel because he was put off his stroke by "This boss-eyed, screaming kid" as he would narrate it to the other bus drivers in the canteen later. The cuff on the ear made Daniel abruptly take in a gulp of air and stop bawling. He'd run out of the front door and he'd disappeared.

It was getting dark early, and Marilyn was worried as the day turned to dusk and still there was no sign of Daniel. She'd walked Shane home from school, holding his hand tightly, but all the time she was looking over her shoulder for Daniel. She had bought Shane flying saucers from the shop and let him eat the rice paper and sherbet treats as they walked. She didn't usually buy sweets from the shops for her kids. She told them it would ruin their teas. In reality she couldn't afford them, but today she had a bit of cash. The bus driver had left her a fiver. "Because he was thoughtful," Marilyn convinced herself. He had told her to treat herself to something, maybe some stockings, he had suggested. Full of ideas, the number 79 bus driver.

The flying saucers had made it worse. Daniel had watched from behind a tree as little Shane walked hand in hand with his mother. He watched as she put his gloves on nicely for him. He watched as she handed him the bag of sweets. She looked over her shoulder furtively, like she was checking to make sure Daniel couldn't see her giving sweets to her favourite son. There was no doubt now, she liked Shane more than him. Maybe she didn't like Daniel at all.

Daniel had thought about running away but he was too scared. It was getting dark and the bogeymen would be out, or the aliens, or the dragons. He went home. His mother had been relieved to see him, although she didn't know what to say. Marilyn had done Marmite on toast for her boys that night as they both loved it. She was relieved that Daniel was eating and that he hadn't gone off his food with the shock of what he'd seen. Shane ate his toast too, and drank his lemon barley water and spit drink. The spit had been Daniel's contribution when Marilyn had turned her back for a moment and Shane had gone to wash his hands before tea.

Later Marilyn had cuddled Daniel and stroked his hair. But it was too late. He'd heard. He knew the truth.

The memory is still very fresh in their minds.

"Fifty quid wouldn't kill you. You want them to find me in the gutter? Rid you of me? That it?"

"Alright, alright. Give me some peace." Marilyn stands up and goes over the road. Her ankle is hurting and it takes her ages to get across the street. She feels cold as she stands outside the Maddoxes' house even though it's July. Billy answers the door, which can only mean that Nancy isn't in.

"Dunno where er is. Wuz expecting er hours agoo."

Marilyn says she'll come back later.

"Should yow be walkin on that foot uv yourn?" Billy says.

Marilyn hasn't got the energy to reply. Daniel Grundy watches from behind the net curtains in the front room as his mother makes the painful journey back.

"Thought you said it wasn't there," he says sulkily as she returns.

"It isn't. I was going to ask her to lend me some, but she's not in." Daniel knows she is lying, but is more furious that his mother has come back empty-handed.

He wonders what to do in the meantime. He thinks about looking for the girl, the one from yesterday. What was her name again? He can't remember. He doesn't realise he hadn't actually asked her.

Daniel rattles off up towards the phone box. He makes a call. His dealer answers. "Fuck off, Grundy. Yuh call again, I'll break yuh neck."

"I need something."

"Yuh got money?"

"I'm getting some later."

"Don't bother me unless yuh got the cash."

Daniel puts the phone down. They won't give him anything. He can't believe it, but what Nancy has said to him appears to be right.

There is no sign of Wass-her-face on the street corner. He feels disappointed so he mugs an old lady as she walks up towards the car pitch which everyone uses as a cut through to the town.

He grabs her handbag and wrenches it off her arm. He doesn't care that forever after the old woman will have trouble with the shoulder he pulls out of the socket. He doesn't care that forever after the old woman will have panic attacks and have to rely on someone else to do her shopping. He doesn't care. If it is anybody's fault it is his mother's for not giving him money when he's in need, and for liking Shane more than she likes him. And maybe it's partly Wass-her-face's fault for not being there to share her earnings and her needles with her cross-eyed soulmate, Daniel Grundy.

Daniel Grundy has dropped lucky with the handbag. He throws it in a waste bin on Sainsbury's car park after removing the purse and its contents. Cash! Nearly £150 in cash the mad old cow had been carrying. Any lingering fear of bogeymen and right and wrong evaporated there and then. Daniel scoots off to ring his dealer again, and this time he says he's got some money. On his dealer's say-so he sets off to the Black Horse car park and buys fifty quid's worth of gear. He decides to use some of the rest of the money to buy a bottle of whisky and then he decides to save some for the next day. Daniel Grundy saving for a rainy day! It's good to know that some people can manage to put money to one side.

Nancy lurks around in the vicinity of the theatre. She knows that the degree ceremonies usually take place there. She plucks up courage and walks up to the doorman. "Is there uh college do on theyer today?" she says, squinting to look past him into the darkened foyer.

"Yes! They'll be out soon." Nancy nods and crosses over the road to stand outside the Wetherspoons pub. The vantage point is better, she will be able to see everyone that comes out easily if she isn't part of the crowd. She lights up a cigarette, and waits. A scruffy man with no teeth panhandles a fag off her. She gives it willingly, but without smiling. Twenty minutes later, they start to trickle outside the theatre in their strange hats and black cloaks. The red and gold stripes on the gowns are garish, and make Nancy think of jesters. The graduates are nearly all Asian and they mill around smiling and chattering with family and friends. Nancy is worried that she won't be able to see the party from the bottom shop. She needn't have been, as Reeta and Nirmal are still puffed up with pride. They strut about like two peacocks. Reeta's sari is expensive and lavishly decorated. Nirmal is making a huge song and a dance about organising his family into a group for a photograph. Pritvi, tall and lean, is pushed to the centre. Her shiny black hair, thick and lustrous, hangs loose over the hood of her gown. Her calves are tight and muscular, she is bare-legged and wearing the highest pair of shoes Nancy has ever seen. Nirmal is signalling for the family to bunch in. He looks through the viewfinder of his camera and then commandeers another man who is wearing a pink turban to do the honours. He puts the camera up to his face. His gold bangle glints in the sun. "Say cheese, please!" he says with an accent which is a fusion of Bilston and the Punjab.

"Cheese, please!" they all chorus, with perfect timing. Nirmal has jostled for position next to his beautiful daughter and his chest is puffed out so much now his shirt buttons strain to contain him. When the shutter clicks they are captured for posterity. The Sangha family and, just in frame, Nancy, the light bouncing off her glasses, her gaze fixed on Pritvi.

The group breaks apart, and Nancy makes her move.

"Yow con do these now, car yow?" Pritvi is surprised to see the woman from up the street, she is a little scared of her and remembers her stern looks from childhood.

"What is this?" Nirmal is confused, and Reeta is embar-rassed, shiftily glancing at the people around them and smiling wildly when she makes eye contact, as if it were the most natural thing in the world for the old white lady from up the street to turn up at a graduation waving a Lidl carrier bag.

"Er con do this now, car er? Certifyin?" Nancy gets out the passport form and the photos. "Ar doh know anybody else," says Nancy, becoming aware of the strangeness of the situation she is creating. Everybody looks at her. She is tempted to reach up and check that she isn't wearing one of the mortar boards like in her dream. Nirmal takes the papers and the photo and looks at them. He cottons on quickly, and ever affable and kind, he saves the day.

"Of course, she can! Look, Pritvi!" he waves the forms, "Still in your graduation robes and already your first job as a lawyer!" The situation defuses and the family laugh.

"Pritvi, you are in demand already?" says Reeta loud enough and proud enough for those within earshot to hear. Pritvi laughs, and very graciously takes the forms and certifies the photographs.

She leans on top of the pillar box outside the post office, her shoes making her just tall enough to reach. And then her father insists on a photograph as she passes the completed documents over to a dazed Nancy. The Sangha family clap.

Nancy slopes off and finds a bench to sit on. She lights up another cigarette and catches her breath.

It is forty-five minutes before she can get herself together enough to head back to the post office. Most of the graduates have gone from in front of the theatre, off to restaurants for family meals. Nancy goes into the post office and pays for a postal order. She puts the forms, the photographs and the money into an envelope and walks outside to the postbox. Before she has time to talk herself out of it, the envelope is posted. Then she marches off to the civic centre and pays the overdue money on the council tax. They give her a receipt. She thinks about the IOU that she's written, sitting on top of the remainder of the bingo winnings, and walks home.

"Wot yow bin doin'?" asks Billy as she comes in, looking at her suspiciously.

"Norralot," she answers. Billy looks at her again as if to say something else, but she is already miles away with her thoughts. About ten thousand miles away.

Daniel decides to do one more lap of the block to see if Wass-er-face is anywhere to be found. He's thinking about how it isn't just her gear that he likes. He's thinking about how he had felt happy when he had sat with her. There was something reassuring about her. He feels that she is lucky for him and the mugging had proved that. It is only right that he should share some of his good fortune with her.

Daniel hadn't had any luck since he had been nine and he'd gone into care. His mother had to have an operation and needed some recuperation time afterwards. They put Daniel and Shane in a kids' home down Windmill Lane on the other side of town. The kids' home was run by a man and his wife and they were nice to Daniel Grundy, and to Shane. Not that it mattered to Daniel if they were nice to Shane because there was no love lost between them anymore. There was a snooker table at the children's home, and the man taught Daniel to play. They gave him lovely food. They read books to him.

There was porridge for breakfast. Hot, milky, and sugary. It was so comfortable there. When he wet the bed, they didn't shout. The lady came in one morning and Daniel was sitting up in the corner of the room crying, facing the wall. She came in and patted his head.

"Shusshhh, shusshhh, Daniel. The sheets will wash. We'll pop you in the bath."

He looked up when she said, "pop". He liked the way she said the word. "Let's pop Daniel Grundy in a nice warm soapy bath and sponge him down," she said as she took his hand and led him to the bathroom. And while Daniel was being "popped" in the bath, the dirty sheets were taken away and the bed was dried out. Clean flannelette sheets were put on that night and Daniel had fresh stripy pyjamas off the clothes horse in front of the fire. They were still warm and they made him feel loved when he "popped" them on. Then Daniel Grundy was "popped" back in bed. Pop. He dreamt of warm milky porridge for his breakfast and going to a school where nobody would know him and where he would work hard and make the nice people proud.

The people liked Daniel Grundy; they were good with little misfits. Lo and behold, Daniel started to try at the school he was at and the teacher gave him a star one day. Daniel Grundy had never had a star before. It was only a red one, not a gold one, but it was still special. He ran his finger over the stick-on shape, rubbed the raised edges. He was as proud of it as if it had been a medal.

When school broke up for summer, the children's home decamped and went on a holiday to the seaside! Daniel Grundy had never seen the sea. The nice people smiled at the way his little jaw dropped open at the sight of the ocean and his amazement at the sound of the waves, his joy at the mysteries of rock pools. They watched him run along the beach, turning round and round every few steps. He was following another little boy. Daniel was attempting to make friends. He was trying to socialise. The boy kept stopping to let him catch up but then he'd run on.

All the time Daniel ran, the nice people kept their eyes on him. They knew the boy was relaxing and starting to enjoy the holiday. Eventually, Daniel Grundy had to stop; he had made himself dizzy with all his twisting and turning. Twist and turn. Twist and turn. The sun blazed down, a hazy globe keeping an eye on little Daniel Grundy.

When Daniel got his breath back, he looked up the beach to where the nice people were. Except they weren't. They'd disappeared! Daniel Grundy looked at the empty space where the nice people had been with the other kids building sandcastles. They were gone. No nice people, no sandcastles, no other kids. No Shane even. Daniel started to panic. The panic rose and rose as he stared and stared along the edge of the dunes. Poor Daniel Grundy had run further than he'd thought. He'd lost all sense of place.

The little boy who he'd wanted to make friends with had come back; he had decided he didn't want to play hard to get anymore. He wanted to be friends too, but he was a good little boy and he'd been to ask his mummy if he could go back along the beach and play with a boy he'd seen, and his mummy had said yes he could, if he promised not to play too near to the waves. Daniel didn't see his would-be friend coming back towards him, he saw the gap on the beach where the nice people ought to have been. He started to scream. Blind screaming. The sun clapped its hands over its ears and Daniel's would-be friend ran away.

The nice people had seen Daniel realise that he was lost and had already made a move to go and fetch him. The nice man stood up off the blanket and hooked his thumbs under the legs of his purple swimming trunks to pull them down from where they'd gone up his arse. His wife stood and put her hand over her brow to shield her eyes from the sun. The man started to walk over the hot gritty sand, the ground burning the soles of his feet. He saw the scream start and he ran, ran like crazy towards the little boy, eager to take Daniel's pain. He grabbed Daniel and lifted him. He held him tight. So tight. The man had been an evacuee during the war, he understood the missing people. He understood the scream. Daniel was locked inside himself. The blind screaming continued.

By the time Daniel and the man got back to the nice lady the screaming had stopped. Daniel was numb, staring blankly. The other kids glanced at him but carried on with their digging. Most of them had screamed at sometime. Only Shane stood and looked at his elder brother with something close to embarrassment.

When Daniel recovered he had a bread and butter sandwich with slivers of cucumber on it. The sandwich was warm and gritty. He drank lemon squash out of hot red plastic cups. Later, when the screaming was all forgotten, the nice man took him paddling and held his hand. The nice man had a nice warm hand. The man bought Daniel a chocolate ice cream (two scoops) and a gonk keyring from the beach shop. The gonk had a chubby plastic face and a tuft of yellow hair. Everything on the holiday smelt nice. Even when Daniel was older, he'd sometimes catch a whiff of that holiday.

It was a shock when they had to go back to their mother. Daniel hadn't realised he'd have to go home.

As Daniel sees a car pull up on Raby Street, he watches as Wass-er-face gets out. "Alright?" he shouts. "I've got some stuff."

"I'm workin," she says crossly.

"I've got some stuff," says Daniel again. "You could come back to mine."

"You mean your mom's," the girl says sarcastically, walking slowly towards him.

Daniel pulls the bag of brown out of his pocket and waves it at her. "I'm going away soon. Moving to the seaside," says Daniel, remembering the rock pools again.

"What with?" laughs the girl.

"I've got money," says Daniel, not liking being laughed at. He turns his pocket out and shows her the notes he's put aside for a rainy day.

"Tell ya what. I'll come back to yours if you reimburse me for loss of earnings." She comes close and snatches a twenty pound note from his pocket, still laughing. Daniel hears the pitter pat of his rainy day slowing in his head, but doesn't argue.

They walk down the street together. Daniel puts his arm around Wass-er-face and she shrugs it off. "Probably a bit too soon," thinks Daniel.

The vet phones the man with the nice smile and asks him to go with him to Kinmel Bay on Saturday. "It's nice there as long as you don't go into Rhyl itself," the vet says. The man with the nice smile is off the idea when he hears that Sebastian Grundy will be accompanying them, but when it becomes clear that the object of the exercise is for Sebastian to be left over a hundred miles away, and for good, he changes his mind and accepts.

Marilyn thinks about the day before, when she had sat with the girl in the lounge and she'd felt the family thing, the cosy thing. She realizes that she too had felt happy, almost wanted. She imagines the girl was Daniel's girlfriend come to visit. She remembers how nice the girl had been when she made her a cup of tea. She lets her mind wander, and has almost married the prostitute and Daniel off as a question starts to nag at her.

When had Marilyn last been happy? Marilyn thinks and thinks and thinks, and comes to the conclusion that it was years and years ago. Daniel must have been about ten, and Marilyn had got herself a steady bloke. He was a bus driver of course. He lived with his mother. He used to like to take Marilyn up to the club every night. They'd play bingo together. He'd cross the numbers off using a very smart Parker pen with a navy blue barrel and silver top. He kept it in the breast pocket of his jacket with the little arrow showing. He always wore a jacket. He would cross the bingo numbers off with very deft, neat crosses. Methodical he was. He did his spot the ball in the same way. Neat even crosses. He made tracings too, so he could check them the next week in the Express and Star. Marilyn put big felt pen rings round her bingo numbers. Big, bold, and bright.

On Sundays they would dance at the club. She would wear her strappy sandals. How Nat could glide. He was very nimble on his feet. His father had taught him. He had, as a little boy, stood his small feet on top of his father's feet and then they'd glide around the front room together. The little boy's feet and legs following his father's every step. His mother, who he was very close to, watched admiringly through the serving hatch before pottering some more in the kitchen. Always in the kitchen his mother, before she went off her legs.

In the three years or so that Nat was walking out with Marilyn he never took her to meet his mother. Somehow he knew his mother wouldn't approve of the bottle blonde in strappy sandals, even though he really liked Marilyn.

Marilyn and the bus driver would take Shane with them up to the club, but Daniel had wanted to stop in the house. Nat said he was old enough at ten. He said he had often stopped on his own when he was ten; he hadn't, he'd been fourteen before his mother would leave him. Well, she did worry so. It was his dad who had convinced her that she was making a "nancy boy" out of him.

Daniel didn't make any trouble when he was left on his own. He sat and watched the TV. Sometimes he drew. Dragons, mostly. One night he had to draw a blue dragon, rather than a green one (everyone knows dragons are green), because his mother had taken his green felt pen with her up to the bingo. She'd won a line that night. Big dragon green rings all over her card.

Daniel liked being on his own in the house. He never went to bed before they got back. He didn't sleep very well anyway. He had never slept very well. It worried his mother. One night Nat said she should take the boy a little bottle of something back to help him get off at night. Marilyn wasn't sure, but Nat was a very persuasive man and she trusted him. Marilyn took Daniel a bottle of Cherry B and he loved it. He loved the warmth in his belly. It did help him sleep. He didn't even wet the bed that night.

"See," said Nat. Marilyn was so grateful for a non-wet bed that she decided to buy Daniel a bottle of Cherry B every night. It became a routine. A bottle of Cherry B and a packet of scratchings. Daniel loved the ritual of drinking it sip by sip, and in between each one he'd take a mouthful of scratchings which he didn't have to share with their Shane.

Marilyn smiled at the memory of Nat. He'd been a good man. She sat back on the sofa and thought about happy days. Wasn't she due some more? Or was that it for Marilyn Grundy?

Marilyn was enjoying her daydream. She remembered how kind Nat was to her boys. Nat was still on the scene when Daniel was eleven, and two days after Daniel's birthday Nat bought him a second-hand record player. "How lovely was that?" thought Marilyn. It was a Binatone stereo with an arm that could hold lots of singles in place. They'd drop down one on top of another and play. Nat had even thrown in a couple of his old singles so that Daniel could have something to listen to. Daniel liked *Heartbreak Hotel* in particular. He played it over and over.

Marilyn hadn't realised that Daniel had to play it every night at exactly ten o'clock nor that he would have to play it three times. Nor did she know that when they came back from the club at 11 he would play it three more times before taking three sips of his Cherry B. And before he could go to bed he had to check all of the plugs. He had to flick the bathroom light on and off three times. And sometimes he didn't feel like he'd done it right and he had to do it again and again, also in little bursts of three. He had to click his fingers three times when somebody spoke to him. And blink three times when he said good morning to his mother. He clicked his spoon against his breakfast bowl three times before he scooped up a bit of cereal. He had to beat cars to lampposts on the way to school. He had to sharpen his pencils over and over. He had to say little phrases to himself, in multiples of three. He had to dip his paintbrush in the water three times in the art class.

His classmates started noticing and saying, "You're a bloody weirdo, Daniel Grundy."

Marilyn had been too happy to see.

When Daniel Grundy comes back in, his mother wakes up with a start. Her day-dreaming had turned to real dreaming. She comes to her senses and she sees that Daniel has Wass-er-face in tow. "Hello, love," she says smiling, pleased to see the girl. Daniel looks at his mother's wistful expression. Her obvious delight at seeing Wass-er-face annoys the hell out of him.

"Wos up with you?" he asks.

"Thinking about, Nat," says Marilyn. "You remember, Nat?"

Daniel certainly did remember Nat. There was one very particular memory of Nat that stuck in his head. Daniel Grundy had not long been a teenager. Terrible teens. Daniel was underdeveloped for his age. He didn't look like a teenager. Now glue was the only thing that made Daniel happy.

He sometimes went too far with it. He often hallucinated. He liked it. He liked not being in control. He didn't have to do his rituals when he was on the glue.

Andy Winterson had introduced him to it. They'd been skiving down the canal together. "You go first, Daniel," Andy had said, and so Daniel did. The bread bag was sticky against his face. He breathed in and the bag pulled inwards against his cheeks. He breathed out and the bag blew out away from him. The sound of it pleased him. He did it three times. Andy didn't much fancy breathing into a bag that smelly Daniel Grundy had been breathing into so he didn't bother, instead he watched with amazement as Daniel started with his antics. Andy laughed and laughed as Daniel burbled about things he could see that Andy couldn't. Andy Winterson watched him, and smiled to himself.

Andy had made, well, not friends with Daniel Grundy exactly, more of a project out of him. He realised that he could, if he wanted to, get Daniel to do lots of things. "Daniel, let's run in the shop and grab a can of coke each and leg it." They both ran in, but only Daniel grabbed a can before they both ran out. Andy Winterson cackled about how he'd tricked Daniel. Daniel laughed too. Andy Winterson drank the pop.

Andy Winterson suggested they climb the highest tree in the school playground. "I'll follow you up," said Andy. He went halfway up the tree and shouted encouragement to Daniel who was above him. "Get to the very top branches, Daniel." So Daniel did. Andy Winterson found it easy to get down. Daniel didn't. The headmaster had to call the fire brigade. Daniel had detention for a fortnight. Andy Winterson had a good laugh at Daniel's expense.

But Daniel could forgive that because Andy Winterson had given him something in return. Glue. Relief. Freedom.

One day Shane and his friends (Shane had lots of friends) went to the park to play Nakey Nakey 123. Daniel Grundy didn't see them until they came right up to him and even then he didn't recognise them. Daniel was whizzing round on the roundabout, lying back, sprawled out, glue bag over his face. He was breathing in and out, in a world of his own.

Shane came over. "What ya doin', Daniel?" Daniel looked at the little creature that had beamed itself into his field of vision. Shane's alien moon face was pulled into an expression of wonder. His friends stood behind with their moony faces.

"Why's he doin' that?" one of the friends said, looking at the bread bag which was clamped to Daniel's face. Daniel was spaced out. Space. He was so in space he thought Shane and his friends were little aliens come to get him. He stared at them and stared at them. They weren't green, but he knew they were aliens. Green was the colour of most aliens and dragons, apart from when your mom takes your green felt pen, then they can be blue. But aliens could be clever and morph into other things; take on flesh tones which were human. Daniel couldn't speak, so he continued to stare at the aliens. He took the glue bag away from his mouth. His mouth was red and sore from constant contact with the plastic and the glue.

"Are you real?" asked Daniel. But what the kids heard was "Arrrueal." Shane wrinkled his nose up and laughed at his brother. What Daniel saw was an alien face wrinkling up and making threatening noises. Daniel tried to get to his feet. He tried to get off the roundabout. It continued spinning after he'd jumped clear.

"I'm going to tell mom," said Shane. An onlooker might have thought that this threat was what triggered Daniel to do what he did next. An onlooker might have wrongly assumed that Daniel was scared of his mother finding out about the glue and that Daniel grabbed hold of Shane and hurt him because of this. But it wasn't that. In his gluey head, Daniel thought he was saving mankind from the aliens. The glue had made him brave. He thought he was tackling the alien leader.

108

A big moon had come out early. It was still daylight but the moon watched as Daniel Grundy the super-human bent Shane's wrist so far round his back he broke it. Snap. The aliens ran away; all of them ran. No laser guns to save mankind, a quick twist of the wrist was all that was needed. Shane ran screaming all the way home. His mother and Nat had to take him to casualty and get his arm put in plaster. All of Shane's friends would sign it over the next week at school.

Daniel fell asleep back on the roundabout after the aliens had gone. It spun, rocking him gently; the breeze singing a lullaby for the hero of the day. Poor Daniel was tired after saving the world. When he finally awoke later, it had gone dark. When he got home, Shane had got a plaster cast on. Shane cried at the sight of Daniel. It was put on for attention. His wrist wasn't really hurting, but Shane could milk it with the best of them; he hadn't been a younger brother for all those years without learning a little of the art of manipulation.

Daniel wondered how Shane had broken his wrist, but he didn't ask. He learned though, when Nat and his mother tackled him about it. Daniel denied any knowledge of the wrist. He had an alibi, not that he could tell anyone because they probably wouldn't believe him about the aliens. Aliens were not reliable witnesses and that was a fact.

Nat believed that he understood the type of discipline that Daniel needed, even though he hadn't been disciplined harshly as a child himself. He'd always been a good boy for his own mother. He'd had the odd smack but it wasn't really the smack that had hurt, it was the displeasure on his mother's face that killed. That's what stopped him doing bad things, things that would displease her, things like having normal adult relationships.

Nat had heard of people giving the belt to their kids. It seemed appropriate. Nat had a belt; he took it off. He wasn't sure how to administer the belt. Did you hit with the buckle end, or did you hold the buckle and lash out with the strap? Nat decided that the buckle would be the weight that carried the strap down. The buckle would add momentum. Daniel Grundy had to pull his trousers down. Nat belted him eleven times. The buckle cut into Daniel's skin. After the eleventh belt, Daniel asked for another. And when it didn't come, Daniel started begging for another. Nat thought the boy was being cheeky. Insolent. It confused Nat. Hadn't he hit the boy hard enough? Was this little lad so tough that Nat couldn't administer discipline? Nat felt inadequate. He was beginning to wonder if bingo and dancing were enough compensation for all this trouble that Marilyn had about her life.

He looked back at Daniel who was still begging for another lashing. Daniel had counted eleven belts. Eleven was a bad number. Twelve was a multiple of three. Nat lost his rag. He belted the boy again and again and again; until they both lost count. Daniel was cut and bruised and bleeding and didn't have a clue whether the number of strikes was divisible by three. Daniel couldn't sleep for worrying that there would be trouble the next day because of the problems with threes.

Nat went home back to his mother. He couldn't look the old girl in the eye for days. He was ashamed of how violent he could be. He became fearful of losing his temper with her. She was getting demanding; it was the start of Alzheimers.

Not long after the belting, Nat began to cool off with the dancing and bingo. Within the month, even though they had been walking out for nearly four years, he stopped calling and for Marilyn there was no more going up the club with her felt pens and her strappy sandals.

There was no more Cherry B for Daniel, but he needed it because it was part of his ritual. He started to steal it from the top shop. One bottle a night. Within two weeks he'd had a crate's worth, and Doreen had been down and told his mother, who had to pay. He started having to steal from a different shop every day. It was another thing he had to do, another thing making life stressful for Daniel Grundy.

Shane's wrist always hurts him in cold weather; this was Daniel's small consolation prize.

"Nat was a right bastard," says Daniel to his mother. On that, Daniel takes Wass-er-face back into the front room. He is like a spiteful child removing a toy from another kid who wants to play with it. Daniel is pleased when he sees the joyful light extinguish in his mother's eyes.

When Nancy wakes up her shoulder is hurting like billyo. The pain is almost unbearable, she must have slept on it funny. Perhaps she should stop sleeping downstairs and go up to the bed once in a while. She tries to stretch her arm out, but it brings tears to her eyes. Billy looks at her from his chair.

"Yow car goo in like that."

Nancy doesn't answer. She tries to stand up. She feels sick. She tries to argue. She feels sicker. She reaches into her overall pocket and pulls out some painkillers. She takes two, crunches them up and swallows them down dry without water. She is eating painkillers like Smarties. Billy says he is going to go up the pub and tell Bernice that she isn't coming in, although he doesn't actually move.

"Be orright in uh minute," Nancy says. She breathes in and her chest hurts. She'd dreamed again last night of flying, or at least trying to. She'd been flapping her one wing against her side frantically. Perhaps she'd acted the dream out and pulled something.

She polishes her glasses to bide herself a bit of time before standing, hoping the painkillers will kick in. She isn't good at waiting.

111

She remembers a little bit more of her dream, where the exertion of flailing her wing had made her cough, and the taste of blood had come to her mouth. She stands up then, more to get away from her thoughts than anything. As she stands, a crumpled tissue falls to the floor. There is a pinkish stain on it. Nancy sees the stain as she picks up the tissue, but chooses to ignore it. She feels hungry and has the urge for something warm and comforting. It is the wrong time of year for mashed potatoes and winter cabbage, but that's what she wants.

"Yow car goo in like that!" says Billy again. Nancy knows he is wrong. Nancy knows she has to. She thinks of the IOU upstairs with the bingo winnings. Not only does she have to go in, she'll have to find more work to help cover her tracks.

"Well, ar'm gooin' in!"

Billy gets up and makes her a cup of tea, insisting she drink it before she goes. Nancy thinks to herself that he's not so bad. Not when it came to a crunch or when a push came to a shove. She swallows two more painkillers with the over-sweet tea.

"Con yow mek Marilyn one, tek it ova to er? With uh sandwich? Ar'm runnin lairt now!"

"Bloody 'ell!" he says as he stamps off into the kitchen. "When did we open uh café?" He does it though. He cuts up a boiled bacon sandwich on a plate, he even covers it over with cling film so no dirt gets on it when he crosses the road.

Nancy slopes off to work while he is buttering bread. She throws the tissue in somebody else's wheelie bin as she goes up the street and then feels guilty, like she is disposing of evidence or landing a curse on another family by way of their bin. Voodoo.

Marilyn is worried. She'd realised that Nancy was late with breakfast but she'd hoped that she'd still come. Her worry is that maybe Billy had told his wife that Marilyn had managed to cross the street and that the act would deem Marilyn active enough to fend for herself. The walking across the street had taken its toll and her ankle was sorer than it had been. When she hears knocking at the door, she struggles to it and sees Billy there. Her heart jumps in her chest.

"What's the matter?" she says, her eyes making her look like a startled deer. Marilyn's mind goes into overdrive. Had Nancy been run over? Had a killer struck? Marilyn hasn't got the sense to think that if Billy's wife had really suffered some sort of ill-fated demise her husband probably wouldn't be up to cutting cold boiled bacon sandwiches for the woman over the road with the damaged ankle and the lazy son.

At that moment the lazy son in question appears behind his mother. He is wrapped in a yellow blanket, which is secured round his waist in the same way a person might wear a towel when they'd got out of the bath. His pasty, bare chest is showing above. His hair is sticking up and his eyes are still gummed together with sleep. Daniel doesn't want to miss out on anything. He squints at Billy through a gummy crack that he's forced open between his top and bottom lids. Billy thinks "Lazy little bastard," but he doesn't say it. Although the look he gives Daniel makes it pretty clear the lines along which he's thinking.

Marilyn is so happy to hear that Nancy isn't a corpse she chooses not to notice Billy's look. Daniel clocks it. He knows that he is being judged. Daniel doesn't think it's fair. He isn't that lazy. He's had jobs. The first one he had was when he was fifteen and still supposed to be at school.

Daniel had sussed that if he got money he could buy as many Cherry Bs as he liked, and as much glue as he needed. One morning, when skiving school again, he'd cut through the market. It was early and the traders were setting up their stalls. They were laughing and joking, shouting to one another. It was still quite dark. Daniel liked the half-light. He liked the transient feel of the market. He started going every morning, and hanging around.

The traders accepted him as part of the market furniture, like an awning or a dustbin. One of the traders eventually told him not to stand around but to help. They'd got to know him. He'd help them unload. Then he got work picking up the litter. Cash in hand. Enough cash to buy all the Cherry Bs in the world. He used to buy three every night. Then he upped it to six every night. He still managed to get up in time for the market though.

Daniel felt happy. He felt happy enough to go to the pub with the traders after the market had shut. By this time he was going back early evening to help them take everything down and sweep up. They offered to buy him a drink and he'd asked for Cherry B. They'd laughed and called Daniel Grundy a girl. That was it; he couldn't drink the Cherry B anymore. They took the piss out of his spotty, gluey face. No more glue. He stopped the glue, but still carried round a bag and breathed in and out of it. He swapped from Cherry B to lager.

The ritual changed to six cans of lager a night. He secretly missed the Cherry B, and felt bad and girly for doing so. Every night, Daniel would go to bed drunk. He wasn't even sixteen. He'd never been kissed, he'd never held a girl's hand, but he was already reliant on drink. Weird Daniel Grundy.

Billy tuts as he turns his back on Marilyn and Daniel. He puts a hand up in a sort of a wave as Marilyn shouts her thanks, but he doesn't turn to look at them. He goes back home and washes up the plates, then he sits back in his chair and goes to sleep again.

Billy had woken Daniel up from a nice dream with his knocking. Daniel was annoyed because in the dream he was snuggled up in a warm bed with the cross-eyed prostitute and

Billy had shattered the illusion. Bang! Bang! Bang! "Shaddup," Daniel muttered, as he woke to find that Wass-er-face had left sometime during the evening, taking the remainder of his hard-earned muggings with her.

Daniel thinks about the cross-eyed prostitute. He thinks he might love her. Not in a sex kind of a way. Not at all. Daniel isn't very good at that kind of relationship. Daniel shudders as he thinks about it. Not very good at all! He decides to forgive Wass-er-face, settling himself that she has probably borrowed the money. He has some of his mother's genes after all.

Next Daniel imagines Wass-er-face going with a punter and immediately gets angry with her. It isn't jealousy, but the idea of her being a prostitute has brought back a memory he'd rather forget.

On Daniel's sixteenth birthday his mother had got up early and wrapped him a digital watch in pink wrapping paper, which was all they'd had at the shop. She wrote a card. It had a *16* on the front and footballers. Daniel Grundy didn't like football. It didn't make any difference anyway, because Daniel Grundy had already gone out before his mother had managed to get the present wrapped or the card written. He had gone up the market to start work. Marilyn felt cheated. It was her boy's sixteenth birthday and she wasn't allowed to demonstrate how much she loved him and how surprised she was that he'd got this far in life without doing anything too bad. She put the present on the mantleshelf and went back to bed. She was having one of her difficult days.

Shane got up and opened the card, checking for money. None. He pocketed the present and threw the card in the bin. At school, he sold the watch to one of his friends. Shane went to school every day and never wagged. He was a good boy!

Daniel told the market people it was his birthday. He was surprised that he told them. They said he must go to the pub after work. They told him he should pop his cherry by the

115

time he was sixteen. Daniel didn't know what they meant, but the word "pop" reminded him of the nice woman in the children's home, and by association it sounded comforting. He half-wondered if it was another tease about his earlier drinking habits. He didn't know what was going to happen. If he had he might not have gone.

After work they stood at the bar. Everybody lined up drinks for Daniel. They were a good-hearted bunch. Daniel drank snakebites that night because TJ, who Daniel looked up to, was drinking them. When they organised the prostitute for the cherry-popping they didn't think about this being Daniel's first sexual experience. They didn't think about making it special.

Esther was tall and strong. Strong as a man. Blonde hair. Good looking. They pointed out the target. There was Daniel Grundy with his back to her, drinking snakebite. She sidled up to him. Daniel was already having trouble focussing. She went in and out of his vision.

She put her hands down the front of Daniel's trousers! His balls turned to ice. Two icy stones and a button mushroom. She tried to work his cock up into some kind of stand. It wasn't happening. He looked around at the men laughing. He looked into the prostitute's strong face. Daniel Grundy wet himself.

The memory of wetting himself makes him think he wants the toilet. He goes to the bathroom but can't pass water. Daniel goes back to the front room and fortifies himself with some of the whisky he'd bought the day before. See, Wass-er-face couldn't be that bad, because if she was she'd have taken the drink too. His thoughts towards her become pleasant again. He remembers how she had administered another dose via needle, and pleasant thoughts turn to loving ones. Daniel gets ready for work, his thoughts about Wass-er-face warming his heart. His need to satisfy his cravings is most definitely becoming a full-time job.

Nancy works hard in a hazy painkiller-induced bubble. Tyrone's barks seem rubbery as they bounce around the empty bar. He is in a buoyant mood as Bernice has finally placed an order for crisps and now the delightful-smelling boxes are ensconced behind the bar. Although sales will prove to be slack for some time as people have got out of the habit of asking for them.

Nancy finishes up. She feels exactly like the wrung-out dishcloth that she leaves to dry on the water pipe behind the toilet. But even so, she knows she needs another job and fast. She shouts a half-hearted "Tarra, cock!" to Bernice, unsure if she is even within earshot and then heads out, turning left and walking the few yards to the top shop. Doreen knows everything about everything, except maybe exact amounts of bingo wins, but if there is work going Doreen is the one to ask.

"Bar staff they're after at the New Inns."

"Cor really see myself as bar staff!"

"Nor me," laughs Doreen. "They'm all topless ones down theyer. Bridie Churchill's girl's one uv em. Er must be 45 if er's a day."

"Cleaners?" says Nancy. "Anyone lookin fuh cleaners?" Doreen looks thoughtful. Three down in the queue shouts, "Harry at the Summerhouse. He only said yesterday his missus was going to India and he'd have to get someone in."

Nancy is off like a shot before somebody else beats her to it. Doreen is miffed that Nancy doesn't buy anything, there is a price for information and that price is a purchase, however small. Some people have no manners these days.

Nancy is soon down onto Steelhouse Lane. She knocks on the door and one of Harry's son's answers. He is a

117

broad Asian lad with a hairdo bordering on bouffant, and a suspicious face.

"Yower Dad lookin furra temporary cleaner?"

"Yeah."

"Ar'll do it. Eight pound fifty un hour. Cash. Burrar'll be wantin uh key cos ar'll need tuh gerrin early afore ar doo up the Dartmouth fuh Bernice."

The lad looks at the little woman. She stares back. He feels compelled to give her the job; it is something about the way she seems to look straight into his soul. Nancy goes home, not happy exactly, but relieved. At least she'll be able to get the money together to repay her debt. And maybe, if things pan out, they might take her on permanently and then she could save for the Australia trip itself.

Harry's son tells his dad when he gets back from the cash and carry that he's found a new cleaner to cover for his mother while she is in India. "What, doesn't your father have a say now?" Harry screeches at his son. He tells his dad, sheepishly, that he's already given her a key. His dad carps on about it for half the afternoon, making comments about references and how he hopes she doesn't rip the till off. He finally gets bored of it. Had Harry gone to the door himself he would have given her the job too.

Daniel Grundy is lying on top of the old pigeon loft which is in the yard belonging to Billy's and Nancy's neighbours, not the neighbours who are growing cannabis in the loft but the ones on the other side. The pigeon loft has a sloping roof covered with a loose tarp where somebody at some time has tried to cover the leaky felt roof. Daniel no longer feels comfortable on the Maddoxes' shed roof since his close call on Sunday night, but the neighbours' roof is ideal as both the slope and the tarp afford him some cover.

He's managed to access the roof via the yard of a boarded-up house in the street that backs on to their street. The alley gate had been left open so Daniel was able to get into the yard easily and then climb up the six-foot wall and onto the roof. He's wriggled himself under the tarp and created a sort of burrow which he is now peering out of.

He's studying the house closely. It's very hot on the roof. He is wearing some sunglasses as a disguise. He'd found them in one of the drawers in the front room at his mother's as he'd been searching for winnings. They had been Marilyn's mother's, they are trimmed in some sort of see-through plastic which contains gold flecks. They have extremely pointed corners, like wings, but Daniel has long since given up on fashion. Like him, they are still just about functional.

He stares through the dark, scratched lenses and tries to imagine where a person might hide a big bingo win. All the houses are the same layout. He imagines his own house but turns it round in his mind. His money is on the cash being in the glory hole under the stairs, or a wardrobe, or one of the upstairs cupboards that are built in. If he can sneak in and get himself in the glory hole and search it, he would then be able to walk out through the front room and back onto the street without being noticed. The only problem with that idea is that Billy never leaves his chair. Or if he does, it is only to stand up and stretch, or to make a cup of tea. When he makes a drink, Billy needs to use the kitchen, and that is the only way Daniel can see of getting in to the house.

Spying is hard work, and thinking is even harder. His train of thought about getting in the Maddoxes' house is interrupted frequently by the whining voice inside his head demanding some sort of high. It is so very hot under the black tarp. Daniel thinks he might rest his eyes. He turns on his back and feels the sun roasting his peanut head. He falls asleep for a couple of hours with the top half of his face showing.

Daniel is woken by a rumbling which he at first thinks is thunder. Then, as he comes round, he realises that the noise is Billy fetching the bins back in. That's it! Bin Day! Bingo! He watches as the old man parks his neighbours' wheelie bin in their yard and then parks his own. Daniel has missed his chance by falling asleep, but next week, next Tuesday, he'll be ready. That was the way in, that was the way to a fortune.

Daniel's face feels tight as he scrambles down from the roof and heads home. When he gets back to his mother's he takes the sunglasses off and puts them back in the drawer. His face is very red but there are strange shapes round his eyes where the glasses have been, almost like a pasty mask which is the same colour as the rest of his bleached, skinny body.

That afternoon when Nancy got back she had a sleep in the chair and, to her surprise, when she awoke she felt better than she'd felt in days. She felt almost as good as Tyrone had felt when the crisps got delivered. It was something to do with the new job. Perhaps her weariness had been to do with worry about the council tax and then the guilt about the IOU. Even the guilt had now been alleviated slightly with the chance to earn money to pay it back. She pushes the nagging thought of the stained tissue out of her mind.

Nancy feels so refreshed, she decides to tackle a letter to Vee. She sits upright on the sofa having equipped herself with a tray to lean on, some writing paper, and a pen.

Billy is in his chair, watching the television. Nancy thinks about her wing dream again as she sits and chews on the lid of the blue Bic biro that Billy has leant her. She steadies herself and begins by writing her address at the top right hand corner, like she'd been taught at school. She asks Billy the date. He doesn't know, and has to look at the top of the paper. She copies the date down. She chews her pen top again.

"Oo yow writin to?" says Billy without taking his eyes off the television.

"I owe ower Vee a letter."

Billy glances at her then. She'd owed their Vee a letter for a good many years to his knowledge, ever since Vee had moved to Australia, in fact. He wonders why she is writing now.

"Dear Vee..." starts Nancy, before stopping and sucking on the pen again. Absentmindedly she scratches her foot, poking down the side of her trainer with the pen top. What should she say? "I'm getting a passport! I'm coming to visit!" No, she can't start it like that.

She puts pen to paper again. "How are you both? Me and Billy are well." She coughs as she writes it and she feels a twinge in her arm. "Chrissie and the kids are fine." She thinks about Sunday and her argument with Chrissie about going to Australia; she hasn't seen her since and she wonders if she's cooled down or if maybe she's passed it off as the barley wine ramblings of her elderly mother.

Nancy stops to think again. Should she say it now? "I've sent for a passport! I'm coming to visit." No, not yet. She couldn't say it yet. She imagines Vee looking pleased. Shocked, but pleased. Then she imagines her looking smug as if to say, "I knew you'd give in, in the end." She imagines Vee wanting to send her the money. Nancy feels bad. She couldn't ask for it. If she wants to go, she'll have to get the money herself. She thinks of the IOU still sitting upstairs on top of the bingo winnings.

She puts pen to paper yet again. "How are things coming along with the new games room?"

She looks at the letter. It's an incredibly short letter. She is ashamed of how short it is. She looks at Billy sitting in his chair. She couldn't leave him. He wasn't a bad old goat. She remembers how he'd made her a cup of tea and taken the boiled bacon sandwich over to Marilyn that morning. She couldn't go without him. Could she?

She adds a PS. "I've sent for a passport now. Just in case."

She packages the short letter up in an envelope, licks the flap, and attempts to stick it down. The envelopes are that old, the stickiness has gone. Nancy rootles round in the drawer of the unit until she finds some sellotape. Billy tuts and winces at the noise, exaggerating how loud it is. Nancy choses to ignore him and bites a piece of tape off, sticking it over the envelope flap.

"All done?" says Billy.

"All done!" she answers.

The kindly vet finishes work at 6 o'clock and nips over to Sainsbury's to grab a few things for his evening meal. He's been deliberating over his decision to off-load Sebastian and had been having second thoughts until he received the call from the young woman a few streets away from where he lived. She'd asked politely if the three-legged dog that had appeared in their garden and eaten her children's sandwiches while they had been playing outside in the lovely sunshine was anything to do with him. She'd phoned the number on the collar, a new addition to Sebastian's ever-growing selection of accoutrements. The vet had missed his lunch and gone over to claim the pooch, who had gone AWOL yet again.

After much mopping up of tears (the woman's youngest child had been labouring under the misapprehension that the dog was going to become the family's new pet and had already re-named him Sam) the vet was able to make his escape but not before making a smallish re-imbursement (small for a vet a least) to the family to cover the cost of one burst paddling pool. Sam had got a little over-excited by the sight of water and had attempted to make the children quack like the ducks he'd seen when he'd fallen into the canal.

The vet had locked Sam/Sebastian in his 4x4 while he worked the afternoon shift, leaving the window slightly down and a bowl of water within easy reach. Although he had been tempted to leave the window up and let the hot day take its toll.

The vet relaxes slightly as he strolls about the aisles of Sainsbury's. Perhaps the fact that the place had once been a church is having a calming effect upon him. He feels almost spiritual as he picks up one or two things with a view to putting together a picnic to take to Kinmel Bay on Saturday. The Scotch eggs look quite appetising. He smiles to himself and goes for it, picking up party food that he thinks might work well *al fresco* should the weather hold. Then he grabs a few necessities, some expensive loo roll, and an air freshener. The air freshener had become a necessity since he'd left Sam/Sebastian Grundy in the 4x4 all afternoon.

He thinks about getting some alcohol. A cheeky little red, perhaps. He wanders to the booze aisle and picks up a bottle of champagne. "Too much?" wonders the vet, thinking not of the price but of the gesture. Would the man with the nice smile and the hopefully less-squashed genitalia think it was a bit over the top? He doesn't want to scare him off with grand gestures.

"Ideal for a picnic, refreshing on a summer's day," reads the vet as he considers the label on the champagne, and then the strangest thing happens. As the vet stands there trying to decide which brand to choose, an odd-looking fellow with a red face and a pair of white rings around his eyes, which suggest a shape reminiscent of a burglar's mask, sidles up beside him, takes a bottle of whisky from the shelf, undoes the top, and attempts to down the contents in one.

"Oi! You!" The shout of a security guard barely puts the man off his stride. His adam's apple bobs up and down as he glugs away at the bottle, whisky running down the sides of his face and on to the floor. As the security guard nears at speed, he slips on the puddle of Bells and goes careening into a bargain display of Pymms. The drinker drops his bottle to the floor with a smash and flees for the exit.

The vet helps the security guard up and, having assured himself the man isn't hurt, goes to pay for his own purchases. That will be an anecdote to tell his mother on Sunday. She does so like to hear about the horrors of living in a midland city.

When the vet gets back to his 4x4 he sprays round the air freshener and waits for the recently re-christened Sebastian to get over his sneezing fit before they both drive home.

Later, after filling in another hole in his garden, the vet sends a flirty little text to the man with the nice smile and warms him up to the idea of a romantic weekend picnic, with Scotch eggs and champagne.

Nancy lets herself in the front door and cleans behind the bar, in the bar, and then in the gents and ladies toilets at the Summerhouse pub. The new job isn't much different to her other one except there isn't a lounge. It is a small pub, mostly used by men. Dartboard and pool table rub shoulders with each other. A noticeboard is cluttered with the season's fixtures, and recent and not-so-recent updates to rules. Nancy had been pleased to find a well-equipped cleaning cupboard, and a new broom which put the tatty one that Bernice had to shame.

Nancy switches the bandit on before she goes. She waits for it to go through its rotations and warm up. When it has stopped she puts in a pound and watches the wheels turn. She doesn't win. She isn't surprised.

As she locks up the pub it is still only 5.35am. The cleaning has taken her nearly an hour. £8.50. Billy had been snoring his head off when she'd got up at 3.30 and snuck out. If he is awake by the time she gets back, she'll tell him that she's been to post her letter to Vee. She takes the letter in question out of her overall pocket and shoves it in the post box outside the bottom shop as she passes, looking over her shoulder as she does so to see if anybody is watching. "There," she thinks to herself. "If ar've tuh use that as un excuse then it wo even be uh lie. Norranymore." She gets the picture of Vee's face in her mind again as she imagines her reading the letter.

She needn't have worried about being caught. The old goat is still snoring away, mouth open and none the wiser that his wife has been moonlighting. Or perhaps daybreaking would be a more accurate description. She wakes him up with a cup of tea and some toast.

Next Nancy shoots off up to the Dartmouth, knocking Marilyn's door on the way with some hot buttered toast and a mug of tea. Marilyn answers much more quickly than usual. She is getting better on her bad ankle. "I ay ad time tuh do yow anythin fuh yower dinner yet. Ar'll drop summat in on mi way back lairter. Abaht 'alf ten."

Nancy is still feeling upbeat and energised as she heads for the Dartmouth. It only takes a couple of hours before her mood is changed.

Chrissie had gone up to the top shop to buy a tin of ham for Neil's tea. As luck would have it they'd run out at the shop that was closer to hers. As Chrissie goes in, all smiles, Doreen says, "Ya mom got the job down the Summerhouse then?"

"Wot?"

"The second cleanin job er was after."

"Oh. Yeah," says Chrissie, not wanting to look dumb.

She forgets about the ham and leaves it on the counter. Doreen puts it back on the shelf and makes a mental note to give it to Chrissie when she comes in again. It is too much effort to run after her and if she accidentally forgets, then she can re-sell it. There is, after all, the small matter of some unpaid for information. All's fair in love and small business.

Chrissie knocks at the Dartmouth. "Where's me mom?" she asks, as Bernice comes to the door.

"Cellar! Havin a sly fag," says Bernice. Chrissie trots off in the direction of the cellar door. "Mom!" she shouts down the steps. Nancy appears, blinking up at her eldest child.

"Shussh! Er doh know arm dahn 'ere."

Chrissie rolls her eyes. "Wot you doin' takin on two jobs with the way yower shoulder is?" Nancy looks sheepish. "Doh tell me it's still this Australia nonsense."

Nancy feels a surge of anger well up inside her. It makes her shout out. "Why shunt I if ar want to?" Her shout is loud and it surprises them both.

"When did Chrissie become the mother?" thinks Nancy as she calms again. Her anger subsides almost as quickly as it has risen.

"Ar've had enough of this. Ar'm tellin dad. Yow've gone saft."

"Tell im," mutters Nancy. "See if ar care."

This is getting silly, they are bickering like young siblings might. A verse from the schoolyard pops into Nancy's head. "Tell tale twit, your tongue will split, and all the little birdies will have a little bit!"

Chrissie leaves, and Nancy finishes the cleaning, but however much she tries she can't get the ditty out of her head.

126

When all the jobs are done, Nancy goes and stands in the street outside the pub to have a fag. Usually she would have gone and stood on her own step, but she feels alienated by Chrissie's threat to side with the old goat. She is feeling defiant. She thinks about the Australia trip. The squelching postman passes, and she wonders idly if he is carrying her passport. How long do they take to come? She isn't sure. It's only two days since she sent for it and already she is getting impatient.

She imagines Chrissie telling the old goat about her madness as the postman knocks the door to deliver the shiny new passport. Cats and pigeons. That settles it, she isn't going home yet. Perhaps she can sort out some of the smaller details of the trip while she waits for the larger ones to fall into place.

Nancy feels hungry, and has an urge for something warm. She decides to pick up two bacon sandwiches and take them down to Marilyn's. They could eat them together.

When the policeman knocks the Grundy's door, it is Marilyn who answers. Daniel stands behind her, earwigging. The copper looks at him. Daniel looks back at the copper. The copper thinks Daniel looks familiar. Daniel knows the copper looks familiar. He recognises him immediately. The copper used to work with him on packing when Daniel got his next job after the market.

Daniel Grundy had missed working at the market. He'd not gone back after the incident with the prostitute and it had taken him a year and a bit to even think about working again. But the rituals were getting too much, he couldn't steal enough lager easily, and the need for money was getting greater.

The lady in the job centre, who he could barely speak to because he was paralysed with fear, told him that a meat-processing plant near where he lived was recruiting. She was big and tall with a strong face. She looked like the prostitute that the market traders had organised for him. Daniel thought he was having weird flashbacks, but it was in fact the prostitute's sister. Small world.

When Daniel went down to the factory they gave him a job. Easy as that. They gave him a hat, overalls, and gloves. He had to get there very early and at the end of the day after he had finished cleaning down, he would go to the pub and spend his hard-earned money. He drank alone. He drank in pubs along the Birmingham New Road, a different one every night until he had been in them all, and then he'd begin the circuit of pubs again. He walked unsteadily to work and unsteadily home. He smelt of meat and alcohol. That was Daniel Grundy's life. Work, pub, home, bed. Work, pub, home, bed. Work, pub, home, bed. He paid Marilyn board, and she did his sandwiches, and a tea which he usually didn't eat until very late at night.

Daniel Grundy wore the same clothes day in and day out. He didn't shower. The backs of his heels were black. His fingernails were grimy and his hair went through cycles of greasy and non-greasy as it tried to clean itself. He had gunky teeth. He was spotty, and picked the spots with his dirty nails. The spots sometimes turned into sores. Daniel Grundy worked hard and trayed up lots of the meat for people to eat. Daniel Grundy could have done a lot to make vegetarianism popular, had anybody known him. But nobody did.

"House to house enquiries, madam," the policeman says, addressing Marilyn and breaking Daniel's train of thought. "You might have heard about the attack last night." The copper is still trying to place Daniel as he is talking, but then all these chav junkie types look the same. Daniel would have made a better copper. At least he could remember faces.

"What attack?" asks Marilyn.

"Last night, on a young woman. Checking if anyone knew the victim or if anyone saw anything suspicious."

"We didn't," says Daniel, butting in before his mother can speak again.

"How do you know you didn't?" says the copper.

"We don't know any pros," says Daniel. "Do we, Mom?"

"Who mentioned anything about prostitutes?" Marilyn thinks momentarily before her concern for the victim takes over. "Are they alright?" Marilyn addresses her question to the police officer.

"Shook up more than anything. She fought him off."

At that moment, Nancy comes down the road carrying the sandwiches. She scowls at the copper as Marilyn smiles a big smile at Nancy; she is glad to see her again. She had been shocked yesterday when Billy had turned up like that. It didn't seem right. Nancy was as tough as old boots. It would be like the end of the world if anything happened to her.

"Ar've cum tuh see if yow've gorra suitcase uz ar con lend," says Nancy, focussing on her mission and ignoring Daniel and the police officer.

The copper repeats his spiel again, this time directing it to Nancy. Nancy looks thoughtful but doesn't say anything. She carries the sandwiches into the house, following Marilyn through the front and into the middle room. Marilyn had assured the policeman that if they heard anything they'd let him know.

"Can you smell bacon?" says Daniel, standing on the step and looking at the policeman. He doesn't mean anything by it. It is just a question.

"Did she have boss-eyes?" he asks before the copper can react. An overwhelming worry has come over him.

"What?" says the policeman, who by this point has sniffed out not only the tempting smell of bacon, but also the notion that something dodgy might be going on.

129

"Shifty looking bloke, capable of anything," thinks the copper as he turns away.

"From pork to pig," thinks Daniel.

Daniel is feeling jittery as he shuts the front door firmly behind the police officer. Something is bugging Daniel. He'd managed to get hold of some whisky last night and decided to search for Wass-er-face. That much he remembered, after all, she owed him some money. He hadn't found her, or he didn't think he had, but he was a bit wrecked once the alcohol had kicked in. He remembered asking one or two of the working girls if they'd seen her and then after that it all went fuzzy. He'd woken up on a bench in the park as the sun was coming up. He was surprised how well he'd slept. Apart from the noise of the damn foxes, he'd barely stirred.

He decides to go and look for Wass-er-face again, and put his mind at rest.

In Marilyn's middle room, Nancy has sat down. This is unusual, but Marilyn is pleased. They sit together and eat their sandwiches in silence.

"You don't have to do this now you know; I'm much better on my feet," says Marilyn, talking about the food deliveries.

"Ar, but berra safe than sorry. A bitta walkin might do it good but yow doh wanna get stondin on it fuh too long."

"Daniel could make me food," says Marilyn. Nancy gives Marilyn one of her long stares. "Maybe," adds Marilyn, unconvincingly.

"I'm goin' out now," shouts Daniel from the other room and the front door slams.

"Still plannin tuh get shut of im?"

"He's not really caused much trouble this week," answers Marilyn. "And," she pauses and looks at the gap in front of the gas fire, "it's a bit of company."

"Uz e givun any clues uz tuh where e's showud up from after all this time? Where's e left that missus of hissen and

130

them kids?" says Nancy, referring to Marilyn's grandchildren. The whole neighbourhood had heard about Marilyn's grandchildren at some time, although they'd never seen them.

"I think they're still in Stockport."

"Ay e mentioned em?"

"No. But I haven't asked him. I don't want to pressurise him with questions," says Marilyn, thinking about tin foil, cupboards, and bad ankles.

"Shuwerly e'd uv mentioned em."

"I sometimes wonder if they're real," says Marilyn with a panic-stricken expression. It was a shocking admission. Marilyn is quite bereft as she realises that she may have killed off her grandchildren with her disclosure of the possibility that they were imaginary. Nancy is surprised that Marilyn is being so frank. It throws her for a second. Then she nods.

"Ar. Did wonder meself."

"I've never actually seen any photos."

"Did e ever av a wench? When e was livin 'ere?"

Marilyn thinks. She remembers that something funny happened after Daniel's eighteenth birthday, something that may have indicated a girlfriend. Daniel had a bath!

It was a long bath, and he attempted to scrub his heels clean. He cleaned his teeth properly. Three times of course. He made his gums bleed because they weren't used to being brushed, and he asked his mother to get him some mouthwash. He started bathing every day. He started putting his clothes to be washed. He even went and bought new clothes. He was in a blind panic and sweating as he bought them but he managed to get the things to the till and pay before running away. He ran all the way home with his clothes. Some of them didn't fit quite right because he hadn't felt up to trying them on, but they were clean and they were new. They were clothes like TJ might have worn on the market. It was the first time that Daniel had thought about the market people in a while. He shuddered. He started taking squirts of Shane's deodorant. He wore clean underwear, although the nylon made him sweat.

The girl's name was Mary-Jane Bilson. She worked in the office at the meat-processing plant. She was on some sort of government scheme. She wore skirts to the knee, white blouses, and blue court shoes with little flowers embroidered on the sides. He'd seen her first when they'd called him over to the offices to talk to him about his holiday entitlement. He hadn't taken any. They told him he needed to take his holiday by the end of March. Daniel said he didn't have anywhere to go so he'd rather not bother if it was all the same to them, and the girl had smiled at him. A girl smiling at Daniel Grundy! He didn't know that she was a nice girl and she smiled at everyone in that way. He liked her hair. It was brown and wavy. It was permed that way but Daniel thought it was natural. Daniel eventually found out her name by doing lots of sneaking around and listening.

One day he followed her to the bus stop and caught the bus to town so he could get on it behind her. He invaded her personal space as she paid and she felt him brush against her. Daniel hadn't meant to get that close, not at all. He jumped back from the touch. When the bus driver looked expectantly at Daniel, Daniel didn't register for a couple of seconds that he was supposed to pay. Daniel didn't have change because he didn't really need to catch the bus, he only lived round the corner. He felt too stupid to turn round and get off. He stuck a fiver in the slot. Daniel didn't sit by Mary-Jane, he sat on one of the side seats near the back. He watched her, though. He watched her until she got off in the bus station and then he watched her as she went to another stand to wait for her next bus. She waited in the Merry Hill bus stop. He noted the bus number as she got on it, and then walked all the way back to work so that he could set off from there and go to the right pub for his nightly ritual.

On Saturday and then Sunday he walked to Merry Hill, following the bus route, and wandered around the streets so he could feel close to his beloved Mary-Jane. He wondered which house she lived in. He wondered if he'd passed it. He had. She lived in Bhylls Lane. She'd seen him go by as she was looking out of the window waiting for her boyfriend Terry to come. Terry had a fancy car and was into Duran Duran in a big way. Mary-Jane didn't really like them, but pretended she did because she didn't want to upset Terry. She wondered what the strange boy from work was doing in Merry Hill. She didn't think that he might be looking for her.

Every night Daniel Grundy caught the bus into town so he could stand by Mary-Jane in the queue. He never spoke to Mary-Jane but he found out more and more about her as she stood chatting to another girl out of the office. He found out she was a Leo. Every night, when he walked all the way back from the bus station to the meat-processing plant and then on to whichever pub was the designated one for the evening, he bought a newspaper. He would turn to the stars and read what the day had in store for him and Mary-Jane. He was looking for a sign or a message. Even if Mary-Jane's stars had said, "Tomorrow you will be asked out by Daniel Grundy and you should say, 'yes'," Daniel still wouldn't have spoken to her.

At night Daniel masturbated while looking at the picture of Mary-Jane that he had stolen from the reception area where a recent display of the office staff and their titles had been put up for visitors to see.

Daniel found out where Mary-Jane lived. He broke into the filing cabinet of staff records. He was good at sneaking about. Years of stealing Cherry B and glue had made him skilful at that kind of thing. He went down to her street and he looked at her house and tried to guess which was her bedroom window. If Mary-Jane had known about this and she had fancied Daniel, it would be called romantic. If Mary-Jane had known about this and she didn't fancy Daniel, it would be called stalking. If Mary-Jane's boyfriend had known, he would have beaten Daniel to a pulp. Had Mary-Jane's parents known, they would have called the police. As it happened, nobody knew, and Daniel Grundy, insignificant Daniel Grundy, was allowed to watch the house in wonderment. Wondering mostly what it would be like in Mary-Jane's bedroom.

The ritual stopped when Daniel Grundy saw Mary-Jane kiss her boyfriend. He felt sick. She wasn't what he thought if she could do that. She'd kissed him in the street, all probing tongues and saliva. Maybe Mary-Jane would have been much better off with Daniel Grundy. Daniel would have been true to her. Terry had other girlfriends who he kissed in the street using tongues. The other girlfriends pretended they liked Duran Duran too.

Daniel stopped the watching of Mary-Jane and the catching of the bus. He threw her picture away. He carried on with the bathing rituals, and the teeth cleaning, which was a relief for all those people that eat meat. Some good came of Daniel Grundy's unrequited love. Mary-Jane was none the wiser about their affair.

Marilyn looks at Nancy. "I don't know. I don't think he did ever have a girlfriend. Not before he left."

"Marilyn," says Nancy after a long silence, "Ar doh think yower Daniel's the full ticket!"

Marilyn realises it is the first time she's ever heard Nancy use her Christian name.

Marilyn sits on her sofa after Nancy has left and realises that she hasn't responded to the mysterious request for a suitcase. The discussion about Daniel had led them both down a side track. She hopes that Nancy isn't going somewhere. She would miss the woman. The idea of people leaving upsets Marilyn. It had been such a shock when Daniel had left all those years ago, she'd not really got over it.

For some reason, not known even to himself, Daniel Grundy got up one morning and his head was telling him he needed to leave his hometown. Daniel followed his bathing rituals, got dressed, but then something changed. He didn't eat his breakfast. He didn't shout "Bye, Mom!" three times, and he didn't head off for work. Instead, he took his wallet and a carrier bag with their Shane's deodorant. He patted the dog, who had become very fond of Daniel since he started smelling of meat, three times.

Daniel looked in the mirror and stared at his reflection, blinked three hundred and thirty-three times before getting three cans out of the fridge and moving to Stockport.

Marilyn missed Daniel in the house. Shane was always out and about and it wasn't long before he moved out and got his own place, a small room in the Dana, Shrewsbury. She had to get used to her own company. The dog was very good to her though.

Now, Marilyn had got used to Nancy coming in and out and she didn't want to lose her new-found friend. All her life Marilyn had to get used to space where people used to be. Her husband had gone, leaving her with two kids. Nat had dumped her. Shane had gone to prison. Daniel had disappeared. The dog had gone. The canary was dead, and even the prostitute had left a small gap in front of the gas fire. And now of course the grandkids had been magicked away by her admission of doubt.

Marilyn would have felt relieved, and possibly a little guilty, to know that Daniel Grundy had indeed had a girlfriend in Stockport, and Daniel's girlfriend had actually got pregnant.

He'd met her in a pub. He was doing his work, pub, bed thing having got a job in a chicken-processing factory. He'd gone all the way up north to do the same thing with different meat.

Daniel was frightened at first about the baby, but Tonya said it was alright, that all he had to do was make sure he gave her money. His job in the chicken factory paid quite well.

Daniel Grundy's girlfriend being pregnant was quite a shock for Daniel. He'd only slept in her bed once. He'd gone back to her place after the pub. He'd been very drunk and he hadn't remembered doing anything with her but she assured him that he had, so he must have, mustn't he?

Daniel Grundy gave up his bedsit and moved into Tonya's spare room. He gave her nearly all of his money. He cut his drinking down to three a night which was hard because he'd got it up to twelve a night without too much trouble and when he cut it down he shook and panicked and woke up with the night terrors.

He did ask if they should be sharing a room but was glad when she said, "No." She explained that the baby would need to share her room. Daniel knew nothing about babies apart from a vague notion that they were demanding and that Tonya wouldn't really want to know him when the baby came. Not that Tonya really wanted to know him anyway, although she did want to be on friendly terms with his pay cheque.

Daniel worked overtime and made lots more money than usual. Tonya was happy. Her bump flourished and grew big. She delivered a son at eight months. She said it was premature. Of course it was, Tonya. The baby was big and healthy and bonny. Nothing like poor Daniel Grundy.

Daniel took a white teddy bear to the hospital for the baby. He looked at the newborn and felt nothing. He knew that he must do his duty. He wrote a card home to Marilyn. "Dear Mom. I am a Dad now. Hope you are OK. And the dog. Form. Daniel."

Marilyn had half-wondered if Daniel was dead, so it was quite a surprise to hear from him. She told everyone she met that she was now a grandma. It was a bit embarrassing when they asked about the baby and its weight. It was awkward when they asked after the baby's mother, because Marilyn didn't know anything. She told everybody that the baby had a shock of blonde hair, assuming that the baby probably resembled Daniel as a child. She said Daniel was doing really well holding down a job, and his girlfriend was lovely. She said the baby was called Nathan. She assumed it was a boy for some reason. Grandmotherly instinct.

The baby was really called Lucas after his dad, who had been called Luke. Tonya had wanted some security after the fair had left town. But she wasn't completely bad because she gave the baby the middle name Danny. If Daniel had been a Danny then life may have been better. Dannys are fun. Girls tattoo names like Danny on their arms and want to stop with them even when the Dannys have other girlfriends and other babies.

Marilyn dozed off for a bit in the chair and when she woke up again she started thinking about her second grandkid that had now potentially disappeared.

When Daniel was twenty-two and Tonya was still carrying fat from the first child, she announced she was pregnant with the second one. Daniel, who was still only on three pints a night, had not been drunk since Lucas was born and he knew that although he had lain in Tonya's bed when she asked him to, they had definitely not done anything that would constitute making a baby. He knew this. He knew it without question. He began to wonder if Lucas was really his. Daniel is a bit slow on the uptake sometimes. By now, though, life with Tonya and Lucas was one of his rituals and he didn't want to stop it, so Daniel kept his mouth shut and waited for the next baby to come.

Daniel was good to Lucas, and when Tonya went into hospital Daniel cared for the boy. He did it properly. He got hold of a double buggy and pushed Lucas up to the hospital in it. Daniel bought a brown teddy this time and strapped it in the other seat of the buggy. The new baby looked like Lucas had. Tonya looked tired. Daniel pushed the buggy with the two kids, and carried Tonya's rucksack so she only had to manage the teddy. They walked home from the hospital, because right then Daniel was afraid of going in cars.

Daniel bought a card from the shop, and sent another message home. "Dear Mom. I am a Dad again. Hope you are OK. Lucas Danny is getting big now. Form. Daniel."

Marilyn was cross to find that Nathan was actually called Lucas Danny. It was too late to tell everyone a new name, so she decided that Nathan was going to stay Nathan. She assumed the new baby was a girl. Her grandmotherly instinct wasn't up to much because it wasn't a girl, it was another boy. Marilyn got a bit more wised up this time. When asked what the baby's name was, she told them they were still deciding. She half-hoped Daniel might send a PS and tell her but he didn't, and in the end Marilyn had to name the baby herself. She called her Dominique. Marilyn had been watching travel programmes and thought Dominique seemed a nice sort of place.

She told everyone that Dominique looked a lot like their Shane. Shane had written her a long letter from the Dana and was in Marilyn's good books. "If the baby was more like Shane than Daniel that would be better all round," she thought.

The baby was really called Luca. The fair had been to town again. Tonya had been to the fair. Luke had spun her around on the Waltzers and, like the last time, he had spun her a line. She went back to his caravan. Luke, who liked Tonya – well, he must have as he'd done it with her twice now – told her she could phone him anytime on his mobile that looked like a house brick to let him know how the kid was. Kids, Luke! Kids. They should have used a condom.

Marilyn is sick of thinking about imaginary grandchildren. She stands up and looks at the space on the wall where her mirror should have been. Maybe Marilyn should disappear and get her own back on the world. But where would Marilyn go? She puts her weight on her foot. It is definitely feeling stronger. She decides that she will go up the shop tomorrow and get some food. The air will do her good.

When Nancy gets home it is surprisingly quiet. She'd half expected to walk in on Billy and Chrissie both sitting there with their arms folded, waiting for her, but there is no sign of her daughter and Billy is staring bleakly at the lunchtime news.

"Yow'm late," he says. It isn't a question, more of a statement.

"Ar," says Nancy without any inclination to provide an explanation, even if it had been a question. She sits on the sofa and puts her feet up to the side of her, sitting like a younger woman might. She leaves her trainers on, too tired to even kick them off.

"There's bin un attack on one uv the girls up Raby Street."

"I know, ar. Sum copper knocked uz ower Chrissie cum dahn. Soon as e towd uz er was off tuh warn the kids. Day even stop furra cuppa!"

That explains it then. Chrissie had forgotten her promise to "tell" in the excitement. Nancy feels guilty for linking the word "excitement" with an attack on a girl and then she feels more guilty as she hadn't even thought of going to warn her granddaughters to be careful. Twenty years ago she would have been straight off, knocking doors and telling everyone. She wonders where her community spirit has gone. Perhaps, she thinks, whatever she does it won't make a difference. Perhaps Chrissie is becoming the parent, the protector.

"There ay bin nothin on the newuz!"

"Fought im off, they reckon," says Nancy as the adverts come on. "Might av five minutes," she says, yawning. She closes her eyes. She hadn't dreamt anything last night. Nancy feels pleased with herself. "Perhaps they've stopped."

"Wot?" says Billy.

Nancy, unaware that she's said it out loud, doesn't answer. She is already asleep.

Daniel is worried. He is worried about three things, but the order of the priority of his worries has recently shifted slightly. The order of worry had been: A, where was Wass-er-face because he loved her? B, remembering when bin day would be because then he would be able to access the bingo winnings and run away to the seaside with Wass-er-face to live happily ever after (he liked the idea of her administering needles of the beautiful brown stuff) C, getting a drink or two to see him through the day. But his alcohol levels are starting to drop rapidly and he feels shaky and itchy and the order of worry begins to get jumbled and confused. He tries to condense his needs. A – get a drink because he loves it. B – he must re-member to take the bins out. C – he needs to find someone but can't quite remember who or why. He tries to think again. There, he has it. "Drink!" says Daniel.

Daniel heads for the shop. He goes in and Doreen watches him. He heads to the fridge and makes a pretext of looking as though he is going to buy an ice-cream. He then appears to change his mind and completely indiscreetly he loads four bumper-size bottles of Frosty Jack's into his coat and zips it up. He has doubled in size and has a little trouble adjusting. He bangs against a wire basket containing some reduced-price bread and mumbles an apology to the loaves before leaving the shop with as much stealth as an alcoholic carrying four cumbersome bottles tucked into a heavy winter coat in the middle of July can muster.

He runs and stumbles ten yards or so before he has to stop. He is panting as he looks back at the shop. Doreen isn't watching him, she has her head down writing something. Daniel congratulates himself on his cunning and undoes the top on one of the bottles which immediately fizzes out in a way which shouldn't be possible for something which calls itself cider. Daniel puts his mouth over the fountain so as not to lose any more of his spoils. The warm cider fills his mouth and comes down his nose. Daniel sits on a low wall in front of somebody's house and gathers his fizzy thoughts. He takes another long swig and a few gulps. Pain relief.

Drink priority sorted, Daniel's attentions turn back to Wass-er-face. He can now afford to be concerned about her again. He would begin his search on Raby Street where he first met her. He wanders off up the road, carrying three bottles, the empty fourth now lying in the front garden behind the wall he's been sitting on. Daniel is aware that he is whistling, but unaware that it is the theme tune to *The Sweeney*.

"Eye, eye. Here's trouble!" One of the girls shouts this to her mate further up the street as Daniel rounds the corner. She makes a cross-eyed face.

"Not him again," the young Asian girl shouts back. "He's bloody weird."

"You want business, love?" the first girl asks, laughing.

"I wanna know..." says Daniel, stopping as the effort of speech takes its toll. He unscrews the lid off his second bottle and offers it to the prostitute. She takes it and has a slug.

141

"What you takin that off him for? You don't know where he's been." The Asian girl walks over.

"Nah, he's only just opened it. Have some."

The first woman passes it to the second, who also has a large swig. Daniel has a beady eye on the size of the swig and feels the urge to grab the bottle off her, but she passes it back to him before he can act. Daniel takes another big swig, then spits a little bit back in the bottle, making sure the girls notice.

"I want to know about the attack," Daniel says. the power of speech coming back as his medicine kicks in. "It wasn't the boss-eyed girl was it?"

"Nah, wasn't her. You was looking for her the other night, wasn't you?" The girl is curious.

"Are you sure it wasn't her? How do you know?"

"It was me!" This throws Daniel for a second. He isn't sure if she is lying. She pushes her hair back and reveals a long scratch running around her neck. Daniel drinks from the bottle again, puts the lid back on and studies the evidence. Then he has a funny feeling, and goes to speak but can't.

When he comes round, the Asian prostitute is standing over him staring, and the girl with the scratch is on her knees at his side.

"You alright?"

"Man, you should've sin your eyes roll. Like *The Exorcist*." The Asian girl does a strange shaky dance and lets her pupils go up into her lids in an uncannily accurate imitation.

Daniel wonders for a second or two if one of them has tripped him up. "So it wasn't her?" he continues, still lying on the floor but looking round for his bottles, two of which have rolled into the gutter.

"No, like I said, it was me!"

"Did you see your attacker?" Daniel is feeling like a real police officer, better than the one that'd come to the door yesterday. He is asking all the right questions.

142

"What are you, some kind of copper?" the Asian girl says, laughing at him again.

"Yes," says Daniel, feeling pleased. "Inspector Grundy."

The girls both giggle and help Daniel to his feet. He starts scuttling about, rescuing his drink. "I never saw the bloke that did it. He came at me from behind. He legged it when I fought back. Elbowed him good and proper and he let go. I swung round and give him a good kick and next thing he was running off. I day bother reporting it 'til the next morning when Manda my drugs worker said I should."

"So where's Wass-er-face?"

"The boss-eyed girl? Dunno. I haven't seen her for a couple of days."

"She sometimes works down Ward Street too," the Asian one says helpfully.

Daniel thanks them and heads off following the lead they've given, taking his two and a half bottles of cider with him.

"Roll up! Roll up! To the greatest show on earth! See the flying woman take to the firmament!" The ringmaster, who looks a lot like Mr Sangha from the bottom shop, cracks his whip. There is a drum roll and the ooh-ing and ahh-ing of a large crowd. A spotlight swoops around the room and Nancy is filled with dread as she looks up at the star-spangled circus tent roof and waits for the beam to find her. She is conscious of the one wing hanging heavily at her side and the spangled, sequinned leotard that she is wearing. The leotard has been made for a woman with curves, not a stick-thin 79-year-old. Nancy tries to re-arrange some of the baggier bits of the costume.

"Ladies and Gentlemen, I give you the amazing, the marvellous, the sensational Nancy Maddox!" The crowd cheers. The spotlight stops swooping and she is standing in a puddle of light. She tries to flap her wing. It lifts imperceptibly and then there's nothing but the roaring silence as the crowd watch, waiting for something to happen. She can see beads of sweat standing out on Nirmal's head. He is looking worried. As she looks at him closely, she realises she's mistaken, it is not Nirmal at all, but Bernice from the pub. The dark curling moustache is fake and peeling off on the one side. "Do something!" hisses Bernice, hurriedly sticking her moustache back down.

"Wot?" says Nancy.

Bernice improvises. "But before that happens, the amazing flying woman will cut a man in half!" A tubby staffy up on its hind legs, wearing a stiff little tutu, enters from the off-stage shadows. It is pushing a magician's case on a trolley. The case is like a painted coffin and is filled with Daniel Grundy, his peanut head poking out one end, his dirty feet poking out the other, wiggling. The crowd seem interested again. "Quick, get sawing! Before they lynch us!" Nancy grabs the saw from the top of the brightly decorated box and starts to cut through wood, sending sawdust floating up into the stage lights. Then Nancy slices into Daniel Grundy like he's butter. He screams, and Nancy worries that if she cuts him completely in half he might not die. Instead, she might create two of him.

Nancy jolts awake gasping for breath. She struggles to get her bearings and thinks she sees a face at the window.

Daniel had headed off in the direction of Ward Street, but then he'd met Pete Something-or-other in the park.

Pete Something-or-other, who Daniel had never met before, had a bottle of whisky and a packet of fags. Daniel was feeling sociable, as he had enough cider to keep him going for a while and Pete, his new best friend, seemed very amenable to sharing his whisky. They talked gibberish for a number of hours, Pete speaking in patois, which Daniel doesn't understand. Daniel had nodded and drooled and laughed, which Pete didn't understand either. At one point Daniel drooled or laughed in the wrong way because Pete (or was it Paul?) cuffed him round the head and looked angry but then just as quickly he seemed to forgive Daniel, and the next moment he was laughing and patting him on the back.

The sun was very hot and they dozed together for a couple of hours on the grass. When they awoke, Pete got a scrumpled five pound note out of his trouser pocket and ordered Daniel to go to the shop and get some more alcohol. Daniel obliged and brought it back. They shared that, too.

Daniel had another turn, which Pete watched open-mouthed. Pete laughed again, and clapped Daniel on the back once he'd come round and was sitting back up. He seemed pleased by the entertainment. Pete told Daniel his life story, which Daniel would have been very moved by, if he could have understood any of it. Daniel's power of speech had gone for a while but it didn't matter as Pete was doing all the talking. Then Daniel's bladder control also went, which disgusted Pete so much that he got up and shuffled off to the other side of the park, where he went to sleep on a bench.

As Pete went, Daniel noticed that there were no laces in Pete's shoes and wondered how he managed to keep them on.

Daniel went to sleep too, clutching half a bottle of cider tightly to his chest like a child might hold a teddy. The night was warm, and as the sun set Daniel was at peace with the world.

When the birds start chirruping and chirping again at 3am, Daniel stretches, sits up, and drinks the rest of his cider. He stands up and carries on along to Ward Street in search of Wass-er-face.

When he finally gets there he sees a girl leaning into a car window. She has brown hair, she is about the same height as Wass-er-face. He is pretty sure it is her. He tries to shout, but can't think what to say. She gets in the car and he watches in the grey morning half-light. The car zooms off. Daniel is cross to see her disappear so quickly, after all he's taken 16 hours to get here, the least she could have done is stop and speak to him. But he is also relieved. "At least she's not dead in a bush!" thinks Daniel. "At least she hasn't been murdered by a crazy man!" says Daniel to the wall.

"Who mentioned anything about murder?" it answers.

Daniel is so pleased she is safe that he almost floats home. He is buoyed up by the thought of running away to the seaside with Wass-er-face. He decides to check up on his investment before going to his mother's. He tries Billy and Nancy's front door in case. He goes round the back and tries the back door. Then he tries the window at the back. Nothing is open to him. He stares in for a while to see if he can see any signs of wealth before turning to go back up the alley.

He notes that they still have their bins in their yard, which is encouraging in terms of his plan. He urinates up against them and then he goes back up the alley, crosses the road and bangs on his mother's door until she answers, bleary-eyed.

Marilyn heaves as he walks past her. "God, he stinks." He goes straight through into the middle room and sits on the sofa where she's been sleeping.

When she comes through, Daniel is back in detective mode. "When is Tuesday?" he says. Marilyn is still half-asleep and doesn't answer, but her son is persistent. "When is Tuesday? When is Tuesday?" he drones on. He makes her write herself a note to remind him when it is Tuesday and then he makes her put it on the mantleshelf.

Marilyn is wide awake now. She decides to take a bath. It's not even 3.30 in the morning and yet she feels strangely dirty.

Even if she could have, after the circus dream Nancy hadn't wanted to go to sleep again. It is 3.20 and nearly time to get up. She slopes off into the kitchen and quietly makes herself a drink. She keeps the cap of the kettle spout lifted so that it doesn't whistle. She pulls the door to so that she can put the light on in order to watch for the bubbles.

Once the tea is done she clicks the kitchen light off and creeps back in to the middle room and sits down on the sofa. She hasn't made a sound, or so she thinks, but the old man still tuts in his sleep.

Nancy drinks her tea slowly to bide time. She looks at the clock on the video blinking away, the video recorder that hasn't been used since the early 90s. She studies the slow minutes passing. Minutes are tricky things. When watched they seem like they take forever to go, like the number is never going to change, like she is going to be stuck forever at 4.34. It's when you turn your back on the minutes that they run faster and faster, hours passing, days, weeks. "79," thinks Nancy again.

4.35 eventually clicks up on the display. Nancy creeps out to start on the Summerhouse cleaning.

Once he'd got his mother to make a note about Tuesday, Daniel sat on his own sofa back in the front. Like Nancy he is aware that he'll need to get to work shortly. His day will be the never-ending task of sorting out some sort of alcohol or drug or both to get him through. He is tired now, though, and thinks he'll allow himself a little rest before getting going. He takes a couple of the painkillers that the doctor had given him. He can hear his mother running a bath and he is glad that she'll be out of his way for a bit, he isn't in the mood for her and her funny looks.

Daniel allows himself a moment or two to take stock. He feels pleased with his previous day's activities. It is good to know that Wass-er-face is still around. He is sure it'd been her getting in the car. Daniel wouldn't have liked to lose Wass-er-face, not now his plan is so close to coming together.

Daniel starts thinking about when Tonya had run away with the fair, taking little Lucas and littler Luca with her. Daniel was twenty-five when that happened and it had thrown him, he didn't like it when people went away and spoilt his routines.

Luke had got Tonya a job on the Mr Sizzle sausage van, and he'd got her a caravan. Tonya would be working with Tia, who was the mother of Luke's other children, Lucia and Lucien. It had all worked out quite well because the two women were a similar age and they'd got on when they'd met, which probably wasn't that surprising. After all, they'd got a lot in common.

Tonya left Daniel a note. It said, "Sorry. You have been a good Dad but I am leaving now." Tonya was about as good at notes as Daniel. Within the month the chicken plant laid him off; a lay-off being appropriate for chickens, but Daniel didn't see the funny side. He lived on baked beans and didn't pay the rent. He ate the beans three at a time, pronging them individually with the end tine of a fork. It was quite difficult. Sometimes it took him all day to get through a meal.

It wasn't long before Daniel got evicted from the house he'd shared with Tonya and the kids. When they came to take possession he didn't argue or make a fuss, within two hours of them turning up he was standing at a motorway island with his worldly possessions in a rucksack. Daniel had stuck out his thumb and got a lift with a truck driver who was well over hours and wanted someone to make sure he stayed awake. Daniel Grundy was ideal company, he was giving off enough nervous energy to light up a Christmas tree and the driver began to feel alert and full of electricity. He managed the journey from Stockport to Norfolk without stopping.

On the way back, without Daniel Grundy for company, the driver crossed the central reservation, killing himself and three other people.

Daniel got a job on a turkey farm in Norfolk. The farmer let him sleep in the barn. He even gave him an old camp bed and as much hay as he could cope with. The hay being to sleep in, not to eat. The farmer's wife made sure Daniel was fed, although he had to eat in the barn. She didn't want the lad in the house; she didn't really know why.

Daniel wasn't bothered. He liked the turkeys. It made a change to be working with live meat. Daniel was usually working with dead stuff. On Sundays, Daniel Grundy would go to the swimming baths in a nearby town and have a shower. He spent all his wages on the drink, but he did his job well, so nobody really bothered about his alcoholic ways.

Daniel starts to nod off as he is thinking of Norfolk. Daniel dreams of the farm. Turkeysdrinkbed. Turkeysdrinkbed. Turkeysdrinkbed. A little smile creeps across Daniel's face as he dozes. Daniel Grundy had been a good little worker. The farmer was happy because he paid him next to nothing to do the job. Daniel Grundy had another good ritual going and he had been happy. Yes, Daniel Grundy was happy once upon a time.

Marilyn feels like a new woman after her bath. She's had a good soak for an hour or so, letting out some of the water every time it went cold before topping up with fresh water from the hot tap. She is becoming extravagant since winning that money, there is no doubt about it. She'd relaxed in the bath and now she feels like she can take on the world.

She gets dressed and puts some weight on her ankle, gingerly testing it out. It feels strong. It feels as though it will at least get her to the top shop and back. Marilyn is jittery at the idea of going out, like the feeling of butterflies that she always used to get on a first date.

She walks from the bathroom into the kitchen and looks at the clock on her radio. 4.36. It is too early to go yet. She makes herself a bowl of soup, not able to wait for Nancy to deliver breakfast. Soup and beans are the only thing she has in the house; she must get out and stock up. Whatever Nancy says, she can't keep relying on her. Marilyn sits with the television on, turning the sound down so she won't wake Daniel or encourage him to come in if he isn't yet asleep.

Before 7.00 she decides to set off. She can't hear anything from the front room and as she opens the door she looks in to see Daniel sitting upright; his eyes are shut but he is smiling. He looks almost human. The sight makes Marilyn smile too. "He's lovely when he's asleep," she thinks, treading lightly as she goes through to the front door. She opens it quietly with only a click, slips through the gap she's afforded herself and pulls it to behind her. She winces when the lock clunks back into place.

Marilyn looks up and down the street. The day is warming nicely, the sky is blue, and it feels good to be out and about.

Well, out at least. She looks at her foot as though it isn't part of her. With one half-hearted glance down the road in the hope of spotting the missing dog, she decides to trust her foot and she makes for the top of the street.

It is an interesting style of walking but it is fairly effective. She gets to the top after a few minutes and makes the turn. She'd been right about the fresh air, it was definitely doing her good. Marilyn waves to an old Asian couple at the bus stop, who wave back cheerfully. She shouts a friendly "Morning!" to the man from the chip shop who is walking his grizzled border terrier. The animal sniffs at her as she passes, and Marilyn pats the bitch's head. The wiry little curls feel reassuring under her fingers.

Marilyn gets to the top shop, opens the door, pulls herself up the step and in a joyous mood, worthy of any mountaineer reaching a previously insurmountable peak, she greets Doreen with enthusiasm and a real sense of her own achievement.

"Oh it's you!" says Doreen grumpily. "Thought ya'd left town after ya win."

"No, I had an accident, hurt my foot. First day out in a while."

"Well, now that ya're here ya can settle up!"

"Pardon!" says Marilyn. Her foot starts to throb.

"£63.49 pence." Doreen presents Marilyn with a neatly itemised list.

"What's this?" Marilyn scans the writing. Doreen has very loopy ys and gs. She doesn't look like a woman that would loop her letters but there they are, unashamedly looped.

"It's what e's pinched since e's been back," says Doreen by way of explanation.

"Oh," says Marilyn as things became clearer. "I haven't got that sort of cash on me. And it's not like I've got one of those debit cards or anything," Marilyn says, going slightly red and putting her hand to her chest. "I'm good for the money though," Marilyn adds quickly as she sees Doreen start to scowl. "I'll bring it as soon as I can. Tomorrow or..."

"Mek sure ya do!" says Doreen. Her tone is unnecessarily sharp, but Doreen feels that Marilyn has to bear some of the blame, after all she'd brought the boy up. "Bring a bit extra with ya. E'll probably have been in again by the time ya get round to coughing up."

Marilyn feels ashamed. She takes some bread, milk, and a little tin of sardines from the shelves. The sardines might do for dinner. Then she remembers Daniel and swaps the little tin for a bigger one, in case he decides to eat something later. As she pays and leaves, she catches sight of herself in the shop window . Her hair is lank, she hasn't had a good cut in years. She feels ashamed again. When did she start to let herself go? Marilyns owe it to their names to be beautiful. She is letting the side down.

The journey home is more difficult and Marilyn gives up waving and greeting people. The man from the chip shop is walking back the other way and this time when the dog sniffs at her she doesn't even stop to pat it.

Marilyn thinks about asking Nancy for some of the money that is in safekeeping and then thinks better of it. She doesn't want to have to own up to the fact that Daniel has been misbehaving again. She lets herself back into the house, sits down on the sofa in the middle room and puts her leg up. She catches herself biting her nail and stops. She looks at her fingers. The nails are all chewed and yellow. She hadn't used to chew her nails. Marilyn sighs. She'll have to go into town. She'll need to rest her foot for a while but if it isn't hurting in the morning she'll go then. If not, she'll wait and go Saturday, but she'll definitely have to go into town.

Nancy had finished the Summerhouse by 5.30am. She was speeding up as she'd worked out a routine. She decided to go back home, have a little kip, and then do a sandwich and some breakfast for Marilyn. She hasn't given up on the idea of the suitcase and wants to ask again. Little steps towards her goal are keeping her going.

She does some cereal and a cuppa, and makes a cheese and onion sandwich, wrapping it in a little bag before putting it in her overall pocket. It is after 7 when she crosses the street carrying a mug and a bowl. She puts the mug of tea on the window sill by Marilyn's front door and knocks using her free hand. There is no answer. That's weird! Nancy knocks again, and then peers through the letter box. It is too dark to see anything. She listens and thinks she can hear snoring, it is quiet and raspy but it is definitely snoring. There is no sound of anybody making their way to the door on a dodgy ankle.

Nancy gets cross. She's gone to all that trouble of making breakfast, tea, and a sandwich and Marilyn isn't coming to answer the door and lend her a suitcase. Nancy starts coughing. She posts the sandwich through the door. "It'd serve Marilyn right if Daniel ate it!" thinks Nancy, uncharitably. The thought is out of character and Nancy immediately feels cross with herself again. She coughs a little more as she walks back over the street. She takes the bowl of cereal and the mug of tea in and puts them down by the old goat's chair, giving him a nudge as she does so. He wakes, blinking.

"Ta, cock," he says, although he doesn't make any attempt to drink or eat.

Nancy goes out on to the step. She lights up a fag with an orange lighter she's found on the floor in the Summerhouse. She smokes half of her cigarette, watching the street and staring hard at Marilyn's front door as if to make it open by force of will. The suitcase is bothering her. She feels like there is no progress being made. There is no sign of a passport and yes, the letter had gone off to their Vee, but what did that mean? It will make her look even more foolish if she doesn't get there now.

It is 6 o'clock in the evening when Daniel comes into the middle room with his hair cocking up, eating what looks to Marilyn like bread crumbs out of a bag. When she came back from the shop, Marilyn had inadvertently pushed the door over the sandwich that Nancy had left for her. Daniel had sniffed it out when he finally woke up, and was now tucking in.

"Is it Tuesday yet?" asks Daniel politely.

"No," says Marilyn.

"Stupid cow," says Daniel as though Marilyn were somehow controlling time. Daniel gives his mother a dirty look as he walks through to the bathroom. He is shaking and shivering as usual and he misses the toilet completely with a dribble of urine. He then makes an attempt to wash his hands without managing to turn the tap on. He carefully "dries" his hands leaving dirty marks on Marilyn's clean but threadbare white towels, and then he heads out into the early evening, aiming for the top shop but being waylaid when he notices the fire door to the lounge bar at the Dartmouth is ajar.

The room is mostly used as a function room, and as Daniel pokes his peanut head around the door to look, there is nobody in there, either drinking or manning the pumps. Daniel sneaks in and makes a quick evaluation. The end of the row of optics is tantalisingly near to the end of the bar. Daniel gets himself a stool, drags it as close as he can to the optics and then sits on it. He puts both his feet on the lower rung of the stool and levers himself upwards using the counter to steady himself. He stretches out an arm and finds he can almost

154

touch the end bottle. Daniel sits back down for a second as the exertion takes its toll.

He leans over the bar and eyes the glasses stacked neatly on the shelves under the counter. The spirit glasses won't be any good. He'll need a pint glass for this. He hangs right over the bar and finds what he is looking for, grabbing it and then returning to his seat.

"Oh, sorry," says Daniel, aware that he's been caught in the act. "I was...." He stops himself from explaining his actions further and apologising again when it sinks in that Tyrone is a dog, and that even with all the staring in the world the dog isn't really in a position to say anything. The dog growls and then barks once. Or maybe he is!

"You want crisps, boy?" says Daniel, in some sort of weird telepathic response. The dog stares at Daniel harder than before. Daniel reaches over the bar again and grabs some crisps out of a basket on a shelf at the back. He opens the bag and tips them on the floor. While the dog is occupied, Daniel puts both of his heels on the bottom rung of the stool again and lifts himself up. Leaning one arm on the bar and the other towards the optic, with his pint glass in hand he can just about manage to reach and exert enough pressure on the dispenser for it to deliver a shot. He manages to milk about ten shots or so before the shaking and burning in the arm he is leaning on gets too much. Captain Morgan looks down from the bottle, proud of Daniel's piracy. And so the evening goes on. Daniel pulling his latest stunt every time his glass gets low and then drinking the rum, Tyrone giving little "Crisps!" barks to his new interesting-smelling friend, and eventually the optic bottle is nearly empty and the basket of snacks is bare.

Daniel has stopped shaking and Tyrone is in serious need of a bowl of water to compensate for his over-zealous intake of salt. Daniel has replenished his glass, having drained the last of the contents of the rum bottle, and is on the verge of working out a plan to reach the next optic along when a police officer comes in through the fire door! He eyes Daniel suspiciously and calls through to the staff working the bar. "Anyone in?"

Daniel creeps off his barstool as the young barman, who Bernice had recently employed, comes through. "Did you know the side door was open?" says the copper. Daniel sidles slowly out towards the toilets taking his pint glass with him, stopping to listen once he is on the other side of the door.

"Thanks, mate," says the barman. "The cleaner must have left it open." Many people in workplaces like to blame cleaners. Nancy hadn't left it open, the barman himself had gone out for a cigarette, and when he'd come back in he hadn't shut the door behind him properly.

"Any problems tonight?" asks the copper.

"No, it's been quiet. Have you got anyone for the attack on the prossie yet?"

Tyrone starts barking for water.

"No, we've stepped up patrols a bit." Tyrone barks again. "What's up with him?"

"Probably wants crisps."

"Get him a bag," says the copper, taking a pound coin out of his pocket. The barman goes into the bar and re-appears with a bag. Tyrone stares in disbelief as another packet of crisps comes his way. "Water!" he barks again desperately. Though he eats them anyway. He can't help himself.

Daniel decides to hole up in the toilets for a bit until the coast is clear.

Yes, it was ridiculous and he knew it, but the vet had decided to take Friday off as annual leave and spend some quality time with Sebastian before he took him off to his mother's house the next day. He couldn't explain why he needed to do this, after all the dog didn't seem to be the brightest of buttons and it would probably not recognise the gesture for what it was. "A sort of feeling of..." he tried to explain himself to his veterinary nurse.

"Guilt," she hooted at him, stopping him in mid-flow.

The vet had laughed and nodded. "Guilt!" he'd said, holding his hands up in a gesture of surrender.

"Where are you taking him? The theatre? For a meal?" And so she continued all day, teasing the vet mercilessly.

The vet had actually decided that he would take Sebastian for a long walk on Cannock Chase, followed by a visit to a pet superstore to pick up a few more necessities for the move, and then he'd cook a steak tea for them both.

He pats the dog's head as he goes up to bed. "A good day planned for tomorrow, Sebastian." He lets the dog follow him upstairs and get on to the bed with him. His duvet cover is developing an odd smell which is definitely of the canine variety. The vet makes a note to himself to change the sheets soon. After all, if the weekend goes well, then who knows what might happen?

Daniel smiles. The gobbling of the turkeys is soothing at first, and then it gets louder. Too loud! Smack! One of the turkeys clouts him round the head. He wakes up to find himself sitting on the toilet seat in the cubicle in the gents at the Dartmouth. His pants and trousers are round his ankles and an incandescent Bernice is shouting for him to "Get out of the bloody bogs, yow dirty little junky!" She starts screaming for Jake, the new barman, to come and help.

Daniel blinks at her as one of her ropey red strands of hair flops off her scalp to hang down to one side of her head. Her turkey neck is swinging from side to side as she shouts.

Bernice and Jake manage to get Daniel outside. His fallen trousers and pants are holding his feet together, preventing him from kicking out or struggling too much. They frogmarch him into the street and cross him over the road to litter the pavement that isn't directly outside the pub. They hang him over the low, wide wall which runs in front of the overgrown gardens of the derelict vicarage.

"Gobble, gobble," says Daniel to himself.

Bernice gives him another clout for good measure, she isn't sure what this "gobble, gobble" malarkey is all about but she thinks it might possibly be some sort of vile junky humour at her expense.

"Call the bloody coppers. Let them deal with im."

Jake gets out his phone and dials. Bernice, aware now that her combover is hanging down the side of her head, rushes back inside the pub to sort it out.

Jake watches, shaking his head as Daniel, his pasty bottom exposed to the moon and the street lights and his trousers still round his ankles, hoists himself up to lie face down on the top stones of the wide wall as though it were a comfortable bed. Daniel yawns, stretches, and turns over before falling off into the overgrown gardens behind the wall. He sprawls under the branches of the fir trees. It has become customary for residents to plant their Christmas trees in the deserted grounds since the bin men stopped taking old trees away after Twelfth Night. The trees are flourishing.

It is a soft landing, and Daniel smiles up at the trees politely even though he doesn't like Christmas. As a kid, he'd been terrified of Santa. The idea of a man who could come down chimneys, showing the way for the burglars, frightened him. A man with a red suit and a big terrible laugh. Not even the fact that the man had presents was any consolation for Daniel. He used to try and stay awake to listen for the sleigh bells so that, should he hear them, he could hide downstairs in the glory hole when Santa got in the house. Their Shane loved Santa. Shane would look up the chimney and stare out of the window. Shane tried to stay up to see Santa. He had a million and one questions about how Santa juggled his preparations for the big day and still managed to be in Beatties department store for all those weeks running up to Christmas, including Christmas Eve. Given the chance, Shane would have asked Santa how he got all the way around the world in one night and what reindeers ate and what happened when they poohed whilst they were flying.

On Christmas morning, Shane would run to open his presents. Daniel would go slowly towards the tree, looking about him to make sure that the weirdy beardy Santa wasn't still lurking about.

Daniel wished that Jesus brought the presents. He could have coped with a nice calm Jesus bringing gifts. Even Jesus's beard wasn't threatening. No raucous laughing with the son of God. Jesus would probably stroke your head while you slept and leave you something special. Jesus would know what you wanted. Santa seemed to get it wrong a lot. Like the year him and Shane wanted a Scalextric and they each got a book and a scarf with matching gloves.

Christmas in Norfolk on the turkey farm was special though. The pub that Daniel used was decorated up for Christmas beautifully. A real tree, so tall the very tip bent over as it touched the ceiling. Gold decorations and gold tinsel.

On one of the days before Christmas there was a hoar frost; that's what the farmer had called it. Daniel thought he said "a whore frost" and wondered about it for weeks. He wondered if it was called that because the whores were the only ones who'd be out in that kind of weather. Daniel was using his

159

experience of the town to understand the country. On Christmas Eve, Daniel didn't drink his usual nine pints. He drank only three and decided to walk back to the barn early. It was so cold, so bitterly cold, but he had hay and blankets. He lay in the hay. He felt quite safe. No chimneys on barns. He imagined Jesus in his barn. He thought about the kids, the kids that weren't his, and he missed them. He thought about his mother. He thought about Shane. He didn't miss them, just thought about them.

The next day, the farmer and his wife had Daniel over to the house for his dinner. It was the biggest dinner Daniel had ever seen. Roast vegetables! Daniel had never eaten roast vegetables, only boiled. There were parsnips and swedes and turnips. There were potatoes and sprouts and turkey. He wondered which turkey it was, but he still ate it. The turkey was a humpy backed one that Daniel had been fond of.

After, they had brandy sauce poured over the Christmas pudding. Weeks before, the lady had put silver charms in the mixture as she'd stirred it. Daniel didn't know about this tradition because he had only ever had a bought Christmas pudding. He accidentally swallowed the old silver sixpence that had been passed down from generation to generation. Daniel Grundy was upset. The farmer's wife was upset too, that the fool Grundy had swallowed a family heirloom, but she didn't say anything because it was Christmas and a time of Goodwill To All Men. Even Daniel Grundy.

The farmer was softer on the lad than his missus. He was old school. He'd not always been a farmer, he'd been a hand like Daniel. He'd started as an itinerant worker. He too had been hard-working and liked a drink. He'd slept in barns. But the difference was he'd had the wherewithal to ingratiate himself with a farmer's daughter and he'd married her and her family heirlooms, inherited a farm. He ran it well and was kind to the daughter. He'd grown to love her, even.

Daniel didn't outstay his welcome that day, and left the couple to enjoy some of their Christmas together, going back to his barn as it was starting to get dark.

Back in the place he used to call home, Marilyn had sat all day imagining Daniel with his little family in Stockport and feeling sad that they hadn't come to visit. Marilyn never for one moment imagined that her Daniel was spending his Christmas in a barn. Daniel Grundy on a farm! She would have been shocked to know that Daniel was now the towny friend of the turkeys and swallower of family heirlooms.

Daniel had spent the rest of that Christmas night thinking about how he would get the farmer's wife's sixpence back for her, and how that would please her. Daniel Grundy tries so hard to be thoughtful. It was the first of many Christmasses that Daniel would spend on the farm, although the sixpence never quite made its way back into the Christmas pudding. Each year the farmer's wife would get the sixpence out, scrub it under the hot tap and look at it thoughtfully but, however much she scrubbed at it, she could never quite bring herself to drop it, plop, into the pudding mixture that she stirred in November, mixing it with her wooden spoon in the light brown, salt-glazed basin used by her mother, and her mother before that.

"Lovely fairy lights," says Daniel.

The beams from the torches flicker in amongst the undergrowth and play amongst the branches of the Christmas trees.

"We've got him," says one of the coppers.

"That's smaller than yours!" says another laughing, as they shine their torches on Daniel Grundy lying there with his arms outstretched, trousers still down and his small shrivelled penis on show to the world.

"Fuckin hell, I don't want him in the car. Radio in for the van."

"Fairies..." mumbles Daniel.

They make quite a fuss of Marilyn in the bank. They give her a chair to sit on in a little side room when it becomes clear that she's struggled all the way there with a bad ankle. A thick-set young man with eczema on his face and a Homer Simpson tie – clearly an attempt to show that bank managers have a sense of humour – orders a cup of tea to be brought. When his back is turned to Marilyn he mouths to the office girl he's put in charge of the tea-making, "It's the bingo-winning woman." Marilyn is given a chocolate biscuit too.

Nancy had not been right about Marilyn not being sensible enough to put her winnings in the bank. The bank had even given her advice, which she'd taken, about upgrading her account. When the bingo cheque had cleared Marilyn had taken some money back out, but not all of it.

The banker demonstrates the use of the cashpoint machine again. He'd shown her last time she'd been in, and the time before that, but Marilyn had been nervous and forgotten exactly what he'd said. The banker assures her that he'd be delighted to show her again and that she isn't "a daft old woman." There is a slightly embarrassing moment when he tells her to put her card in the machine and Marilyn has to turn from him to firtle around down the front of her blouse and remove it from its hiding place. She's been keeping it in the cup of her bra, under her right breast.

Together, they stand at the cashpoint machine as Marilyn tries to remember the sequence of moves the man has demonstrated. The bank manager watches approvingly, turning away as Marilyn cautiously puts in her pin number, pressing each key slowly and deliberately. She takes out £100 to pay Doreen off, and a little extra to get a bit of shopping in, another roll of tin foil (for emergencies), and a new bottle of Febreze.

As Marilyn limps from the bank, passes Argos and heads towards Sainsbury's, her attention is taken by a little shop that she'd not noticed before. Through the window she can see a masked Chinese man, who seems not much older than a boy, working very intently on the nails of a young woman. Both the mask, and the precision with which he works, put Marilyn in mind of a competent surgeon. If Marilyn hadn't got embroiled with bus drivers, her ideal man might have been a doctor; she'd liked Dirk Bogarde in *Doctor in the House* very much. She daydreams a little about handsome interns and watches for a while longer as the boy works. The whole shop is there for the sole purpose of decorating nails. Marilyn looks down at her nibbled, yellow fingernails in shame. She bites the nail on her forefinger thoughtfully for less than thirty seconds before she makes up her mind and goes in the shop.

When it is finally her turn she sits while the beautiful Chinese boy panders to her every need, rather like the bank manager had. She has pearly pink nails done with a little swirl of cream. And then the boy adds some dots and dashes that make a flower head. Her nails are quite simply beautiful. Marilyn gets out her cashpoint card which is also a debit card and pays for her new squared-off fancy nails.

The boy has to put her card into the machine the right way round for her and it is quite difficult to key in the pin number with the new nails, but she masters it eventually. "Yes," thinks Marilyn Grundy. "I could get used to this." The boy, still masked, passes her a receipt.

At Marilyn's request, the Chinese boy instructs one of the girls working in the shop to call a taxi. When it arrives, Marilyn asks the driver to take her to the top shop. She asks him to wait while she goes in and settles up with Doreen, who is a little disappointed that she isn't able to say that Daniel has been in again as she'd predicted, but she can't lie as she hasn't seen him.

Doreen raises her eyebrows and turns her mouth down as Marilyn hands over £70 in crisp ten pound notes. Marilyn then plucks something from the sweet trays and puts that down on the counter. An impulse buy. Doreen's eyebrows stay raised as she takes in Marilyn's fancy nails.

"If Daniel comes in again and takes stuff, then call the police as I won't be paying next time. Keep the change," says Marilyn, and with that she goes and gets in her waiting taxi to be driven the few hundred yards or so to her door.

If she is honest, the bingo win had all been a bit of a shock to the system, but she is rapidly coming round to the idea and rather liking it.

Nancy has knocked at Marilyn's door on her way back from cleaning at the Dartmouth. Still no answer. It is a relief in some ways, at least she doesn't have to go fetching and carrying anymore. It is good that Marilyn is back on her feet.

Then Nancy has a pang of concern. What if something has happened? After all, she hasn't seen either Marilyn or Daniel for a couple of days. She knocks on the neighbour's door.

"Yow sin er next do'ar recently?" she says, without even greeting the young lad that answers.

"Sin er yesterday. Comin back from the shop."

Nancy, happy to hear that Marilyn is still alive, crosses the street and goes in for a sit down.

"Come back, Sebastian!" the vet shouts, as Sebastian shoots off across the Chase. For a creature with three legs, he can certainly shift. The vet has thrown a stick, and Sebastian is running after it but then keeps going. The vet sprints after him, struggling over some boggy ground. He slips and falls sideways, landing on his arse in the mud. That particular pair of chinos will never be the same again. Sebastian has run back, keen to see why the chasing game has finished, but not before he's found something unmentionable to roll himself in.

The subsequent trip to the pet superstore, which had been planned as an excursion of treat buying, ends up as a visit solely to purchase pet shampoo. The vet and his pet are back home by 11 for an early bath which goes about as well as their quality time together. Breathless and red in the face, the vet fights and struggles with Sebastian until he manages to get him clean. He then turns his attention to himself and has a long soak in a Radox infusion, which the label assures him is intended for stress relief.

When the vet comes back downstairs in his towelling robe to find the casserole dish broken, and the two steaks which had been put out "to rest" before cooking now missing, his stress levels return to normal instantly, and he is completely resigned to the fact that taking Sebastian to live elsewhere is the best thing all round.

The police left Daniel in a cell to sleep it off over night. They checked up on him a couple of times and heard snoring. At about 10 o'clock next morning they took a photo, his fingerprints, gave him a slap on the wrist for being drunk and a bit of a nuisance and readied themselves to send him on his way.

"I doh feel well," says Daniel to one of the coppers.

"I'm not surprised," the copper answers, "the amount you must have put away. You'll be alright once you get outside and grab yourself a bit of fresh air."

"Can I stop here a while longer?" says Daniel.

"It's not a hostel."

"I'm not well."

"Nor a hospital. There's nothing wrong with you."

But Daniel couldn't argue anymore because he was having one of his turns.

"Jesus! Shit! Get an ambulance!" shouts the copper. "And quick!" A death in police custody would be a paperwork nightmare.

Marilyn decides to rest for the remainder of the day. She puts the TV on and finds a film. With her tired foot up on the sofa, and a cushion behind her, she watches her namesake trade banter with Jack Lemmon and Tony Curtis. She's done herself a cuppa and cut up a small bar of Turkish Delight into squares, allowing herself one at regular intervals. She doesn't know why she's chosen Turkish Delight or why she's chosen to cut it into squares; it seems right for a bingo-winning woman of means. Wealth.

In the ad breaks, Marilyn admires her nails and idly wonders where her son has got to. Perhaps he's left again. She wouldn't be surprised. Is she bothered? Is she relieved? Marilyn decides to avoid thinking about him and spoiling the mood. She thinks she might like to get Nancy a present for being so helpful, but what would somebody buy for Nancy?

The film comes back on. "Glamour," thinks Marilyn, "that's what's been missing from my life." She gives a little sigh as she absentmindedly tries to encourage volume into her hair with her right hand. With her left, she helps herself to another square of Turkish Delight off the china saucer set on the occasional table.

Nancy had left a note for the bouffant-haired landlord's son on Friday morning. She'd started it with "Dear" and then she'd had to scribble that out as she realised she didn't know the lad's name. She went for a more formal approach in the end. "The work is taking under one hour a day. I would like the money for Tuesday, Wednesday, Thursday, Friday and Saturday to be left for me on Saturday morning." She'd put a heavy full stop, and then thought. "Please," she'd added. Then, not wanting any room for error, she'd put on the bottom "Total - £42.50".

She prided herself in her honesty. She could have easily told them that it had taken her two hours but it wasn't her way. Well, it hadn't been her way. Nancy thinks about the money she owes Marilyn for the passport. What was that if it wasn't stealing? Nancy feels gloomy. What on earth has she become?

On Saturday morning, when Nancy arrives to do the cleaning, there is a note on the bar. "Dear Nancy, money in brown envelope in till. We are very pleased with your work. Do help yourself to a couple of bags of the out-of-date nuts." The boy has drawn an odd smiley face at the end which has the opposite effect on Nancy.

"Out-of-date nuts!" she mumbles. What is that saying about monkeys and peanuts? The cleaning takes her over an hour and then she goes home.

Billy is snoring, so she sneaks upstairs and puts the money back in the trolley. She crosses out the total on the IOU and replaces it with the new one. She is now less of a thief, £42.50 less to be precise. But it is small consolation. Nancy's head is telling her straight, "A thief is a thief," and it won't allow her to feel any better.

Nancy goes back downstairs, glances at the old goat still snoring, and then goes off to work up at the Dartmouth. The morning passes uneventfully, but instead of heading home after her cleaning stint has finished, she takes her wages from Bernice and heads to town, full of purpose and determination.

Nancy gets to the travel agents, and this time she goes in. She walks up to the desk and she asks about Brisbane. She asks how she would get there. She asks where she would fly from. She asks how much it would cost. The travel agent looks at the old lady with the oval glasses, the salt-and-pepper hair, the blue cleaners' overall, the crimpline A-line skirt, the American tan tights, the dirty trainers, and her idea of making holiday salesperson of the month goes right out of the window. She sighs, but keeps it inside and very politely, as if Nancy is her most valued customer, she explains the ins and outs of getting to Brisbane.

Nancy takes in all of the information; she gets up and mutters something to the travel agent about needing to think, and then she leaves the shop.

On the way home, Nancy realises that once she's paid back Marilyn and started to save up it will take her months and months and months to get enough money together. Nancy thinks about the possibility of getting a third job. On the evening, maybe.

Today Nancy avoids knocking Marilyn's door to ask for the suitcase. Ironically, today Marilyn is in. Had Nancy knocked Marilyn would have come downstairs and answered the door. She would have looked a bit dusty and flustered, the slight redness in her face not unattractive. Marilyn was upstairs sorting out the clothes in her wardrobe, putting things into

168

black bin bags (including a large plastic red letter D. Where on earth had that come from?).

Why doesn't Nancy knock? Is it guilt? Had the wind been knocked out of her sails when she heard the price of getting to Brisbane? Nancy is too tired to think about the reason, she needs a sleep.

Two hundred years ago it would have all been so much easier. Two hundred years ago they transported thieves. Transported them all the way to Australia. Nancy could have gone for nothing.

The man with the nice smile, who had thought a trip to Rhyl to dump the three-legged mutt would be a good idea, changes his mind slightly when the loathsome creature is sick. Sebastian Grundy is literally as sick as a dog, and less than twenty-five miles into the journey. The sick stinks. They have to drive with the windows open.

The vet looks at the man with the nice smile and the way he is over-exaggerating the smell, the way he turns his nose up to the open window, which he doesn't want open too far because it is drizzling. The vet finds himself having to suppress a smile.

"Ohh, disgusting!" says the man with the nice smile at regular intervals, getting seemingly camper the more he goes on. Sebastian pukes another three times.

After a while the vet thinks that the man with the nice smile is being a bit of a baby, but doesn't say so. But then the vet is used to smells.

When they get there, the man with the nice smile is impressed with the size of the vet's family home. It is up on a wooded hill surrounded by grounds. The man with the nice smile had lived in a reasonably affluent middle class neighbourhood as a child, but there had been nothing like this. The vet's mother lives on her own.

The man with the nice smile assesses her. She is about eighty, but strong. Proper country sort. Sea air and long walks have made her that way. She meets them with tea and biscuits. She shakes hands with the man with the nice smile. She talks local gossip with her son. She pats Sebastian's head. Sebastian isn't one to miss out on biscuits and the nice lady makes doubly sure that he doesn't.

The vet has introduced his friend as just that, "his friend". His mother is in her dotage and the vet isn't ever going to start worrying her with things like that. The friend doesn't mind being introduced as a friend.

"Show your friend about the grounds," says the vet's mother after a while.

Sebastian Grundy growls at the friend when he stands up to go for a walk about the grounds.

The vet and his nice-eyed friend are glad to get outside away from the formality of the day. They have another open-air fumble in amongst a particularly voracious strain of rhododendron which gives cover from the spying eyes of the house. Not that anybody is remotely interested in spying, the vet's mother is more concerned with getting to know her new charge.

From the fridge, she gets some best ham that she's been saving for tea, and gives it to Sebastian in a silver-plated bowl. The trinket had been some nonsense that her husband had won for his golfing. Sebastian slobbers the meat down quickly and then goes to sit at the old woman's feet. He puts his head on her lap and snuffles at her hands. She pats his head. "You're a fusspot then," she says. She hasn't realised that her hands still smell of ham and that Sebastian Grundy wants to get another taste.

170

When she hears the two men returning from their walk, she leans over and whispers into the dog's ear, "He's gay you know, like his dad."

Daniel was out for the count on the medical assessment ward. He was hooked up to wires and monitors and bleeping machines and there was a drip running into his arm. It was a hot windowless ward and the drip wasn't of an alcoholic nature but Daniel was in no position to complain.

In suburbia, some people are pottering in gardens and cleaning their cars, and some people are going for pub lunches before walking off their over-indulgences alongside a canal.

The vet would do all of these things later, but for the moment he is enjoying a lie-in. He's propped himself up against a pillow and the man with the nice smile is sleeping quietly in the crook of the vet's right arm. They'd had a late night.

He smiles as he plays back the events of the evening. Once they'd got back home, they'd cracked open the bottle of champagne to celebrate the start of Sebastian's new life. Secretly the vet had been hoping that this would be the start of a new life for him, too. Then they'd had a picnic on the vet's lounge floor with the food he'd bought but not eaten during the day on account of his mother filling them full of homemade scones and potted meats. The vet smiles down at the sleeping form. He'll give it five more minutes before he wakes his new lover and offers him some breakfast.

In the urban regeneration area that is All Saints, Nancy is fast asleep on the sofa and has been since she got back from her stints at the Summerhouse and the Dartmouth. Chrissie has come down and let herself in with her spare key. She is perched on the edge of the sofa, in the gap between the arm and her mother's dirty trainers.

"Thought ar'd cum an see'f yow wanted to cum to dinner again."

Any hope of a repeat performance of the previous week's attempt at happy families is quickly squashed.

"Yow wo wake er. Be like this now all afternoon," says her Dad grumpily.

"Why doh yow cum then?"

"Leg's playin up." He turns back to the telly.

"Ar might uz well be off then," says Chrissie, waiting for him to talk her out of it.

"Orright cock," he says, without even looking at her.

Chrissie leaves. Her mother doesn't know she's even called.

Billy decides if he can't beat his old girl then he'll join her. Without putting the television off, he leans back in his chair and starts snoozing.

Marilyn is asleep too. She'd stayed up half the night sorting clothes and then started again at first light. What did they say on that daytime television show? "If you haven't worn it in the last two years then let it go." She'd been through her vast amount of clothing and discarded nearly all of it. In her day

172

she'd bought things that were the height of fashion. What she hadn't spent on her boys, she'd spent on cheap and cheerful clothing, but she'd had the figure to make it look good.

Marilyn had worked quite hard and had always managed to keep the money coming in one way or another, sometimes aided by bus drivers and sometimes not. Once the boys had been in school she'd got herself part-time work for Chubb's and when they'd been old enough she'd gone full-time. She'd stuck with the company, and they'd stuck with her until the last change of name, when they'd laid her off.

That's when she'd lost interest in herself. There wasn't much to get up for. Nobody seemed to want to employ some-body who was three years shy of 60. She'd never managed to save while she'd been working, of course. She'd lived hand to mouth. The benefits had almost been enough to eat and pay the bills, well, apart from the phone which she'd had taken out to avoid temptation. The council tax and rent were covered, and every four or five weeks, if she squirrelled enough away and went easy on the electricity, she could afford a tenner for a game of bingo. It wasn't so bad, but she had to admit that now was the time to get a grip.

She'd got one chest of drawers left to go through, but she'd come downstairs and stopped for a quick cuppa and that was when she'd fallen asleep, one elbow leant on a stuffed bin bag, head resting on the crook of her arm.

Perversely, the only person that isn't asleep anymore is Daniel Grundy. He's come round to find himself hooked up to wires and tubes and a drip that isn't alcohol in a windowless and airless room. The pains in his chest and stomach are horrendous. Now he feels he is in a position to complain.

"NUUURRRSSE!" Daniel gasps. "Need sumfin to drink!" He passes out again with the exertion.

In the distance is a big wheel turning round very slowly, the little carts swinging slightly as it rotates to let more people on to the ride. She can make out Billy and Chrissie waving from one of them. There is a helter skelter too. Children are dragging up bristled mats to the top before sliding back down. There are swing boats and a coconut shy. It is like a proper old-fashioned fair. Marilyn is there buying a candyfloss, pink and fluffy. She is wearing a white, belted dress and is smiling. Nancy can hear the *plink, plink* of airgun pellets hitting metal ducks, and then the music starts.

The sounds of the barrel organ send a wave of nostalgia washing over Nancy. She is sitting on one of the painted cockerels on the carousel, both hands gripping the barley sugar twist of a pole that spears the creature through. The ride starts to move. The horses either side of her flare their nostrils. The insides of them are painted pinkish red like open sores. Nancy finds the colour disturbing amongst all the gaiety. She tries to ignore the horses and enjoy the ride. This had been her favourite as a child. Her dad had always taken her to the fair when it came to town. She'd always begged him to let her go on this ride.

Up and down the cockerel goes. Up and down and round and round. She closes her eyes and tries to pretend she is six. She opens them again and looks for her dad in the crowd each time she comes round to the place where she thinks she's left him. Instead, there is a girl with orange ribbons wearing a yellow summer dress with a white crocheted cardigan over it. She thinks she recognises her. It's Vee...Little Violet. She looks at the white shoes the little girl is wearing. She recognises the shoes and realises it isn't Vee after all. It is herself. Little Nancy Metcalfe, serious-faced, and looking worried.

The next time the carousel turns and the cockerel passes the same spot, the child has gone. Nancy thinks she sees a glimpse of yellow heading towards the cake walk, but she can't be sure. The music speeds up, and the movement of the carousel increases with it. Up and down. Up and down. Round and round. Round and round. Nancy feels ever so slightly sick. As a child she'd have ridden the ride forever and would have never have got queasy but now, as an adult, the up and down, up and down, round and round, round and round is unsettling.

Nancy is woken by the sound of her own coughing. She is immediately aware that it is Monday again. Up she gets, down to the Summerhouse. Up and down, round and round.

Had Daniel Grundy not come round, then things might have stayed the same. Up and down, round and round. Nancy would eventually manage to pay off her debt. Up down, round and round. She might then have been able to put the thieving incident behind her. Marilyn, not needing to bother Nancy for any of the money because Daniel was no longer there costing her and running up debts, would be none the wiser. And when she finally asked for the money back, Nancy would be able to return it all intact. But Daniel has come round. He hauls himself off his pillow.

"NUURRSSEEE! I need sumfin to drink!" One of the nurses comes to see what the shouting is about.

"Please," says Daniel, smiling at her.

"I'll see what I can do," she says.

Daniel falls back on his pillow. The sweat is coming up in beads on his forehead. The pain in his chest is still bad, although his stomach ache has subsided.

"Perhaps I'm having a heart attack," thinks Daniel.

He remembered how the farmer had clutched at his chest before falling and sending a splash of turkeys into the air. Daniel saw it from over the other side of the compound. For a second he thought maybe the farmer had tumbled over but he hadn't, he dropped like a stone. Daniel walked towards him. He didn't run. Only as he got nearer to the man did he panic. He didn't know what to do; didn't know how to try and save his friend. Daniel had come to think of the farmer as that. Even though the farmer gave him orders and paid him little or nothing, sometimes he went for the occasional pint with Daniel, or took him a can and sat with him on a bale of hay for half an hour.

Daniel didn't try to resuscitate his friend. He didn't know how to do that. Instead, he ran all the way to the farmer's wife and shouted in her face. It took her minutes to understand what he was shouting.

"Hesfellhesfallenonthefloorhesfellinthecompoundhesfell- hesfell." The wife wondered why a fall into mud could be so bad. Something about the panic in Daniel's voice made her call an ambulance before she ran up to see for herself.

The turkeys had calmed and were no longer rippling from the splash the farmer had made when he dropped. They were feeding around the farmer now. One large hen bird stood on his back as if he was some kind of rock. It wasn't the hen's fault, he'd fallen like a stone and the bird had no reason to believe he wasn't. Daniel followed the missus up to the compound, he watched her drop to her knees in the mud and try to turn her husband over. Daniel knew he was dead.

When Daniel got back to the barn he sat for a while and looked at the floor. He cried a little. Then Daniel picked up his bag of belongings and two of the old army blankets that the farmer had given him, and he left the farm.

Daniel Grundy was barnless. He walked all night until he got to a main road he liked the look of, and then he stuck out his thumb again like he had years earlier when Tonya had left him. A transit van stopped. Daniel Grundy hopped into the front seat and went where he was taken.

The transit was going to Leamington Spa to make a delivery. The driver said he'd drop Daniel by the railway station. Daniel chose a direction and bought a ticket. He ended up in Birmingham and then he got on another train to Manchester. The train went via Wolverhampton. It also went via Stockport. Daniel got off the train in Wolverhampton and walked from the railway station. He walked to the top of his mother's street and stopped. He looked down the road towards his mother's door. He imagined his mother and Shane in the house. He imagined them saying, "Oh God, it's Daniel." He imagined them not wanting him. He imagined the dog growling at him. There was always a dog. It hadn't registered that years had passed, that Shane was long gone, and the dog he was imagining had succumbed to distemper a year after he'd left.

Daniel turned round and walked away. He decided he should have stayed on the train and gone to Manchester, so he went back to the station and caught the very next one. But he couldn't help himself and decided to get off at Stockport and find his real family. Now he was respectable and upright and had been working on a turkey farm, surely Tonya would want him back.

Train travel was very expensive; when Daniel got off in Stockport all of his money was gone. He had no choice but to find a hostel. The first night there he was offered heroin, weed, crack, and a blow job. Daniel Grundy turned it all down. Well done, Daniel Grundy. He wanted to keep himself respectable for Tonya and the boys.

The nurse comes back with a plastic jug and a plastic see-through tumbler.

"What's that?" asks Daniel.

"The water you asked for," answers the nurse, puzzled.

"Fuckin water!" says Daniel. His stomach ache starts to come back and compete with the pain in his chest. He'd need to do something fast. "Am I dying?" Daniel asks.

"You will do if you keep drinking," the nurse says, cutting the warm heavy air in two with her sharp tongue.

Marilyn's foot is stiff again. It is inconvenient not having a phone anymore. Marilyn thinks about getting it reconnected. She imagines Daniel on it, phoning all sorts of dodgy people who might phone back and shout threatening things into the earpiece like they had through the letter box. She decides to wait to see if he's gone. Or if he hasn't gone, she'll wait and see if he settles down a bit. She is still keen to give him the benefit of the doubt. Perhaps if she did get the phone put back on, in case of emergencies, she could get one with a lock so that only she could use it. She could hide the key. She is surprisingly good at hiding things when she wants to be. She puts her hand to her right breast and checks for the oblong of plastic nestled above the wire of her new pale pink bra. It is a lovely lacy thing that Marilyn had found in the back of a drawer yesterday. It'd still been in the packet, although the price on the packaging had been in old money.

Marilyn stops prevaricating and decides to go to the phone box. Billy is on his step as she comes out of the house.

"Cooeee!" shouts Marilyn, waving. "How is she? I haven't seen her for a few days."

"Er's bin cuffin well," says Billy, who is – on the quiet – a bit worried about his wife. It's making him fidgety. This is why he's standing on the step today, hanging around on the edge of the real world.

"Oh dear," says Marilyn, who would have struck up more of a conversation if Billy hadn't lost his nerve and gone back in.

Marilyn carries on up the road and calls herself another taxi. They recognise her voice this time. The base operator knows the address before she says it. "I'm becoming a regular customer," thinks Marilyn proudly.

The taxi driver waits impatiently as Marilyn loads up his boot and his back seat with black bin bags. Seventeen of them! They are piled so high that when he goes to look in his mirror, which admittedly isn't often, he can't see over them.

"The charity shop at the bottom of Cleveland Street," says Marilyn. They drive around the city's one-way system in the heavy traffic until they finally manage to access Cleveland Street from the correct end. There is nowhere to unload so they block a bus stop while Marilyn humps out the bags one at a time and hauls them into the shop. Once Marilyn has taken the last bag in, she stops to finish her conversation with the girl who is taking the bags from her. The taxi driver honks and hoots. The bus drivers honk and hoot. And Marilyn waves a dismissive arm until she's finished what she wants to say. She is a bingo-winning woman, and they can whistle.

When Marilyn gets back in the taxi, she instructs the driver to drop her round to Beatties. Beatties is the sort of shop that she would have liked to have shopped in all those years ago when she was trying to make ends meet. The taxi driver grunts. Marilyn could easily have walked round to the shop in two minutes, and well she knows it, but today she is going to do everything with style. They head off into the one-way system again, passing the nail shop which Marilyn looks at fondly, before circling the city centre to gain access to Worcester Street from the right end.

The taxi rank outside the shop itself is full of black cabs, so the private hire taxi driver has to stop in the street, blocking the road again. Marilyn asks the driver to wait while she visits the cashpoint. He growls. Marilyn gets out and goes to the nearby hole in the wall. She gets out three crisp ten pound notes, trots back to the taxi, and uses one of them to pay the fare.

A bus comes down through the lights, the driver hooting the horn. Marilyn, who would normally have scuttled away in embarrassment, waves a manicured hand at the driver while she waits for her change. The driver tuts to himself as the woman finally heads towards Beatties' steps and then up through the revolving doors which lead to the perfume department. As he watches her go he feels like he knows her from somewhere and tries to recall a vague memory. Then a second bus coming through the lights starts honking its horn, and the driver shakes himself out of his reverie and moves on.

The perfume girls, who are usually very good at working out who to offer samples to and who to ignore, are in a state of confusion. The look is washed-out and bedraggled, but then there are those nails. Not cheap. And there is something about the walk. Marilyn puts them out of their misery. "May I have a little spray?" she says to a tall girl with long black hair extensions. The girl has enough orange foundation to provide the footings for a block of flats. She manages a smile, and obliges with a squirt of something very, very expensive. "Thank you," says Marilyn. "There used to be a hair salon in here," she continues.

"Yes," says the girl. "A very good one. It's still here."

"That's exactly what I want," says Marilyn. "A very good one." She looks at her nails as she says it.

When she goes into the salon, the girl in charge of the appointment book eyes Marilyn suspiciously. "I'd like an appointment," Marilyn says confidently. "Do you have anything this morning?" The girl looks unsure. Marilyn puts one of her hands flat on the counter as though the fancy nails were currency. "I don't mind waiting," says Marilyn, smiling.

The girl remembers they've had a cancellation. "11 o'clock," she says.

"45 minutes to wait," says Marilyn. "Time to treat myself to a cuppa." She goes to the coffee shop and orders a big mug of hot chocolate with cream and marshmallows. Then she notices the muffins with chocolate chips and asks for one of those too. She sits in the window. She's usually on the other side of the glass, watching the suits and the smart women sipping their expensive drinks and nibbling at the overpriced cakes. She sips, enjoying her little foray into decadence. She looks at her reflection in the window and smiles at her lank locks. She passes half an hour looking at all the passers-by as she drinks.

A woman waiting in a bus queue is holding a bright bunch of flowers, orange gerberas. Maybe that would be a good thank you for Nancy. "What kind of flowers would she like?" wonders Marilyn. A vision of a cactus comes unbidden into Marilyn's mind. Perhaps not.

She stares into the dregs of her hot chocolate and readies herself to go. How had she managed to end up like this? One son in and out of prison, the other wavering on the verge of lunacy. It's not what she'd have chosen for her kids. Men, they were now. At least Shane was out of her hair. But Daniel! Well, what could be said about him? Drink, drugs, missing dogs, dead canaries, prostitutes, and imaginary kids.

Marilyn feels a little sad for him as she stands up, and heads for the hairdressers with every intention of making herself bottle-blonde again.

Imagine her surprise when the hairdresser suggests that this might not be the right kind of look for the more mature woman, suggesting instead that she opt for "Champagne Fizz".

181

Marilyn sits back and lets it all happen, drifting off as the stylist works, imagining what delights might lie in store in the various fashion concessions she plans to explore later. The debit card feels hot and exciting against her skin.

Cough, cough, cough. Cough, cough, cough. This is how it goes all day. She keeps sipping water as she cleans, but it has no effect. The cough is dry and tickly. Cough, cough, cough. Cough, cough, cough.

"Gerrit up, girl. It might be uh gold watch!" says Bernice.

Daniel is fermenting in his own juices. Every time he moves in the bed he releases some kind of new and interesting smell. He'd been in the police cell for a night and then on the ward for couple of days, and nobody has cleaned him up.

The patients in the next beds have gone off their food, and their visitors, not wanting to criticise overworked nurses, don't like to complain on their behalf. And in the darker recesses of their minds they want to avoid, should there happen to be any deviant nurses on ward, some kind of Beverley Allitt, Harold Shipman type of incident happening at the expense of their kith and kin.

At afternoon visiting, the son of the elderly lady in the bed to the right of Daniel pulls the curtain across between his mother and her neighbour. Psychologically at least, the smell improves. Out of sight, out of olfactory reach. The visitors on the other side follow suit. Daniel doesn't mind, it all helps his plan.

Under cover of the curtains, he pulls out his drip and his wire and his bleeping machine. He stands up, slips on the green foam slippers they'd issued him with, pulls his gown down to cover his embarrassment, peeps out from the curtain and scurries for the door. "Going to the toilet," he shouts to a nurse who is on the phone at the desk. And off he shoots, through the corridors, down to the exit, heading for the main road and the nearest off-licence, not far from the entrance to the hospital.

Strangely enough, nobody stops Daniel. A couple of people look after him as he passes, slightly intrigued, but they quickly look away again in embarrassment once they've caught sight of the pale bottom on display to the world through the open back of the gown. Even the off-licence owner, who hadn't noticed Daniel come in the shop, isn't particularly surprised to see a half-dressed figure disappearing out of the door clutching four unpaid-for cans of Tennants Extra. It isn't the first time it's happened and it probably won't be the last. He doesn't bother to give chase.

Daniel feels woozy. He doesn't know that he isn't going to be chased, so he ducks in between two cars in the long row which snakes round the circumference of the hospital grounds. These days the sick and injured like to drive to within crawling distance, preferring to die trying to get to their outpatients appointments rather than pay the extortionate amounts the hospital charge for parking. Daniel opens a can and proceeds to self-medicate. The nurse had probably meant well with her water, but he had known what he needed.

The can does actually steady him somewhat. His pains seem to subside. Daniel is still fully aware he isn't well, and intends to go back to his bed. They are feeding him and putting a roof over his head, so now that he's got what he needs he'll be OK there for a little while. He peeps out from between the cars. There is no sign of any angry off-licence proprietor, so he comes out of hiding and begins walking back towards the hospital, and then he sees it. The bin lorry!

He remembers his plan. The bingo winnings, Wass-er-face, the happy-ever-after he'd promised himself. The lorry is waiting in a line of traffic which runs up to the lights. Its flashing indicator shows it's heading towards the city centre. "What day is it?" Daniel asks a woman at the bus stop.

"Monday," she answers.

Daniel tries to think. Bins are part of his plan, so it all makes perfect sense. He clambers into the back of the lorry with his cans and waves to the woman, who looks cagily about her as though searching for hidden cameras, before waving back. The lights change to green, and the lorry heads on towards the depot.

Later that night, when the nurses remembered Daniel and went to check on him, all they found behind the drawn curtains was filthy bedding and a lingering smell.

Marilyn is exhausted. She's shopped until she's nearly dropped. She is loaded down with bags. She's been treated like royalty by the women in the hairdressers and on all the little stores. They've styled her hair, suggested figure-flattering outfits, matched shoes to bags, and kitted her out. She looks like a million dollars and it has only cost her eight hundred pounds. "That has to be a bargain," she thinks as she catches sight of herself in a mirror.

One of the concessions has even given her a bag to put all her old clothes in so she can wear her new ones to go home. Marilyn sinks into the back seat of a black cab and gives her address. The taxi does a three-point turn and heads towards All Saints. The taxi driver keeps glancing in his mirror, unsure if the lady knows quite where she is going, it is such an unlikely destination for somebody as well-off as his passenger appears.

The taxi has to pull in a few doors up, as there is a bin lorry outside Marilyn's house. She pays with another crisp ten pound note and tells the driver to keep the change, which gives her another thrill.

Two of the lorry crew are helping Daniel out of the back of the truck as she is busy paying the taxi driver.

"There you go, mate. Safe and sound."

"Cheers," says Daniel as they pass him his two remaining cans.

They'd discovered him at Broad Street lights when a car driver had pulled up alongside them, gesticulating wildly for them to roll the window down. "You're carrying a passenger," she'd said. "In the crusher bit!" They'd got out to check and found him sitting there drinking his second can. The bin men couldn't help laughing.

"Where to, mate?" one of them had said. Daniel told them his mother's address like it was the most natural thing in the world for them to take him home, and so they played along. It wasn't too far out of their way, and who knows what trouble they'd be in if they took him back to the depot. There would be at least four different regulations being breached.

When there is no answer at the door, they ask him if he'll have long to wait for someone to let him in. He assures them not. They don't seem to notice the smell, but they had kept their gloves on when they were helping him out of the truck.

As they walk away from the door, the younger one of the two gives a low whistle as a glamorous woman walks past them, and touches his baseball cap in a gesture of respect. His mate barracks him. "She's old enough to be your mother!"

"I still would, though."

Marilyn isn't offended because she knows she is actually old enough to be his grandmother, and she blushes pink from the top of her Champagne Fizz-coloured head to the tips of her rose-pink kitten-heel shoes and allows herself a girlish glance over her shoulder towards her new admirer.

"Oh Lord!" she says as she turns back round, realising that the bin lorry appears to be dropping off rubbish rather than taking it away. "Daniel!" she says. He is sitting on the floor leaning up against the wall, rubbing his stomach. There is no point asking him where he's been, it's pretty obvious from the gown and the tag on his wrist. She steps round him, and opens the front door. Daniel gets to his knees and holds the door for her. It is unusual for Daniel to be helpful, but she is clearly struggling with all of her bags. He looks at his mother. There is something different about her. She looks taller. Admittedly he is kneeling down, but she definitely seems to have grown.

"Mom, can you lend me twenty quid?" he says. It's a shame to waste an appropriate begging position.

"No, Daniel. No. I'm not giving you money for drugs or alcohol." Daniel looks up at his mother. He knows she isn't going to cave in. Something about the look in her eye tells him. She isn't going to give. There is a glint there. A look he hasn't seen for years. Ever, maybe.

"Bath, now!" she says sharply. Daniel scuttles to the bathroom and does as he is told.

While he is in there, Marilyn puts her purchases away in the empty drawers and wardrobe. She opens the upstairs windows and lets in some air. Or maybe she is letting something else out, who knows. She comes downstairs in her old housecoat, a chiffon scarf tied over her new hair, and she cooks them both some tea, over which she and her son will talk.

Cough, cough, cough. Cough, cough, cough. While Nancy waits in the queue for a packet of fags, the man behind her – who has been planning to give up smoking at New Year – quits the queue and leaves the shop. He also quits his twenty-a-day habit there and then, without the aid of a patch. Had Doreen known she'd lost a valued customer due to Nancy's cough, she would have been furious.

Cough, cough, cough. Cough, cough, cough. Doreen puts the fags on the counter and names the price.

"Yuh should give it up!" The voice is deep and menacing. Nancy knows who it is before she turns.

"As vices goo," says Nancy, with a pause, "tay too bad. Ony me uz suffers." The comment is loaded.

He purchases a pack of chewing gum with the right change and beats Nancy to the door, holding it open for her. She passes under his arm, coughing as she does so.

He watches her go and shakes his head.

When Daniel comes out of the bath, Marilyn turns the television off. He eats his tea even though he isn't hungry and doesn't want to, and she watches him do it. When he's finished he opens his third can. "You need to stop that!" she says firmly.

"I can't. It hurts."

"I'll pay for you to go to rehab. I'll pay for you to get better. If you come with me to the doctor's tomorrow, we will sort it out." Marilyn has taken the advice from the fount of all knowledge, the hairdresser who'd done her hair. She knew a woman whose daughter had been on drugs and they'd got her into a clinic and she was now as right as rain, got a kid of her own, and married to a dentist.

187

"Cost them about three thousand pound, mind," the hairdresser had added. Marilyn is prepared to invest it, but it is to be a one-time offer.

"It's a one-time offer," says Marilyn.

Daniel looks at his mother. "Yes. I'd like that," he says. But in his mind he is picturing Wass-er-face administering drugs to him. The seaside. A life with no worries.

"I've got no clothes," says Daniel, attempting to change the subject. "I've left mine at the hospital." Marilyn recognises it as an attempt to change the subject. She goes upstairs. In the front bedroom is a wardrobe with some of the boys' old things in. She pulls out some jeans and a jumper. She goes back down.

"Here, they're clean." Daniel puts them on. The jeans divorce his ankles, and won't stay up.

"I need a belt," says Daniel.

His mother is inclined to agree; she goes back upstairs but all she can find is a pair of red braces. She takes them to him and he puts them on. The trousers stay up now but the gap between his ankles and the bottoms of the jeans is bigger. Daniel slips his feet back into the hospital-issue slippers. It is a strange look, and Marilyn is pretty sure it won't catch on. "At least he is clean and covered," she thinks.

"First thing in the morning, we go. If you don't come, then that'll be it, you're out. I'll have nothing more to do with you until you're sober. You can sort your own life out. Lecture over," says Marilyn, looking at the clock and realising it is time for the soaps.

"By the way," she adds, taking the piece of paper off the mantleshelf and passing it to him, "it's Tuesday tomorrow."

"Yes," says Daniel, "the start of my new life." Daniel smiles a winning smile, and Marilyn smiles back. She has to stop herself in her tracks as she starts to feel almost hopeful.

"We shall see," says Marilyn. "We shall see."

The only chance Daniel has ever really stood of getting his mucky paws on the bingo winnings stashed in the Maddoxes' house is bin day. Although it's been unlikely that Daniel was ever going to be organised enough to put his plan into action, the fates, the gods, the bin lorry and Marilyn's reminder that it was Tuesday had all played their part.

Daniel is up early as his stomach is aching. He ambles round getting ready. He pulls his jeans up and puts his braces over his shoulders. He can't find his new jumper, but while he is looking for it he comes across his mother's make-up case and paints his face with stripes of her mascara in some sort of attempt at camouflage. He gets carried away with his brilliant idea and paints some on his chest too. He puts on his hospital-issue slippers and goes down to the bottom shop. His disguise works, as Nirmal doesn't even notice the smutty-faced, stripy-chested Grundy boy come or go. Daniel gets himself a big blue bottle of cider and heads for his preferred position on top of the shed roof next door to Billy and Nancy's yard.

Daniel doesn't have long to wait, which is a relief as he is starting to feel quite tired. The pain in his belly is dull now and he wants to sleep. He hears the bin lorry turn into the top of the street.

Marilyn hears it too, as she comes downstairs. She is – optimistically – dressed up to the nines for a trip to the doctor's. The optimism is in part that Daniel would be ready and waiting, and in part a hangover from the previous day's success with the young bin man. It wouldn't hurt to see what talent was on offer at the medical centre. She's been awake half the night rehearsing her speech about the help that she'll require for her son, and planning her outfit.

She goes into the front room and sees that Daniel is missing. "One-time offer," she says to the empty room, and returns upstairs to change back into her housecoat. No point wasting her glad rags on the inside of her house. She feels sad. Very, very sad. She ties a chiffon scarf over her new hair to keep the stepped-out-of-the-salon look for as long as possible. "What now?" thinks Marilyn, as she sits on the edge of her bed.

Billy had also heard the bin lorry, and Daniel starts to sweat like crazy when he sees the old man stand up, leave the comfort of his chair, and head for the back door. It's all happening in slow motion. Billy walks towards the alley between the houses. "Come on!" mutters Daniel. "Come on!" The adrenalin starts pumping.

As he is about to move from his hiding place in the rolled-up tarp, the woman from the house whose shed roof he is hiding on appears, and goes through her gate. She is also going to fetch her bin back in. Billy stops to talk to her. Daniel gets agitated. "Fuckin stupid woman!" He thinks his heart or his head is going to explode. Finally, Billy and his neighbour both continue up the alley and head to the street. Daniel takes his chance.

He leaves the neighbour's roof with his cider tucked under his arm, and crosses over the fence to clamber on to the Maddoxes' shed roof before swinging himself down into the yard and reaching back up to grab his cider. He goes through the Maddoxes' back door, through the Maddoxes' kitchen, and through the Maddoxes' middle room, getting tangled up in the curtain hung between middle and front room to stop draughts. Daniel then pulls open the Maddoxes' glory hole door and throws himself into the darkness, shutting the door behind him again. He sits still, trying to catch his breath. Daniel is in! He pats his cider provisions to settle himself. All he has to do now is wait. When the Maddoxes have gone to bed he will sneak around the house and find where the woman has put his mother's bingo money. He opens his cider and it fizzes out a bit. "Sssh!" thinks Daniel Grundy.

Daniel tries to keep his mind occupied thinking about the new life he'll have with Wass-er-face. Perhaps they'll even have kids together, like the ones he had in Stockport. It is very dark in the cupboard and Daniel isn't sure if his eyes are open or closed, which freaks him out. He puts his fingers up to feel. "Ow!" says Daniel. His eyes are open, so he shuts them and tries to picture his kids. He thinks back to the time he had last seen them.

Daniel had stopped at the hostel in Stockport for six months before he plucked up enough courage to look for Tonya. He refused crack every night. He refused brown every night. He refused weed every night. He refused to give blow jobs every night. He didn't manage to refuse drink every night, and took what he could get where he could get it.

When he walked up the front path to the house that he had shared with Tonya, everything looked the same. He expected to knock the front door and have her open it and let him in, like he'd been a sailor returning from the sea with a kit-bag over his shoulder. Daniel had grown his hair long since he'd been on the turkey farm and he had it in a pony tail. It made him feel older and more interesting.

A young bloke in a baseball cap opened the door. "Where's Tonya?" asked Daniel politely.

"Fuck off!" shouted the man in the baseball cap. He slammed the door. Daniel was cross. He was cross that the young man had spoken in that way to upright, clean Daniel Grundy who refuses heroin, crack, weed, and blow jobs. He knocked again. Daniel Grundy was confident.

The young bloke answered the door again. "I'm looking for Tonya and Lucas and Luca," said Daniel. "Do you know where they are?"

"Never fucking heard of them," said the young man.

"They live here," said Daniel.

"I think I'd have fuckin noticed them," said the lad.

"They used to live here," said Daniel.

"Watch my lips. Never-fucking-heard-of-them."

"Thanks anyway," said Daniel as the door slammed in his face. Daniel had finally got the message, although not enough to stop him lifting the flap to look through the letter box in case Tonya and the kids might really be in the house but hiding from Daniel, the way he and Shane and their mother used to hide from the Shoppercheck woman on Friday nights. He scanned the hallway. No sign. Maybe the young man was right.

Daniel Grundy went to Tonya's mother's house. She hardly recognised him. For one he looked her in the eyes, and for two he had this silly pony tail. Why should she recognise him? She had only met Daniel twice. Tonya had told her mother he was the lodger. Which he was. It was only Daniel who didn't realise that.

"Hello, Mrs..." He couldn't remember Tonya's surname. "Where's Tonya and my kids?" Tonya's mother was a bit thrown by the "my kids" but she didn't say anything.

"Still living with the fair, Dameon." Daniel was too polite to correct her. And anyway he couldn't remember her name, could he?

"The fair," he repeated. A memory was forming. He had forgotten about the fair. "Is there any way I can contact her?" asked Daniel. Tonya's mother looked at Dameon. He'd been a good lodger as she recalled, and she couldn't remember Tonya saying anything bad about him; she'd probably want to see him.

"I can give you a telephone number," said Tonya's mother doubtfully. "Or," she said, "you could pop along and buy a hot dog off her." Daniel looked confused. "The fair. It's in town the week after next."

192

"I'll do that then," he said. "I'll pop along and visit her. She'd like that," said Daniel.

"Bye, Mrs."

"Bye, Dameon."

Tonya's mother half-wondered if she should phone Tonya on her mobile, and warn her about the imminent arrival of her ex-lodger, but she got caught up in a TV programme about serial killers, and after that she forgot.

Daniel went back to the hostel and made his nightly refusals. He snuck a bottle of whisky that he'd stolen from the supermarket into the hostel and went to bed. He dreamt of the waltzers. He woke up in the night and was sick from the spinning.

Back in the here and now, in the Maddoxes' downstairs cubby hole, Daniel has nodded off and is snoring, but Billy can't hear it over the telly.

Nancy has stopped coughing, but her chest is hurting her. She's come back from the Dartmouth and is standing on the step but she hasn't gone in the house yet. She's been feeling despondent about Australia, but can't give up on it.

The postman with the squelchy shoes comes down the street and gives her a stare as he passes. He delivers post to the doors either side, but there is nothing for her. She is tempted to tackle him about the passport, to challenge him about its whereabouts. She must have looked like she was going to have a go, because he glances at her and says, "What?"

"Waitin fuh summat tuh cum," replies Nancy.

"Well it hasn't," says the postman and he goes on his way. She feels furious, as if everything is impossible. She has to

193

do something; she has to make some sort of progress, however small. She thinks about spontaneous combustion again. The idea of it seems somehow reassuring. She strides over the road and hammers on Marilyn's door, fully expecting there to be no answer.

Marilyn appears, wearing a threadbare housecoat and a headscarf. She looks sad, but Nancy doesn't notice as she is building herself up to say something.

"That time uz I asked yow abaht uh suitcase...Yow ay got one ar can lend have ya, cock?" Marilyn looks a bit surprised. She'd forgotten about the request, it had slipped her mind in amongst Daniel's tomfoolery and her own shopping sprees.

"Come in. I've got an old one on top of my wardrobe. Had it for my honeymoon." Marilyn gives a big smile as the memory of her honeymoon comes back. She looks distant, and then reddens as she feels the other woman's eyes on her. She thinks Nancy is giving her one of her stares, but she isn't.

"Where d'ya goo?" says Nancy, following Marilyn through to the middle room.

"Morecambe." Marilyn smiles again. "Danced the whole time away."

"Not the whole time, ar bet!" Nancy forgets herself, giving one of her legendary cackles. She stops herself short. She doesn't laugh like that anymore, and the sound makes her jump. The noise turns into a cough. She looks away at the bird cage.

"What about you? You and Billy, where did you go?"

"Rhyl!" Nancy goes back to Rhyl in her mind. She'd always liked Rhyl. They'd been on the fair a lot and stopped in a lovely hotel. On the front it was. Good times.

"I haven't used the suitcase since then," says Marilyn. "Might be a bit musty. You going somewhere?"

That throws Nancy. She hadn't pre-empted the question, although it should have been obvious that Marilyn would ask.

194

"Fuh ower Chrissie. Er's gooin away furra few days. Oliday. Er an Neil," Nancy says, rather too quickly.

"Abroad?"

"No! Weston," says Nancy, thinking of another seaside place that isn't Rhyl or Morecambe.

"I've never been abroad," says Marilyn.

"No. Nor me."

"Got myself a passport though, six or seven years ago..."

"Ow long did it tek tuh cum?" says Nancy, cutting her off in mid-flow.

"I went up to Liverpool so they could do one there and then. I needed one quick as our Shane was going to treat me. He wanted me to go over to where he was stopping in Spain and bring a couple of cases with me, some of his belongings, because he'd left in such a rush."

"Con they do passports in uh day?"

"Oh yes," says Marilyn. "I had a lovely day out. Went up by rail and saw the Liver Building. They have purple dustbins in Liverpool. I saw some off the train." There was a pause. "Abroad never happened though," says Marilyn, feeling sad again.

"Ow cum?"

"Changes in the extradition laws, apparently. I think I would have liked Spain," Marilyn says as she starts up the stairs. "Come on up," she invites Nancy to follow her, "I'll need some help getting it down."

When they go into her bedroom, Marilyn gets the sturdy wooden box she uses as a washing basket, and stands on it. "Here, catch hold of this," says Marilyn as she pulls the cumbersome suitcase off the top of the wardrobe. Nancy reaches up to take it from her. She has trouble taking the weight of it, the underneath of her arm is hurting. Dust bunnies slide from the lid of the case. "Oh dear," says Marilyn laughing. "What a slattern I am."

Marilyn climbs back down and timidly takes a clump of dust from the top of Nancy's head. It is barely distinguishable from Nancy's hair. Marilyn lifts up the box and puts it back at the end of the bed, its wooden feet slotting exactly into the dents it has worn in the carpet during the forty years or so it has stood there.

The case is hard, not flexible like a lot of the modern cases. The locks have rusted slightly and the key, tied to the handle, won't turn to open them. Marilyn says there is some 3-In-One oil under the kitchen sink, so they take the case back down. Marilyn also fetches a duster and some Pledge.

Nancy sets to work to free the locks, and once they've got the case open, Marilyn begins dusting it both inside and out. There is a tapping at the door. Marilyn stands. "I'll go. Exercise'll do me good." Nancy picks up the duster and carries on dusting. She is surprised when she recognises her Chrissie's voice.

"Dad says er should've bin back two hours since."

"Come through, love. She's here. Cleaning up the suitcase. It's a bit old-fashioned, but you're welcome to borrow it. When you going, anyway?"

Nancy looks up in time to see Chrissie shoot Marilyn an "Are you demented?" look.

"I ay gooin anywhere," says Chrissie.

Marilyn shoots a similar but more discreet "Are you demented?" look in the direction of Nancy, but she doesn't say anything.

Nancy stares at Chrissie. Chrissie stares at Nancy. "Yow ay serious! Am yow still gooin on about that bloody Australia trip?"

"Cum on," says Nancy, standing and stretching her shoulder. "Yower dad'll be bletherin if we doh get back quick. Tarra a bit!" she shouts over her shoulder, not turning to look at Marilyn as she says goodbye.

196

Nancy and Chrissie leave, taking the suitcase with them. As they cross the road Chrissie hisses angrily at her mother. "The only reason I ay said anyfink is cuz I thought yow'd cum to yower senses."

When they get over the road, Nancy opens the front door quietly and lugs the suitcase into the front room. She puts her finger to her lips and gives Chrissie a look. Chrissie looks back defiantly as if she is going to walk off. Nancy grabs her arm and makes eye contact with her. She makes the warning look count. "Yow doh say uh word!" whispers Nancy. Chrissie relents. She isn't sure she wants to be the one to start an argument between her mother and father over something that was probably pie in the sky, something that never would happen. Thinking about it logically, how the bloody hell would her mother afford it? Since her Dad had got ripped off in the insurance scam he paid a large percentage of his hard-earned cash into while he'd been working, the couple had been skint. They couldn't manage on their pensions half the time, which is why her mother insisted on working. It doesn't occur to Chrissie that if she and the grandkids weren't quite so often in need of this or that, then her parents might well have been able to manage. Looking at the mood her mother is in, there's no telling what might happen if she mentions the suitcase to her dad.

Quietly and quickly, Nancy opens the door to the glory hole and throws the suitcase into the darkness without taking her eyes off Chrissie. It smashes Daniel Grundy in the face; he is too drunk to even stir.

Daniel wakes up at about ten o'clock in the evening. For some inexplicable reason his head is bruised. He is used to his head hurting when he wakes up, but this is new. He feels the bridge of his nose. "Owww!" says Daniel. A hangover that causes bruising? He sits very still in the glory hole and listens to the television blaring. The inside of the glory hole magnifies the sound. He listens hard. *Big Brother* is on. Billy can be heard bemoaning the licence fee, but he is still watching it, yawning often.

If the Maddoxes had been aware of Daniel hiding in the glory hole, would they have been scared? It's difficult to say. After all, it's not like he's some knife-wielding maniac lying in wait, ready to slit their throats. He's a petty criminal, a feeble-minded alcoholic. In some ways, perhaps they should feel sorry for him.

The television finally clicks off and is followed by the middle room light. "The Maddoxes are going to bed," thinks Daniel. He decides to give it an hour or so before he comes out of his lair. He drinks some more of the cider and tries to keep himself awake, and thinks some more about Tonya and the night he'd gone to see her at the fair.

He had recognised her straight away. She had got fat. She had shorter hair too, but it was definitely Tonya. The fat was down to a mixture of eating her wares, and giving Lucas and Luca three more brothers. She had called them Tony and Anton. The first two named for him, the second two named for her. The fifth baby was called Jackson, after Luke's brother Jack; perhaps we shouldn't go into the reason for that name.

Daniel queued up, and watched her working amongst the flashing lights, doling out hot dogs at two pound fifty a time. He watched a gold clown necklace swing at her neck as she moved about picking up huge sausages with a pair of tongs and putting them into the bread rolls. With the same tongs she'd take a grab of fried onions, letting the water that they were cooking in drip off a little before layering them on top of the hot dog. He watched sovereign rings glitter on her fingers as she handed over the food and then turned one of her hands palm upwards to take the money.

He went to the counter and asked for a hot dog. She served him. He looked at her as he passed her the money. She took it and said nothing. "Can I have red sauce?" said Daniel. Not even the sound of his voice seemed to trigger recognition.

"Over there," she said, and pointed a manicured finger. Daniel hadn't got the nerve to say anything. He squeezed red sauce from the plastic container and it made a loud farting noise. Daniel was embarrassed. Two little kids leaning against the side of the caravan keeled over, giggling. The kids scared him.

Daniel walked off into the dark. He stood with his back against a generator and ate his hot dog. He wasn't sure what to do. Strong and tall, Daniel. Don't give up.

He went back over and queued again. "Tonya!" he said as he reached the front of the queue. She looked at him, squinted out of the light into the dark to where Daniel was standing.

"Hello, Daniel." She smiled. Daniel felt warm inside. "How's it going?" Before he could answer, she said "Hang on. I'm due a break." She waved him away, pointing round to the side of the kiosk. He watched her take out her mobile and make a call before he headed towards where she had pointed. After a few minutes an older woman appears and relieves her. Tonya came out, wiping her hands on a tea towel. "Hello, Daniel," she said again. "Still living in Stockport then? You married or anything?"

Daniel looked confused for a second. Married? Why should he be married? Tonya was his woman. Tonya and the kids were his family. In that second, he knew that he was kidding himself. He remembered now. "Yes," he said. "I'm married. Two kids." Tonya looked impressed. He told her the kids' names. They were the names of the turkey farmer and his wife.

"Thought I'd come and say hello. How are my boys?" Tonya didn't pick up on the "my". The fairground was noisy.

"They're about here somewhere." Daniel looked around confused again. He looked for a double buggy. How could she leave them out in the dark when she worked? He was beginning to think Tonya wasn't a very good mother. Don't be daft, Daniel Grundy. Years have passed. She catches sight of her eldest and yells him. "Lucas! Lucas, get here!" A tall boy, almost a man, comes towards her.

"What, mam? I've got to go and run the Waltzers. Dad's got some business to sort out." Daniel looks into the eyes of an eighteen-year-old. Daniel had thought he would look into the eyes of a five-year-old and a three-year-old.

The two lads who laughed when he was making the sauce bottle fart came over. "Here's two more of mine. Say hello to Daniel," says Tonya to the boys. "He used to lodge with us when Lucas and Luca were little." The boys were still giggling; taking the mickey. There was no recognition in Lucas's eyes as he glanced at Daniel before ambling off, uninterested. Daniel didn't know what he'd thought would happen. Had he really imagined they would still be children? Had he really thought that he and Tonya would pick up where they left off?

They shook hands. The boys still giggling. "Bye," said Tonya. It was nice to see Daniel again. Daniel had been OK to her. She watched him go, disappear into the dark. She was glad Daniel had done alright and that he was married. She'd worried about him after she'd left, thought he might crack up, go downhill. "Fair play, Daniel Grundy," she thought to herself.

Daniel went back to the hostel and made his nightly refusals. The next morning he cut off all his hair, left the hostel, walked to the motorway and stuck out his thumb.

It had been the right thing to do, to leave all the memories behind.

Daniel sits in the cupboard in the Maddoxes' house and shakes his head. He shakes the farmer and Tonya and the kids out of it. He replaces them with Wass-er-face and the seaside. That is his future.

He stands up; unsteady on his feet, possibly down to the shaking of his head, but more likely the emptying of the bottle of cider down his gullet. He comes out of the glory hole warily. The house is making slow ticking noises. Everyone is surely asleep. He clicks on the front room light so that he can see back into the hole he's been hiding in. He immediately thinks he's dropped lucky. Right on top of all the paraphernalia he's been lying amongst is a suitcase he recognises! It is the one off the top of his mother's wardrobe. As a kid, he'd used it to play in. He would pretend it was a car or a boat and sit in it. The thing is definitely his mother's; the size, the shape, the texture are printed indelibly on his memory. He laughs to himself. "Too easy!" He opens the newly oiled locks and finds inside... "Fuck all," says Daniel crossly.

Daniel systematically goes through everything in the glory hole and finds no evidence of bingo winnings, although there is a bingo dabber in the pocket of an old coat which makes him think perhaps he is getting warm, but there isn't a sniff of cash anywhere.

He puts the stuff back fairly neatly and leaves the empty cider bottle in the suitcase. Next he stands at the middle room door and listens. He creeps into the dark room. The house is the same layout as his mother's. He finds the light switch and clicks it on. He nearly screams out with the shock.

There in the armchair is Billy, and lying on the sofa is his scary-faced wife. He clicks the light back off immediately and stands in the darkness. Didn't the stupid old bastards sleep upstairs, like normal people? What is going on?

Daniel's heart is beating so loudly he's sure it's going to wake them. He stands stock still and tries to calm himself, listening for any movement. The old couple's breathing remains unaltered. There is nothing for it, he'll have to search upstairs next. The bedrooms, the cupboards, the chests of drawers. He creeps to the stairs door and opens it, slinks through and then pulls it silently to behind him. It is cold on the stairs as he makes his way upwards. The third from bottom creaks ominously. "Is that yow, ower Davy?" a sleepy voice mumbles. Daniel doesn't hear exactly what is said, but the adrenalin rises inside him; readying himself for fight or flight. Nothing else is muttered. No more sounds.

Daniel gets to the landing without any more creaks. He goes towards one of the three bedrooms which he now knows will be empty. In his mother's house this would have been his bedroom, the one with the cupboard that leads to the loft. In the Maddoxes' house it must have been Davy's old room. Daniel sees graffiti on the wall, names of punk bands. He can make it out in the light from next door's security lamp as it shines through the thin curtains. Daniel hadn't liked Davy. He looks around the room. Empty, except for a bed. He looks at the cupboard. He opens the door. He feels about and finds something square and canvas. What is it? A shopping trolley! He puts his hand inside and feels paper. He lifts it out of the trolley and holds it closer to his face. Money? He can't see.

There is a click, and on comes the light to help him out.

Bernice is stuck behind the bar. She isn't exactly run off her feet, but she can't leave things unattended. Jack the young barman hasn't shown up for his evening shift. "E better av uh bloody good reason," says Bernice to Unsteady Freddie who is propping up the bar, one hand round the pint glass that he's been nursing for an hour and a half. The tattoos on his fingers spell out the word hate.

"Ar could help ya behind there, Bern," says Freddie, who has run out of drinking money and is about to start on his electricity cash. He is sort of hoping that if he gets behind the bar he might either be able to pull himself a sly pint or that the landlady might give him drink by way of reward. Bernice looks at him. The offer of help is tempting.

Tyrone is barking again. He is driving her mad. "If yow really want to be helpful yow could tek Tyrone aht furra bloody walk. E ay shut up today at all." Since Bernice took him to the vet's because he'd been off his food – the cause being Daniel's over-feeding frenzy – the dog had been on a junk-free diet at the vet's behest.

"You're a little fatty aren't you, sweetheart?" the vet had said. Bernice looked at the vet, unsure if he was talking to her or the dog. "A little fatty staffy," the vet had clarified, chucking Tyrone under his wobbling chin. Since the diet had started, Bernice hadn't had a moment's peace from his barking and whining.

"Crisps! Crisps! Crisps!" barks Tyrone. "Crisps! Crisps! Crisps!" She'd taken the vet's advice very seriously. She'd even put a sign up: Please don't feed Tyrone, he is getting fat. He'd still managed to steal a couple of packets of unattended snacks, though, and a meat pie somebody had brought in from the chip shop.

Unsteady Freddie looks at Tyrone. He doesn't want to go out in the dark. It is a chilly night in spite of it being summer. "There'll be uh pint in it for yow, uv course."

"I'll get mi coat," says Freddie, draining the last bit of ale from his glass and slamming it down on one of the drip trays.

Tyrone strains at the lead as they set off. He doesn't like walking much. It takes him away from the source that feeds his addiction. He doesn't ever like to be too far from a box of smoky bacon crisps. Tyrone cocks his leg up a telegraph pole, moodily. Unsteady Freddie walks very slowly and Tyrone is getting fed up. They walk down Maxwell Road towards the park. Unsteady Freddie also needs to urinate. He goes up an alley between a couple of houses and relieves himself. Tyrone waits at the end of the lead in the street, panting.

When they get to the field by the kids' park, Unsteady Freddie lets Tyrone off the lead for a run. Tyrone bounds about the field before stopping and looking about him in an embarrassed way. He reassures himself there are no other dogs watching and then he starts bounding about again. Once he gets into the idea he quite likes leaping about. He paws the grass and barks, then stops to defecate.

Unsteady Freddie lights up a fag and watches. He is cold, but if he stops out a bit longer Bern might stretch to two pints. Tyrone runs off into the bushes, forcing his way deep into the overgrown tangle of council shrubs, weeds, and brambles. He is scuffling in the dirt with real enthusiasm, he can smell something tangy and tasty. A fox, maybe? A rabbit? Don't be silly, Tyrone, they don't have rabbits in All Saints. Unsteady Freddie walks in unsteady circles. When he has finished blowing smoke rings from his fag, he starts trying to blow rings of his own breath, but the night isn't as cold as he's been making out. Tyrone is still going the game in the bushes. Freddie can hear his snuffling.

After ten minutes Tyrone still hasn't reappeared. Unsteady Freddie walks over, swinging the dog's lead. "Come on, boy. ar've ad enough now."

Tyrone comes out of a hole in the bushes. He is chewing something yellow. "Wot ya got there, lad?" Unsteady Freddy tries to take it off Tyrone. "Worris it? A toy of some sort?"

Tyrone crunches it up, yelping and dropping it when he tastes the acidic juices. Freddie laughs as it lands on the ground at his feet. "It's a Jif lemon, ya fool!" Freddie turns and starts to walk way. Tyrone runs back in the bush. Freddie calls him again, but he won't come.

"Come on, boy." The dog barks, but still won't come. "Dammit!" thinks Freddie. "Er wo give me that pint if ar lose yow, ya bugger." He walks towards the bushes, peering into the darkness. "Where are ya?" Freddie gets his phone out and uses the screen to give a bit more light. There is nothing for it, he'll have to go in and get the stupid dog. Syringe barrels crunch under his foot as moves into the bushes. He doesn't see the bag lying open, its contents strewn in the dirt.

Freddie bends himself up almost double and with one arm up in front of his face he forces his way through into the middle of the shrubbery. Tyrone barks somewhere near his left ear. Freddie turns to look, and holds up his phone. It lights the space just enough. Or maybe it lights it a little too much for Freddie's liking, and at the expense of any pleasant dreams he'd hope to have any time soon. He feels more unsteady than he has in years. Tyrone has hold of a hand! Admittedly, it is attached to an arm but Tyrone is doing his level best to un-attach it. He is shaking it by the wrist. The girl's face wears a fixed expression of shock, like she is traumatised by the appearance of a dog in the bush where she's been hiding. Except she isn't hiding, she's dead. Wass-er-face has had her throat cut.

"Wot the bleedin 'ell? Yow little shit!" shouts Nancy.

Daniel stands blinking in the sudden light. He looks down at the money in his hands. Crisp ten pound notes. Bingo!

"Billy! Billy!" shouts Nancy.

Daniel is stuck to the spot for a second. He looks at the shouty old woman. He looks at the money. Nothing is going to stop him now he's got this close to getting what he came for. He stuffs the money into the pocket of his jeans and makes a grab for the trolley with its untold riches, wrenching it free from the cupboard. Nancy comes at him, barking, spitting, and snarling.

"Yow ay avin yower mother's money!"

Daniel uses the trolley as a shield, and puts it between him and the old woman. She grabs it too, and they both try to shake each other free.

"Billy! Billy!" she shouts again, calling for reinforcements. Daniel shakes the trolley so hard that Nancy thinks she can feel her teeth coming loose in her head. She clamps her jaw shut and holds on. But Daniel is stronger, she loses her grip and she shoots backwards, ending up on the floor on her arse. Daniel swings the trolley back and hits her with it. The blow isn't hard, but it is a shock. Daniel takes his chance and makes for the door. Nancy is too quick. She grabs him around his left leg and clings on. He tries to shake her off with all his might, but she isn't budging. Her glasses are gone off her face. She has her eyes tightly closed. She looks like a newborn pup. Blind fury. He lifts the trolley up again with the intention of hitting her harder this time, and that's when she bites him. She sinks her worn down sheep's teeth into the back of Daniel Grundy's calf. Her bite is worse than her bark.

Daniel screams. And that's when Billy bursts into the room with the TV remote in his hand. In truth, it had been the nearest thing to him when he woke; perhaps he'd thought the fracas was the sound of the TV and he'd grabbed the remote in order to turn it down. Whatever the reason, Billy is greeted with a most peculiar sight, like nothing he's ever seen on his telly. It is almost as if he's paused the action with his remote.

The "good-for-nuthin" Grundy boy is stripped to the waist, daubed in some kind of war paint and about to club Nancy, possibly to death, with a tartan shopping trolley. Nancy, his wife of nearly sixty years, has her jaws clamped firmly around the boy's leg.

"Wot the blue blazes is gooin on 'ere?" Billy shouts as he bounces the remote off Daniel's head and the action starts again. Daniel twists round and brings the shopping trolley down towards Nancy's head. There is a crack as Billy launches himself between the trolley and his wife, taking the full force of the blow.

"Fookin 'ell!" says Billy as he puts his hand to his back. Underneath her husband, Nancy has started to cough. She slackens her bite and Daniel kicks free of her. His foot makes contact with her brow. One of Daniel's braces pings loose as he stands there staring at the wreckage of a couple lying on the floor.

"Mad bastards!" shrieks Daniel. He legs it with the trolley and heads downstairs. Never one to miss a trick, he grabs the three-quarters full bottle of Bells by Billy's chair, and makes for the front door.

He is free, he is rich, he is the man with the plan that has worked. He runs for the park where he plans to lie low until morning with his whisky and his winnings, and then he'll find Wass-er-face and they'll be gone for good.

As he turns the corner into Maxwell Road he hears sirens, and he dodges into an alley. There are blue lights, and there seem to be police cars everywhere he looks. Daniel feels uneasy. Surely the Maddoxes hadn't been able to call for help this quick.

The suitcase, and the talk of holidays, has set Marilyn thinking. It is late, but she can't sleep. She sits up in bed, propped against her pillows. She isn't as sad as she'd felt that morning. Now, she is cross. She'd offered Daniel the chance to change and a new life and he hadn't taken it, so if he didn't want it then maybe she should take it herself.

Marilyn gets up and goes downstairs. There is no sign of Daniel anywhere. She rummages through the kitchen drawers until she finds the passport that Shane had insisted she got. It is still in the envelope it came in.

The passport is with Shane's letters. There are loads of them from various prisons and young offenders' institutes, and all of them very loving and thoughtful. There are some with poems in. She takes the letters and the passport back up to bed with her, and spreads them out on the cover. She looks at them and considers how many times he's been to see her when he has been out of nick. The answer, she decides, is twice.

Once, he'd stopped for a week and taken her out every day and spoilt her rotten. The second time he'd come and hidden for a day and a half. He'd told her not to say anything if the police came. She didn't, but was very embarrassed when they found him hiding behind the bath panel. She acted her surprise very badly. "Oh, hello, our Shane. Fancy seeing you there," she said, as they brought him out of the bathroom in handcuffs. Shane had made some sort of face at the policemen as if to say, "How bad is her acting?" and he and the coppers had laughed at her. He'd gone politely and quietly though, which she was pleased about.

Of course, she knew why Daniel had come back, but why on earth was he stopping around? It wasn't like she was giving him money anymore, and the last few days he'd stopped asking with any real intent.

What Marilyn doesn't know is that Daniel hadn't really meant to come back, not to his mother's at least. When he got back to Wolverhampton at first it was a sort of homing instinct, but he had headed for a hostel called the Good Shepherd, not for Marilyn's house. He still had the idea of her and Shane laughing at him stuck firmly in his head. He thought things would be OK in the hostel. Jesus was the Good Shepherd and the name also reminded him of the farm and the farmer. Daniel knew the farmer wasn't a shepherd – you couldn't shepherd turkeys – but the idea reminded him of the rural life and his home in the barn.

There was no room at the hostel the first night. He ended up sleeping down at the old Low Level station. He crept in behind some boards that had been used to block up a doorway. It was cold. He tried to cover himself completely with the farmer's army blankets he'd still got with him. He had no food.

The second day he went back to the Good Shepherd. The Good Shepherd wasn't in so he had to make do with a priest. A loud Irish fellow. He scared Daniel. There was still no bed. They gave him some food though. They gave him a sleeping bag too. He was warmer that night.

The third day he went back again. This time he was luckier. Someone had OD'd and he could have their bed. Daniel got a bed and food for the night. That was all he needed. The hostel nurses gave him a check over. They said they thought he might be depressed. They sorted him out with a doctor. Dr Ram.

He told the doctor that he was in pain. He was talking emotional pain, but he couldn't express its whereabouts effectively so he told her it was in his leg. He also told her he'd been on very strong painkillers when he lived in Norfolk, although he hadn't actually taken tablets for a while, not since he'd been living in Stockport when Tonya had left. Now he was back in Wolverhampton, the pain had started again. She said that he had to take three a day. Daniel made up his mind that he was in a lot of pain so he decided to take three, three times a day. It was a similar dose in Daniel's head, but as his version contained more 3s it would be better for him.

At tea time he went to eat in the dining room. It was noisy. He looked around. Where should he sit? There were a couple of tables of men laughing and joking. They would be the lads. They would be the ones who would offer him things. He'd got used to the system in Stockport. There was a table of three on their own, talking quietly. They would be the nonces; they always managed to find each other; sniff each other out. If they came in new to the hostel at breakfast, by tea time they'd have found their level. Daniel shuddered, and looked for a table on his own.

He spotted a great big man sitting in self-imposed solitary confinement. He would be the one that nobody messed with. If Daniel could perch on the end of that table without getting swatted like a fly that would be the best thing. The man might let him sit there. He wouldn't speak to Daniel of course, but that wouldn't matter. Daniel wouldn't have to mix with the lads and he wouldn't get labelled as a nonce. The big man could be Daniel's shark and Daniel could be like one of those fish that swim around and make themselves useful.

Before he could walk towards the table he heard a sound that chilled him to the bone. His balls went as icy as the day the prostitute had tried – and failed – to pop his cherry. "Fuckin hell! If it isn't our Daniel!"

Shane called him over. He called Daniel to sit with the lads. Shane had got out of the nick again. Shane was back in Wolverhampton too. Later, one of Shane's friends offered Daniel a can. They all stood over the road from the hostel by the bushes. Daniel took the can and drank it, but because it was only one can Daniel had to go off into Broad Street and steal two more from the offie. He drank them on his own behind a large steel bin where The Moon Under Water threw their waste food.

A rat the size of a cat stared at Daniel Grundy as he drank. The rat seemed to be judging him, Daniel thought. "Fuck off, rat!" said Daniel. But only quietly, so the rat couldn't hear. If the rat didn't bother him, then he wouldn't bother the rat. The rat must have had the same idea, and it carried on feeding.

The next night, Shane had told him to come down the canal with the lads. Some of them were going to inject their heroin, and some were smoking it. "Try this, Daniel," Shane had said. "Don't worry, you won't get addicted. It's only smoking."

Daniel had done as he was told. He liked it, and it became a nightly ritual. What with the tablets and the beer and Shane buying him more stuff to smoke, all the pain he felt started to subside. It was yet another routine.

Shane introduced Daniel to his dealer when he went to buy some stuff. And after that, when Shane wanted stuff he'd send Daniel to get it. Shane was always up to something and too busy to go. He always had some plot or plan, some scheme to make money, which was just as well as Daniel was hooked on smoking it now, and he needed Shane to get it. His little brother was watching out for him.

Each night Daniel sat with his tin foil and his lighter, and when he watched the other lads with their syringes he was envious of their ritual, but too terrified of the needles to make it his own.

Shane left the hostel on a Monday, without telling Daniel he was going. All Daniel had left was Shane's phone with the dealers' numbers, and a habit he couldn't feed.

Daniel went to Doctor Ram's for more help with his pain, and that's when he heard about the bingo win. Two women gossiping about his mother and how she'd won the national game. It seemed like all his prayers were answered. He hadn't waited to see the doctor, but had made a decision there and then to go and see his mother. That was when Daniel had rattled all the way to his mother's front door, less than three weeks earlier.

But Marilyn didn't know any of that. And if she had, what could she have done? She'd offered him the once in a lifetime chance and he'd turned it down. She looks sadly at the passport.

They lie on the floor until they get their breath back. There is an uncomfortable silence. The sound of their breathing fills the space between them. Billy stares incomprehensibly at his wife as if she is something foreign, something else. She feels around for her glasses. One of the arms is broken but she puts them back on and realises, as she peers through them, that she is under scrutiny from her husband. She stares back at him defiantly through her lopsided frames.

Billy takes a deep breath and then goes up like a bottle of pop. He doesn't hit the roof, he goes through it and into orbit.

"Wot the cowin 'ell's bin gooin on?"

Nancy shakes her head. She tries to speak but her voice has gone. Perhaps Daniel has taken it with him. Her eye is throbbing, and she puts her hand up to her brow. It is swollen. Misshapen.

"Yow berra start talkin, woman." Billy is so full of anger he looks as if he might burst.

"E's took er bingo winnins. Er gid it me fower safe keepin. In the trolley."

"Ar doh believe it! Wot the bloody hell d'yow av tuh gerr involved for? Doh yow ever learn?"

Nancy thinks it is a strange thing for him to say. When had this ever happened before? She watches her husband ranting on, but the words become a blur. She is trying to imagine

212

where he'd got the idea that this sort of thing was a regular occurrence. He is still raging. He has the uncanny knack of making it sound like it was the hundredth time she'd done something as daft as this. It wasn't like he'd caught her before, wrestling with petty criminals and biting legs. He is making it sound like a habit.

She doesn't respond or reply. She lets the barrage wash over her. She is conscious only of the fact that her mouth tastes horrible and she is starting to feel dizzy. She pulls herself to a sitting position, then over on to her knees, and she crawls to the wall, using it to steady herself. The wall feels like a reality. She rests her cheek against it for a moment or two, and then gets to her feet.

"Where yow gooin now?" says Billy, who has stopped for breath.

"Tuh rinse me mouth aht."

"Right," he shouts after her. "An when yow've done, we'll goo up the phone box un call the police. Sort this bloody mess aht."

Nancy wearily drags herself downstairs. She imagines the IOU fluttering about in the shopping trolley with the tenners. How the bloody hell would she manage to stop him phoning the coppers?

When she comes back from the bathroom, having washed herself and brushed her teeth with bicarb twice, the old goat has come downstairs and is sitting in his chair. He looks pale, but the remote is back in his hand, so some sense of normality is being re-established.

"Yow cor call the coppers! Ar took sum on it, day I!"

Billy stares in shock at his wife. "Tuh pay the council tax and..." she stops. She focusses on a flower in the wallpaper pattern before she continues, "...an tuh buy miself a passport."

Billy is shaking. "Fookin 'ell," he says. That was the second time he'd used the F word in a day.

The telephone box at the top of the street gets more use in the two hours before breakfast than it has in a week. Just after 5 o'clock, Daniel crawls out of the Christmas trees opposite the Dartmouth, dragging his trolley behind him.

He had decided to lay low during the night. When he finds Wass-er-Face he'll need to make sure that his supplies of brown are enough to keep them both going for the journey to the seaside, and until they establish themselves. Daniel checks his pockets for change. Nothing! He grabs one of the tenners from his pocket and looks thoughtfully at the coin slot. He wanders off to the shop in the hope of getting change, but it's still shut.

Perhaps the crack house would be able to provide. After all they'd said not to come to them again unless he had money. And now he did. Lots of it. He'll get the respect he deserves now. He sets off, pulling the trolley behind him. One wheel turns, and the metal where the other should have been sparks occasionally as it catches the pavement. He glances down the street that leads to the park as he goes. He can see a lot of police activity. Something about it all makes him uneasy, as if he almost knows what is going on.

At 6ish, Billy walks slowly and deliberately up the road and makes a call. He looks tired. His legs feel heavy. They are as leaden as the sky that hangs over him as he goes back down the street.

At 6.30 Marilyn, who is dressed up like a dog's dinner again, heads up to the box and makes a call. She flirts a little with the base operator before asking him to book her a taxi for 8 o'clock, going to the railway station. "Going anywhere nice?" he asks.

"Oh yes," says Marilyn. "Definitely!" It has started to rain as she walks back home, but Marilyn doesn't notice. She is singing to herself.

Unsteady Freddie had been up the police station half the night, helping them with their enquiries. He'd gone home at about half four but – not surprisingly – he couldn't sleep. Before six, he heads to the top shop. Doreen is sorting papers out when he goes in. He asks for a packet of fags.

"Ya look a bit peeky," says Doreen, peering at him. And that's when Doreen gets the news scoop of a lifetime. Once she's heard all the gory details she gets her husband up and tells him to look after the shop. This nugget of information doesn't need to be spread quietly from behind a counter, this is the stuff of door-to-door. She puts on her outdoor shoes, grabs an umbrella, and heads for the streets. She starts every conversation the same way. "Av yarr'eard?"

She isn't a gossip; she is doing a duty.

Chrissie turns up not long after the call from her dad. Neil had answered the phone and taken a garbled message about robbery, passports, biting, and not being able to phone the police.

As her Dad opens the door he starts on immediately. He is fuming, she can see that.

"Er's gorrerself uh passport!" he rants, going off on one at his daughter as if she'd had something to do with it all. It seems as if the housebreaking, the biting, and the fact that his wife has been nicking money have all become secondary to another more pressing issue.

"Er wouldn't goo. Not without yow. No way."

Billy looks unsure. "Er's in eya." He leads the way through to the back room and points at his wife in disgust as though he no longer recognises her in her new role as a criminal.

Nancy is sitting staring at the floor.

"Er wouldn't goo, not without yow," Chrissie repeats. "Would yow, mom?" Her mother, living dangerously, shrugs.

"Er's gorrerself uh passport. Er as! Ask er!"

Chrissie looks at her mother.

"Tay cum yet!"

Billy started cussing and swearing. "Wheyer is it?" He starts chuntering, and goes to the drawer where the important papers are kept. "Probly bloody idden it."

"Ar towd yow, it ay bloody cum yet."

"Arm goin' to phone Vee. Ar bet er's got summat tuh do wi' this. Give uz that phone uv yourn."

"You ain't phoning Australia on my mobile." Chrissie is incredulous. She's not long put a ten pound top-up on it which is supposed to last the month. She imagines her credit eaten up in seconds.

"Gis it bloody eya." There is no arguing. He goes to the dresser to find Vee's number.

"You woh gerra signal in eya," says Chrissie. She folds her arms, and pulls her face into an expression that she has inherited from her mother.

Billy continues searching for the number. "Ar'll goo ahtside then!" he shouts, as he roots about in the drawer.

Nancy slopes off while Chrissie and Billy are arguing. Now it has all come out, she thinks she'd better face the music. She isn't really bothered what they think, but she feels sad that she's let Marilyn down. She wouldn't want her to hear it from someone else.

Nancy can't look up at Marilyn properly as she opens the door. She feels ashamed. "Ar've ony cum tuh tell ya..."

"Come in, come in," says Marilyn. There is something excited and jolly about her voice. Giddy. It makes Nancy feel worse about what she's got to do. Yes, Nancy hates Daniel but she doesn't want to tell his mother that he's been breaking and entering. She doesn't want to crush the poor woman's heart. And then to rub salt in the wounds by telling her that the person she'd trusted has let her down too. Nancy sighs.

"Do you want a Baileys?" says Marilyn. "I'm having one."

"Pardon?" Nancy is shell-shocked. A Baileys! It isn't even 8 o'clock in the morning. What on earth is Marilyn doing, drinking in the day?

"I thought I'd treat myself out of my winnings," says Marilyn as she pours Nancy a glass and hands it over. Nancy isn't even sure why she accepts the glass. "Ar doh like Baileys," she whispers to herself. She's never actually had a Baileys before, but she is pretty sure she won't enjoy it. She takes a sip to find it's actually quite nice! Chocolatey, even.

Marilyn flashes her fingernails at Nancy. Nancy can't believe her eyes as she takes in the long squared-off nails, just like the woman's in the post office. "What do you think?" Nancy really doesn't know what to make of them. She starts to feel confused and worried, as though she might have entered a parallel universe.

Then, Marilyn directs her attention towards Nancy. "You look tired!"

Nancy doesn't answer, she shrugs. "Started another job dahn the Summerhouse."

What on earth did she want to go taking another job on at her time of life for? Are they in debt? Marilyn wonders. Then she remembers the suitcase, and the mention of Australia. "You saving for something?" Nancy looks at Marilyn with a cagey glance. "Sorry, didn't mean to pry. It's just that yesterday Chrissie said something about Australia."

"Australia, at my age. Must be jokin." The old woman has gone slightly red, Marilyn thinks. Nancy sighs again. "Ar've cum abaht yower bingo winnins. Ar've ad sum trouble. Sum uv it got took."

"Oh! your eye!" says Marilyn, noticing the woman's injury.

Nancy feels very, very tired. "Poor Marilyn," she thinks. But poor Marilyn doesn't look so poor anymore. Nancy has a proper look at her through her skewed glasses. Marilyn looks twenty years younger. She looks stronger. Maybe it is all the porridge, and the boiled bacon sandwiches that Nancy has been providing.

"Daniel took it, didn't he?" Marilyn says. "You don't have to tell me." Nancy looks at Marilyn harder still, and then nods.

"I can't do anything to stop either of them, can I? They're men. I'm sick of wasting time worrying." Then Marilyn adds quietly, "Look at you. You haven't lived since your Davy went and died." Maybe it is the word Davy that does it, but Nancy has to sit down.

Her reaction isn't hysterics, it isn't over the top, but it is momentous. A tear wells up in her left eye and slowly makes its way out on to her cheek, as though a mechanism has been freed and is slowly starting to work again. Marilyn has to give her the hanky, the one with the little blue *M* on it that she'd cried into when the canary died. Marilyn is stunned. The world must have ended. Nancy Maddox is on her sofa crying out a tear.

The situation doesn't last long. Not long at all. It might have been a minute or two, but the point is there has been a release.

Nancy pulls herself together, as she would have told somebody else to, and sniffs. She takes a breath again. She coughs hard before she speaks.

"Ar took sum too." Marilyn looks at her, not understanding. "Ar took sum uv yower money too! Furra passport, an tuh pay the council tax. Ar left un IOU burrit doh mek it right. Yow trusted me an ar let yow dahn."

"It doesn't matter," says Marilyn. "It really doesn't. You would have put it back. It was only borrowed. I'd have given it you if you'd asked."

"It does matter," says Nancy. "Ar let uh friend dahn."

Marilyn is both taken aback and thrilled by the word *friend*. For a second she thinks Nancy is going to cry again, but she doesn't.

Marilyn looks deeper into Nancy's hardening face. "You're ill, aren't you?" Marilyn thinks. She doesn't say the thought aloud. She doesn't dare. She has a sudden revelation that denial is the very thing that keeps Nancy going.

"Ar'll mek shewah as yow get wot's owed. The second job is tuh pay yow back. Burrar'm gooin away furrabit." Nancy starts to cough. "A couple uv days."

"Where?"

" Away." Cough, cough, cough.

"Australia?"

"Pah!" says Nancy. She goes quiet before speaking. "It wuz jus summat tuh think abaht. Summat else, summat other than this. Ar couldn't goo tuh Australia. Ar'm 79." She hardens some more, becomes flinty. "Ar'm gooin…" She leaves a long pause. "Ar'm gooin anywheyer away from im an is bastard chair." She stands up and makes like she is about to leave.

"Sit down!" says Marilyn.

Nancy narrows her eyes and looks at Marilyn as though she is about to get angry. She doesn't sit again. She remains standing, but she doesn't leave.

"Yow ay gunna stop me."

"No, I'm not going to stop you. I'm coming with you."

Daniel is sleeping the sleep of the innocent, drifting on brown waves. Colin had let him in to the crack house when Daniel waved a fistful of tenners at him. Half an hour later Daniel was sorted.

Now he is sitting in a comfy sofa, slumped forward with his face down on the lid of his shopping trolley.

Colin is watching him thoughtfully when his boss comes in.

"What the fuck is that bad smellin bwoy doin' here? He's trouble. We said we wouldn't sell to him no more."

"He paid cash, and I reckon there's more in that trolley of his." Colin goes over and pushes Daniel off the lid. He doesn't wake. Instead, he resettles himself, leaning his head on the arm of the chair.

Colin lifts the lid and delves inside. He pulls out ten pound notes and an IOU. Colin shrugs as he reads it, and throws it back in the trolley. He counts the notes. "There's nearly nine hundred eya," he says after counting it twice.

"Where did that skank get that kind of money?"

"We should put it up for safe keeping!" They smile at each other as Colin makes the suggestion. "Probably won't even remember he came with it." Colin puts the money back in the tartan trolley and takes it out to the boot of his boss's car.

When the door is knocked, Marilyn looks at the clock. "That'll be my taxi. Are you ready?"

Nancy isn't sure if she is ready, but she goes with Marilyn to the door, half-expecting it to be Billy on the warpath. As they open it, they are greeted not by a taxi driver or Billy, but by Doreen from the top shop.

"Av yarr'eard? They've found one dead in the bush over the park." Doreen can tell by their reaction that they haven't heard, and she puffs up a little inside when she realises she has knowledge that they don't possess. "One of the prossies!" she adds. The rain pitter-pats down on her umbrella and her face is an unnatural hue, coloured red by the reflection from the underside of the brolley. "The dog from the pub and Unsteady Freddie found the wench. Stone dead er was! Reckon some kind of madman ad er. Throat slit!" "

"Which one was it?" asks Marilyn, horrified.

"One uv the young uns."

"Poor wench," says Nancy.

"Sad!" says Marilyn, thinking of the body in the bush. Over the years she'd often wondered if her Daniel was lying dead somewhere. She thinks about the girl's mother and father. She wonders if they know yet that their child has been murdered.

"Unsteady Freddie reckons it was er who stood up on the corner of Raby Street. Boss-eyed one," says Doreen.

Something registers in Marilyn's brain. "Brown hair?"

"Ar. That's the one."

Marilyn goes pale. Nancy doesn't notice, as she is thinking about their Chrissie, and about how she'd feel if someone had attacked her daughter or one of her grandkids. She has a sudden urge to go over the road and warn Chrissie not to go out on her own, to warn her that there is some crazed throat-slitting maniac on the loose.

"Wait theyer!" says Nancy to Marilyn.

Doreen makes off towards the next house leaving Marilyn on the step, feeling uneasy. She remembers something that Daniel had said when the copper had come to warn them after the first attack. "How could Daniel have known that the first attack had been on a prostitute?" she wonders. "Lucky guess?"

Nancy stands in her lounge. She can hear the old goat chuntering outside. He is on the phone to Vee. She can hear Chrissie chirping up too. "Tell er we think er's gorra passport un everythin." They are that intent on their conversation, they don't seem to notice the rain.

Nancy gets cross again. They haven't been listening to her. "The passport asn't cum!" she says to the empty room. They are treating her like a child. She starts to feel petulant. If they're going to treat her like a child then maybe she'll act like one.

The old goat's voice starts to rise. "I doh bloody care wot time it is. It's mornin 'ere an ar want tuh know wot yow pair've bin concocting behind mi back. Doh bloody lie, Vera Metcalfe." He uses Vee's maiden name in his excitement.

Nancy runs upstairs, and grabs the hanger which holds her best skirt, blouse, and jacket. She takes the cameo she always wears on special occasions from the dressing table, and she gets her court shoes from under the bed. She comes back down. She can still hear him shouting as she passes through the back room.

"Ay yow listening? Er's gorra bloody passport un everythin! Whaddya mean, good for er?"

Nancy grabs the suitcase that Marilyn has lent her from the glory hole, and hurriedly throws in her things. She doesn't notice the empty cider bottle. She goes towards the front door. She decides she isn't going to tell them about the murder; she'll leave that to Doreen.

As she gets to the door she notices her grubby work trainers. She re-opens the case, gets out her court shoes, and forces her feet into them with a groan. She pulls her overall over her head and turns it back the right way before folding it and leaving it on top of the trainers.

Marilyn is still standing on her step as Nancy comes back out. She is looking up the street. She seems more anxious than she had done. "No sign of the taxi," she says nervously. Nancy struggles across the street with the case.

"If we'm gooin to goo, we goo now," says Nancy, taking control. "They'll notice ar'm gone in uh minute, an then all hell'll break loose agen."

Marilyn imagines her own version of all hell breaking loose. It involves Daniel, and coppers. It involves hassle, and shame. She nods. The two of them head up the street. Marilyn totters in high heels, carrying an overnight bag, and Nancy clip-clops along in her court shoes, lugging a large suitcase which contains a skirt, a blouse, a jacket, a small piece of cheap jewellery, and an empty cider bottle. It makes for an odd sight.

They are both out of breath before they get to the end of the street. How on earth they think they'll get all the way to the station isn't immediately obvious. Nancy bends over as a fit of coughing takes her. When the car stops against the curb they look at each other. What now?

"Where yuh goin'?" asks the deep, malevolent voice. Neither of the women answer. "Yuh want lift?" Again neither of the women answer. He gets out. "I don't bite," Daniel's dealer says, almost softly. Nancy feels a little embarrassed at the mention of biting. "Come on," he indicates the case and Nancy passes it to him. Marilyn looks at her as if she's gone mad, and clutches her own overnight bag tight to her.

"It's ower ony chance," says Nancy, still wheezing slightly.

"Get in!" He pulls the seat forward and Marilyn gets into the back. It is a tight squeeze, the car is really only meant for two people even though it has back seats. She puts her feet up on the upholstery. Nancy gets in the front. The man with the malevolent voice puts the suitcase next to the shopping trolley in the boot, and gets back into the driver's seat.

"Wh'appen?" He points to Nancy's eye. The bruise is getting worse by the minute.

"Fight with uh shoppin trolley!" says Nancy, gruffly. The man sucks his teeth and shakes his head.

"Where to then, ladies?"

"The station," says Marilyn who has decided that she is going to "go with the flow". It is a phrase she's heard on the TV and she rather likes it. She is partial to sporty cars when it comes down to it. It feels right, what with her new outfit. She looks at her nails again, and thinks about the dog. Dogs, she reluctantly admits to herself, can be a bit of a tie.

They get to the station quickly. Very quickly. They pull up by the glass doors and he gets out and helps the two women out of the car. They stand and wait in the rain as he goes to the boot and lifts out the case and then a shopping trolley. "I think this might belong to yous."

Nancy looks at him, but doesn't ask any questions. "It's er's!" she says, taking it from him and pointing to Marilyn. Nancy lifts the lid and rummages inside to find the IOU. "This is er's too." Nancy passes it to Marilyn, who looks at it before nodding, taking it, and putting it in the pocket of her overnight bag. She knows the old woman will want to pay it back and she isn't going to stop her. It will be a matter of pride.

Marilyn looks inside the trolley. "There's still money in here?" She is surprised. Their unlikely knight in shining armour looks embarrassed, and changes the subject.

"So where yuh off den?"

"Somewhere else," says Nancy. "Somewhere other than 'ere." The man nods to them both and gets back in his car. He watches them as they head into the station with the suitcase and a one-wheeled trolley in tow. Nancy turns in the doorway, and nods in a gesture of thanks.

He sits for quite a while after they disappear.

"Somewhere other than 'ere," he says to himself, laughing. He starts the engine, turns on the windscreen wipers, and drives off, unsure where he is going to go.

Billy hands the phone back to Chrissie. Something about Vee's laugh before she hung up made him think of Nancy when she'd used to laugh. He realises he doesn't hear it anymore. It had been a loud cackle. Too loud, perhaps. But it had been genuine. Sometimes he would be in the bar and she would be in the lounge up the club and he'd hear her. A smile would come to his face. Billy tries to smile now, tries to pull one out of the bag. The effort is too much. Chrissie checks her credit and pulls a face, but doesn't dare say anything.

"Vee says er don't know nothing about it then?" says Chrissie as they come back in from the yard together. She grabs a tea towel on the way through the kitchen, and starts towelling her hair. They look at the chair where they'd left the badly behaved Nancy.

"Where the bloody 'ell as er got to now?"

"I bet er's gone tuh work," says Chrissie, looking at the clock. "Yow want a cuppa before ar goo?" Billy nods and sits back down in his chair. Chrissie tells her dad to try and calm down a bit, that it's probably best if her mom has gone to work, that it gives them a bit of breathing space. Taking her advice, Billy turns on the television and watches a breakfast programme quietly until they do a feature on an Australian movie star and then he flares up all over again.

When the door knocks, Chrissie goes to answer it. Her eyes are glazed over when she comes back.

"Wos the marra now?"

"It was Doreen from the top shop. One of the prossies've bin murdered!"

"Tut," says Billy. He always feels worried for the girls on the streets, even though most people would say they were baggages and rubbish and that if they lived that kind of life then what did they expect? Perhaps if he didn't live amongst them he would have thought the same thing, but he imagined individuals, faces of the kids he saw on his street corners.

For a second, he thinks of their Chrissie as a little girl. "Best be careful when yow goo back up wum," he says softly to his daughter.

"That ay all!" Her dad shakes his head as Chrissie speaks. She beckons her Dad to follow her. They go through into the front room. Chrissie points to the mat beside the front door. Billy looks down, and sees a pair of dirty trainers, and a work overall folded up on top of them. He bends down and picks up the overall, and as he does so a Bic lighter falls out of the pocket.

"Doreen says er saw mom 'eadin off towards the town with er over the road. Says er was carryin uh suitcase!"

Billy thought he'd seen and heard it all last night, but this latest bit of news really takes the biscuit.

When Tyrone opens his eyes, the world smells different. It is later than he usually wakes. He usually awakes when the woman who clanks about downstairs knocks the door. He usually cons her into a packet of smoky bacon crisps, and a polish of the collar, and a smack or two. With his lolling tongue and his soft brown eyes he could coax her into that. Tyrone looks so harmless and cute. He hadn't looked so harmless and cute the night before when he was trying to rip Wass-er-face's hand off. Human flesh or crisps – it is a hard call.

Tyrone barks. Bernice wakes with a start, remembering the events of the previous night. She'd been up till late making tea for coppers, and answering questions. She sticks her head out of the window ready to drop the key. She looks down onto an empty space in the street where Nancy should be. Something isn't right. She looks at her alarm clock, which she always sleeps through. Half past eleven! What the bloody hell was up now? Nancy had only missed once in the last ten years, and then she'd sent her Chrissie.

The butch dray woman pulls up in the brewery wagon. She looks up at Bernice. Bernice is embarrassed to be seen hanging out of an upstairs window in a purple towelling bathrobe, and without her trademark slash of red lippy. She shouts to the dray woman to wait, and runs to get ready. The Nancy problem will have to wait.

There is a small queue of bar flies at the door when Bernice gets there, and the butch dray woman is off with her because she will fall behind with her round which will make her late finishing and she is going out for a meal with her mate and his new boyfriend. A vet. She calms down a bit when she hears about the murder and Tyrone comes out to greet her. "Crisps! Crisps!" he barks. The bar flies come in. Unsteady Freddie gets behind the bar and offers to help Bernice out a bit until the useless barman, who is late again, gets in.

Johnny the Maggot is moaning about the place being unclean. He steps over a pile of sick on the front step. "Bloody disgusting!" he says, unaware that it is his own pile of vomit from the previous evening.

Tyrone taps about the quarry tiles sniffing at anybody who might be carrying smoky bacon crisps about their person. He goes behind the bar and barks at Unsteady Freddie. Freddie nearly trips over him as he goes to serve another customer. After pulling a pint, he grabs hold of the dog's collar and takes him out into the yard. He locks the door behind him. The dog unnerves him. Freddie is getting gruesome flashbacks of the night before, keeps seeing the poor girl's dead face leering up at him. The dog makes him think of death.

When Bernice comes back from overseeing the beer delivery, everything is back to normal in the pub. The young barman has finally showed his face and is being rude to the customers. Unsteady Freddie is on the correct side of the bar, supping a pint. Johnny the Maggot is telling stories of when he was in the nick. Tyrone is barking outside, and everything was how it should be. Apart from the missing Nancy.

Johnny has even mopped up his own sick. Perhaps Johnny could have Nancy's job. "She was unreliable anyway," thinks Bernice. Bernice tends to judge people on their most recent behaviour. It is the only way to run a boozer in All Saints. There would be no customers if misdemeanours more than a week old had to be taken into consideration.

Once the word gets around about the murder, Tyrone and Freddie become the heroes of the hour. Tyrone is brought back in from the yard when his potential for drawing in punters is realised. The dog is now pure novelty value. Bernice had been quick to realise this when two traveller kids had come in off the street and said, "Oi missus, where's the dog wot found er?"

By early evening, Bernice has put on her best top, a bat-winged sequinned number, and is also basking in Tyrone's glory. Unsteady Freddie has forgotten his flashbacks and has begun to play up the horror of it all, and score a few pints off those who like a good tale.

The Wass-er-face circus has begun. The police have rigged up high-powered lights around the crime scene, and taped off the bushes. They start their house-to-house enquiries, and interview the working girls. They ask if any of them have seen anybody suspicious, if the victim had been known to them, and when had they last seen her. Some of the girls mention a strange man with a peanut-shaped head who'd come round looking for her a couple of times. None of them know his name, but they think he lives somewhere nearby.

Doreen had finished her rounds and had been back behind the counter of her shop by early afternoon. She reckoned the killer had struck twice before. She stopped open until half ten so she could maximise the gossip potential and make much of herself being the third person from the area to find out about it.

Reeta from the bottom shop reckoned the police thought the killer had struck five times before. On hearing this, Doreen hedges her bets and ups her rumour to three times before telling her customers that the dead prostitute had always been in and out of the shop for twenty Benson.

Everybody claims to have a Wass-er-face story.

"Ar, er always used to say hello when I went past," someone says in the pub. Unsteady Freddie has partaken of a few more freebies by this point and feels compelled to compete.

"Er only used to charge me a tenner!"

Unsteady Freddie was never charged "only a tenner" by Wass-er-face or any other prostitute; although he had been rolled by a colleague of Wass-er-face's and her pimp one night. They'd taken him home, tied him up, and nicked his wallet and his DVD player. He wouldn't have minded as the DVD was only a cheap one from Asda, but it had his favourite porno in it at the time.

Johnny the Maggot puts in his fourpenn'orth and says she offered him business only the day before, which Freddie knew was a lie, as she'd been dead much longer than that. He shudders at another flashback, and drinks a bit more quickly.

The kids on the street reckon she was the one that legged them when they shouted stuff after her.

But the truth was that Wass-er-face had never said anything to anyone much. Marilyn and Daniel were the only two who had really had anything to do with her, and neither of them were saying anything about it.

When Daniel Grundy wakes up in the crack house, it is dark. He has trouble remembering where he is. He's had a dream about getting hold of the bingo money in a tartan shopping trolley. He asks one of the guys in the lounge if they'd seen a trolley. The man looks at him blankly.

Daniel goes into the kitchen, where Colin is cursing a mobile. He is dialling and re-dialling a number, and is clearly agitated. He hasn't heard from his boss all day and the line which had been ringing out is now dead, as if it has been disconnected.

"Have you seen my trolley?" asks Daniel politely.

"You're fuckin off your trolley!" Colin returns, and he gives Daniel a crack up the side of his face with the back of his hand like he might hit one of his girls.

Daniel decides that it probably had been a dream after all, and scuttles off with his ear ringing. He makes for the door and heads for home. He sniffs the air, there is something fresh in it, as though things have changed. On the way home he looks over at the Maddoxes' house. Something tells him it is over. He's lucked out. The meal ticket is gone.

Daniel knocks at his mother's door. There is no answer. Daniel is a grown man but he has to knock at his mother's door like a child. A sing-song voice goads him, as though it is narrating his story. He peeps through the letterbox.

Daniel Grundy needs a drink, and plans to pester the living daylights out of his mother until he gets one. Except his mother doesn't seem to be there. It's dark. Where would she go? He calls through the letterbox like a big spoilt baby. "Where are you?" he shouts. "Where are you, mom? Mom! Mom!" His whine is a hair's breadth away from becoming the long drawn-out wail of a child. Mommy! the voice in his head goads again.

In the end he goes round the back of the house. He looks in at the darkened window, but there is no sign of life. He's cold, and he wants to get inside. He grabs the empty wheelie bin and throws it against his mother's window. The glass shatters and he climbs through, not caring if he cuts himself on the shards that are left in the frame like jagged teeth.

Daniel goes in the kitchen and has a nosey around the cupboards. Old Mother Hubbard went to the cupboard to get her poor doggy a bone, but when she got there the cupboard was bare and then the poor doggy had none. The rhyme runs through Daniel's mind. There is nothing there to eat. There are two unwashed glasses on the draining board. He sniffs at them. Alcohol! He licks the glasses clean of Baileys. The drink is cloying on his tongue, and Daniel turns on the tap and drinks water straight from it. He goes through the drawers and finds some tablets. He takes them, thinking they are painkillers, but they aren't. They are the dog's tablets used to calm him down around Diwali and Bonfire Night. Fireworks. Toby had needed tranks to help him. Living with the Grundys was difficult at times.

When Daniel goes back in the lounge, he puts the fire on full. He snuggles up in front of it on the floor. He lies amongst broken glass for what might be hours or days or weeks. Daniel Grundy's lost all sense of time. His nose gets dry. Toby Grundy sat in front of a gas fire for seven years. His nose went dry too.

When Daniel gets too hot, he takes all of his clothes off and goes back to sleep, curled up in a naked ball. When he wakes up he is whimpering. He doesn't realise that he's had a stroke. Not a massive one, a small one. His lip is droopy. "Mom!" he howls. "Mom!...Mom!" He says the word over and over, but his mother isn't there. She's gone.

Daniel squats and opens his bowels, shits on his mother's hearth rug. That would be one of the messes Marilyn would have to come home to. If she came home.

Daniel doesn't hear the police come for him a little after midnight. It hadn't taken them long to make enquiries about the strange peanut-headed man with his bottles of cider and his fascination for the fourteen-year-old girl found dead in the bushes. When the forensics come back, Daniel's prints will be all over the Jif lemon, along with Tyrone's slobber.

Daniel won't remember the night he'd witnessed the murder, when she'd passed him sleeping on the bench. She was walking with the man in the red baseball cap, the man who had long gone. Daniel had heard the screams in his sleepy stupor. Thought they were foxes. Maybe he would remember one day. Maybe he'd remember taking the bingo money, too.

Perhaps prison would save him from himself. He might get help. He might get off the drink and the drugs. He might.

Perhaps his wrongful arrest will be a blessing in disguise. Admitedly the real culprit is still free to murder prostitutes in other parts of the country, but that wouldn't be here. Everybody here can sleep safely in their beds again if Daniel Grundy is under lock and key.

The door frame splinters as the policemen batter their way inside.

Billy Maddox stands on the step. He breathes in deeply. The sound of gulls overhead makes him smile. He finds it difficult, as if the muscles are too tight. As if the muscles have forgotten somehow. There is something familiar about his surroundings. There is something familiar about the people that pass by. There is something familiar about the sea and the sky and sand.

He doesn't feel sad. He feels free. Like a bird, he thinks. He looks up at the gulls and listens to their screams. The souls of sailors lost at sea, so some said. It is sunny. He can't believe how sunny. How hot.

He looks up and down the street. He looks for a familiar face. A familiar face on top of a familiar body and familiar legs. He thinks about familiarity, and how they say it breeds contempt, but there is no contempt, not now. He feels like smiling again. He tries it out. He tests a smile and then stops himself. Is he going to get his smile back? It is better than that. He lets out a little chuckle. "Chuckle!" he thinks to himself. The word chuckle makes him laugh a bit more. "Where is the silly cow?"

He looks at the signs over the hotels until he spots the one he's looking for. He stares at the frontage.

"Looking a bit run down now, isn't it?" a woman says.

"Still 'ere though, ay it?" he turns towards her and pulls off a half-smile.

"Yes, I suppose it is." The woman sounds thoughtful. There is silence for a moment. The woman looks at the elderly man and it registers with her that he is lost in his memories. Memories of happier times, maybe.

"Ar've missed yow!" says the old man. Is he addressing the sign? Or the sky? Or the beach? The woman thinks he might be addressing her! She pulls her dog to heel to protect him from the man who may well be a krank. The dog's wiry electric fur ruffles in the sea breeze.

"Come on, Dai Bach." The dog trots behind the woman, who spoils him with doggy chocolates and bones and toys and love. The woman smells nice. They walk away from the man. Dai Bach Grundy cocks an imaginary leg up against the pillar box and heads homeward.

Billy moves from the step, and goes off in the opposite direction along the seafront. He walks slowly. His legs hurt. They are stiff. The joints have locked. Seized. He needs to oil them. Like his smile. Like his chuckle. Everything needs oiling. When he finds her, when she comes back to him, it will be OK.

"Ar've allus liked Rhyl," he says, and then he practises his smile, tastes the sea in the air, and continues along the front towards the fair.

The vet answers the door to the man with the nice smile. The vet looks a little nervous as he invites him in. "Come in. Come on through." The man with the nice smile follows his lover into the lounge.

"It's only for a day or two," says the vet hurriedly as the man with the nice smile notices the tiny moth-eaten beige dog with a scabby tail. "Just over the weekend." The dog is looking up at them with unwavering dark brown eyes. He is wearing a protective collar to stop him licking himself. It looks like a lampshade.

"You've got to be kidding me!" says the man with the nice smile. As he looks at the creature, its left eye appears to wink.

"Isn't he a sweetheart?" the vet replies.

Marilyn smiles at Nancy. They sip their drinks. Nancy feels calmer than she has in years. Maybe it is something about the crying she has done. She hasn't coughed that much today, either. Marilyn feels more alive than she has in years. Maybe it is something to do with the champagne.

When Marilyn told her friend that the thousand pounds in the shopping trolley had been for emergencies, Nancy had needed to sit down on the bench on the station platform. She'd shaken her head in disbelief. Nancy had explained to Marilyn that she thought it was all of the winnings, and Marilyn had laughed.

Marilyn found it quite hard to persuade Nancy that she'd actually been quite sensible, and invested the rest until she had the confidence to do something with it.

It had been even harder to persuade her that a trip away was going to be her way of repaying the kindness, the food, the support. It was to be a one time, once in a lifetime offer.

They sip their drinks again. Nancy feels free. Marilyn looks at the woman's lined face, and her salt-and-pepper hair, and she smiles at her.

Nancy isn't looking back at her, and her face has taken on a grim expression. She is feeling guilty again. "Ar'll pay yow back. Fuh the money ar took." As she speaks, she thinks she'll phone Chrissie and get her to put the old goat on so that she can tell him she'll be back soon, tell him that she missed him a bit already. She doesn't know the old goat isn't sitting at home in his chair, which is where she's imagining him. If she did know, she would be happy for him.

The old goat will probably never tell her he's gone all the way to Rhyl looking for her, thinking she'd go back to the place where they'd had their honeymoon.

When he'd got to the railway station, one of the guards remembered seeing the unlikely travellers who matched Billy's description, and had reliably informed Billy that they'd boarded a train to Liverpool. And when Billy asked, he'd been told that it also stopped at Crewe. Billy had put two and two together. Change at Crewe for Rhyl! He didn't know that Liverpool was where the passport office was, that the runaways would head there and talk a nice man called Mark into helping them get hold of Nancy's passport before it got posted out. He didn't know that they would then find an equally nice travel agent to sort their visas and business class travel.

As a couple, Billy and Nancy had underestimated time. They'd underestimated the passing of the years. They'd underestimated the damage that empty spaces can do if they aren't spoken about. They'd definitely underestimated each other.

At this moment, Billy is enjoying a slap-up fish and chip supper in a seafront café, feeling happy to be alive. He's decided to stay on for a few days. He is wishing his wife was with him, making a pact with himself that he'll bring her here when he finds her. He swears to himself that he'll make her laugh again, and he will do his quiet chuckle while she cackles as loud as she wants. He imagines that they'll walk along the seafront holding hands. Well, maybe not holding hands but close enough so their fingers will brush against each other's as their arms swing. And there will be oil, and the mechanism will run right again.

Nancy clinks her glass against Marilyn's and they both look apprehensive for a second. "It ay like I expected," Nancy says. "Ar've ad dreams abaht it. It ay as much ard werk as it is in dreams." Marilyn looks at her friend. Maybe it is the champagne making her talk nonsense.

"How long till we get there, miss?" asks Marilyn, leaning out into the aisle as she speaks.

"Brisbane's a couple of hours away yet," says the flight attendant as she tops up their glasses. Nancy settles back in her seat, and smiles.

It is a worn down sheep's teeth kind of a smile, but a smile nevertheless.

Ignite Books is a small, independent publisher. This book is the latest in our series which we hope puts fresh, thought-provoking, entertaining writing before a new audience. We have a lot of fun doing this, but we also survive on a shoestring budget and a lot of graft. So, if you've enjoyed this book, please tell your friends about us.

You can also find us on Twitter, so drop by and say hallo. And to learn more about what we do, or shop for our other publications, just visit our website at ignitebooks.co.uk

Thank you.

Independent bookshops are wonders. Each and every one of them run by people passionate about books and the reading of them. Please support them when you buy, and help keep your high street thriving. Pop in and visit them, or do it from the comfort of your own home via either of these websites:

www.bookshop.org
www.hive.co.uk